The Golden Pact

The Golden Pact

a novel by

Howard Eaton

FITHIAN PRESS, MCKINLEYVILLE, CALIFORNIA, 2020

Published by Fithian Press
A division of Daniel and Daniel, Publishers, Inc.
Post Office Box 2790
McKinleyville, CA 95519
www.danielpublishing.com

Distributed by SCB Distributors (800) 729-6423

LIBRARY OF CONGRESS CATALOGING-IN-PUBLICATION DATA
Names: Eaton, Howard, [date] author.
Title: The golden pact / by Howard Eaton.
Description: McKinleyville, California : Fithian Press, 2020. | Summary:
"On 23 June 1977, an oil heiress dies from complications of alcoholism. She was only 50 years
old. She died as a spinster without children. Her name is Caprice Jordan Taylor. She left a will.
The will is straightforward: most of her estate [about $20 million U. S. dollars] is to be divided
between the local hospital, the art museum, the museum of natural history, and the botanic
gardens. However, her will stipulates that none of the charities can receive such gifts until they
settle with her husband. The charities are stunned and enraged. Husband? What husband? Is he
alive? Where does he live? If alive, what claims does he have? After a colorful search discovers the
so-called husband, key facts emerge. His name is Dante Montepulciano and he lives and works
in Milan, Italy. Although Dante possesses several university degrees, he lives in poverty in a Milan
slum and works as an underpaid physical education teacher. Further, he has a severe head wound
suffered as an officer in the Italian army in Rommel's North Africa campaigns. His wound causes
him migraine headaches and, sometimes, cerebral commotion. They meet in the mid 1960s and
fall in love in Italy. But after three years, their relationship ends on a sour note: Caprice resumes
her destructive drinking habit. However, they sign a pact [The Golden Pact] wherein
    Dante promises to care for her. By this time Caprice has slipped back deeply into alcoholism.
Then Caprice drunk and in a rage commits a most offensive act, causing Dante to leave. Four days
of depositions are arranged. They are held in Milan but under California law, starting in October
1979. The charity lawyers intend to destroy Dante's claim as the husband. Dante wants to make
certain that the charities honor Caprice. [By this time, the estate has a stock market value of about
$60 million U. S. dollars, heightening the charities' interest and adding pressure on their lawyers.]
The ending is about settlement, honor, and Dante's death"— Provided by publisher.
Identifiers: LCCN 2019042894 | ISBN 9781564746153 (trade paperback)
Subjects: LCSH: Inheritance and succession—Fiction. | Alcoholics—Fiction. | Promises—Fiction.
Classification: LCC PS3605.A873 G65 2020 | DDC 813/.6—dc23
LC record available at https://lccn.loc.gov/2019042894

For those who have failed trying

IN MEMORIAM

Whatever we inherit from the fortunate
We have taken from the defeated
What they had to leave us—a symbol:
A symbol perfected in death.
And all shall be well and
All manner of thing shall be well
By the purification of the motive
In the ground of our beseeching.

—T. S. Eliot
"Little Gidding," *Four Quartets*

Contents

I: Endings and Beginnings

1

Caprice, the Oil Heiress

June 23, 1977

CAPRICE SCOWLED at her reflection. Although she was only fifty years old, she thought the woman in the mirror looked years older. She didn't like what she saw—the aging and all of that—but she knew the years of alcohol abuse had taken their toll. At least she had been sober for the last seven years, and the henna she used weekly kept her hair the same flaming red it had always been, giving her a bright look. But she knew her face showed the bad years.

"It's a good thing you can't see me," she said, speaking in Italian, talking to someone far away, remembering better days and a precious love. "How long has it been, my heart? Nine years? Ten years? More? Less? I can't remember."

Clarissa Crane, a nurse, her employee and friend, was already pulling back the bedcovers. "What would I do without you, Clarissa?" Caprice said. "You are so dear, so dependable. Through all my years, the sicknesses and recoveries—my God, I can't remember how many—you've stood by me."

"You have been my good friend too, Caprice," said Clarissa. As she walked past Caprice to retire to her own quarters, she said, "Don't forget, tomorrow the driver will pick you up at two, to get you to the board meeting at the art museum on time."

Caprice rose from the vanity seat and walked over to the bed and lay down. The blanket warmed her weary body and, feeling comforted, she gratefully accepted whatever repose she could find. "Oh, god," she said, in gravelly gratitude for relief from the day's pain and for the evening's peace.

A roof joist creaked. Caprice paid no attention. It was only the movement of wood adjusting to the night's coolness after the scorching heat of an early summer day in New Mexico. She thanked God for air conditioning.

She opened the book she'd been reading, Pat Conroy's *The Prince of Tides,* an old friend, a book she had read many times. She loved Tom Wingo's troubled twin sister, Savannah, the tragic but popular suicidal poet. She loved both Savannah's brightness and her broken places. Savannah reminded Caprice of herself: a victim of destructive family relationships.

She shut off the reading light and uttered one word, "Dante," and lay her head on the pillow. She hoped no nightmares would haunt her. Sleep came quickly.

At exactly 2:12 A.M., Caprice's body convulsed violently, desperately trying to wake, trying to live. But it never wakened.

Caprice stopped breathing.

The clock showed 2:14 A.M.

Clarissa was the one who discovered the body. At dawn she entered the room to wake Caprice and leave a cup of steaming black coffee. When Caprice did not respond to her cheerful "good morning," Clarissa shook Caprice's unresponsive shoulder, until she had to accept that her friend would never again awaken. She knelt beside the bed and wept.

Then she rose and went to work. She bathed Caprice, toweled her off, dressed her, and lovingly combed her hair. She even put a little lipstick on her lips. Last, she covered the body with a clean white linen bed sheet. She made three phone calls, then kept a vigil by the body as she waited.

The first call was to John Butler, Caprice's estate lawyer, in Santa Barbara, California. A large sum of money would have to be settled—more than twenty million dollars. Butler instructed her to call Caprice's local physician there in Santa Fe, and the Santa Fe police; those would be her next two calls. Butler promised to catch the next plane to Santa Fe to help Clarissa with the details. When the call was finished, Clarissa called the physician, and then the police, who brought the coroner. They asked questions.

Yes, Caprice Jordan Taylor was the oil heiress. No, there was no husband, as far as Clarissa knew. Years ago Caprice had married a lawyer named Taylor, who had committed suicide. Yes, most unfortunate. No, there were no children. The doctor examined the body and determined the cause of Caprice's death to be massive renal failure, complicated by emphysema and a failing heart.

When the doctor had finished his examinations, he and the coroner placed the corpse in a white-zippered black vinyl body bag and lifted it onto a gurney. The coroner, with the help of a police officer, wheeled the gurney out of the house and to a waiting ambulance. Clarissa thought of how life was over for Caprice, finally. No more pain. No more agony. There would be a lot of gossip but, mercifully, for once Caprice wouldn't hear it. Gossip had plagued her all her life.

In death, finally, Caprice was at peace.

When the ambulance had gone, Clarissa suddenly felt alone, abandoned. She recalled two lines from T. S. Eliot's poem, "Little Gidding," in *Four Quartets*.

And all shall be well and
All manner of thing shall be well....

But that would not come easily, Clarissa suspected. Four days of depositions in Milan, Italy would prove "all manner of thing" to be anything but easy.

2

The Memorial Service

SEVERAL WEEKS LATER, a memorial service was held at the Santa Barbara Mission. John Butler and Clarissa Crane had scheduled it for three weeks before the reading of the will was to take place.

No one in the Jordan family attended the service, preferring privacy. Nevertheless, it was well attended—not because Caprice had been particularly social or popular, but because the sheer size of her wealth made it an important social event. She had been, after all, the daughter of the founder in 1920 of Jordan Oil, and heiress to a quarter-share of a considerable oil fortune. After her father died in 1963, Caprice's brother Dudley, the second oldest son, ran the company.

The historic Santa Barbara Mission anchored the western slope of what was called the Santa Barbara Riviera. Two bell towers flanked the mission's entrance. They were severely damaged in the massive earthquake of 1925 and the restoration marks were still noticeable. Across the street to the southeast was a broad lawn graced with a gorgeous rose garden.

Butler escorted Clarissa to the service. He liked Clarissa. She was trustworthy and able to keep confidences, and he admired her dedication. She had ministered to Caprice during her last years, helping Caprice through painful days, sharing conversations, and cooking for her. As a last duty, she and Butler had arranged a Requiem Mass as a memorial service for Caprice. Clarissa was Caprice's truest and best friend. And that was how she grieved: as a friend. No children grieved, for there were none. Few friends grieved, for there were few. Death is something we do by ourselves, something everyone faces.

Butler and Clarissa entered the mission chapel. Stopping at the back row of wooden pews, he asked her if she would mind sitting in the back of the chapel. She said she didn't mind at all and, in fact, preferred it. After facing the altar and genuflecting, they entered the last row and sat down.

After a few moments of small talk, Butler leaned back and thought of Caprice. As her estate lawyer, he was of course thinking about her last will and testament, which he had helped to draft, and people's likely reactions to it. His stomach twinged with anxiety. A chaotic rush of memories chattered in his brain. After this memorial service, a storm of legal issues would sweep down like a cold wind—one that could transform the warm respect on display at this memorial to a cold-blooded money-grab.

Given the impregnable veil of privacy that Caprice had drawn around herself, it wasn't surprising that so little was known about her. No one attending the memorial knew much about her private life, particularly during the 1960s. But Butler, as her lawyer and confidante, knew enough to make him concerned about the impact of her will. Several charities, the principal legatees of Caprice's estate, would be shocked. But Caprice Jordan Taylor was nobody's fool, and even less inclined to suffer fools lightly. Her wicked sense of satire and fatalism were well known.

Although her body had been ruined by alcoholism, Caprice in her sober moments had been as sharp as a tack. Actually, the last years of her life had been completely sober. But by then it was too late. Already important organs had been irreparably damaged.

Butler turned to Clarissa and excused himself, saying he wanted to go outside and stroll around until the service started. Clarissa was content to be left with her own thoughts. Butler walked through the tall wooden doors and out onto the Mission's spacious stone-stepped entrance and looked out over the lawn and rose gardens, and the sleepy town beyond.

Luxury cars, including a few Rolls Royces and Bentleys and a greater number of Mercedes and BMWs, drew up one by one to the steps of the Mission and unloaded their occupants. The attendees stepped out and looked around to see who else had shown up, seeking confirmation of their own importance and influence. Then they walked up the stone steps and shook hands with Peter Stern, manager of the Jordan Family Foundation and financial advisor to the Jordan family, and Father Francis Brantingham, the pastor of the Mission, who had posted themselves before the entrance. Next they sought out friends and not-friends alike. They wanted to socialize. Memorials are like that—planned and held for the living.

The dead are gone—they can't be seen, Butler mused. *Those of us still remaining seek reassurance of at least our earthly meaning and affirmations of life.*

Stern turned and, seeing Butler emerge from the chapel, reached out a hand. "John, good to see you. I didn't know you were already here. Caprice was like a sister to us. You two knew each other so well, and she liked you so much."

Butler smiled inwardly at Stern's self-flattery. Stern and Caprice had hated each other. She had thought him a bullshitter, and Butler agreed. "Thanks, Peter. Yes, Caprice would have appreciated this turnout." He knew that was a lie; Caprice had never liked pomp and circumstance.

Butler and Stern had spoken by phone the previous day to confirm the date and time of the reading of Caprice's will. In the course of the conversation, Stern had raved on about how he remembered Caprice as an elegant, fashionable young lady, if perhaps a bit old-world, old-fashioned, romantic, not comfortable with modern America. Perhaps a little out of step with the times. Pure bullshit. Stern had ended their phone conversation saying that Caprice— *sober*—was a lady, and that was how he would always remember her.

Butler turned his attention back to the arriving crowd. Stern smiled, looking past Butler, and caught the attention of a group approaching the steps. "Excuse me, John," he said, "I have to greet some people."

Butler smiled, said nothing, and moved on. He recognized Stern for what he was: a high-pressure dilettante, a successful fund-raiser, and a self-serving advisor loyal to the Jordan family, not to Caprice. For years, Caprice's family had tried to buy up her shares of Jordan Oil, and it was Stern's job as manager of the Jordan Family Foundation to wrest them from her. The company was preparing itself for a merger, and the share price was sure to skyrocket. The family foundation would prosper, and Peter Stern would secure his position as a leader in Santa Barbara society. But Caprice had refused to sell, infuriating the family, and none more than Stern.

With Stern gone to greet other guests, Butler was free to

eavesdrop on people's not-so-private conversations. Their chatter formed a biased mini-biography of the deceased.

"I wish Caprice could have stopped drinking. It wouldn't have come to this. I told her so. She had a lot of money."

"Yes, oil money."

"Jordan Oil money."

"Really?"

"Yes."

"But she was generous. She gave a fortune to the hospital and the botanic garden."

"She did so much for our art museum. Her father would have been so proud. The museum's collection of Impressionist and modern art is absolutely priceless."

"I don't think she got along with her family."

"I've heard the same thing."

"She was always so private."

"Dear, I know. She hoarded privacy, and she went to such extremes to avoid publicity."

"It was the alcohol, I swear."

"I think the press drove her to drink."

"No, my dear, it wasn't the press. It was her family."

"If you ask me, it was that bastard Peter Stern."

"Peter Stern?"

"Yes, Stern, the family's financial advisor, that one over there."

"Really?"

"He's so fucking full of himself—excuse my French."

"And what about that red hair? That wasn't her natural color was it? That wasn't *any* natural color!"

"Was it even her own hair?"

"If you ask me, she was always a little crazy. Don't you think so?"

"That's a terrible thing to say! This is not the place or time—"

"Well—"

"I agree. This isn't really the place or the time to bring that up, not at her memorial service."

"Well, she was different."

"None of us really knew her."

"I think she suffered terribly. I mean all that wealth. Everybody was after it."

"Did she ever marry?"

"Once, to a lawyer named Taylor."

"He died, right?"

"Years ago—suicide. There were no children."

"She never remarried?"

"Not that I ever heard, and that's something difficult to hide."

"Well, after all, she moved from Santa Barbara years ago. I think she traveled the world and then settled in Santa Fe, New Mexico. A friend of mine told me. She never remarried."

"Good Lord, with all that money she could have had the pick of whomever she wanted."

"Well, dear, we all know she wasn't a beauty. I mean, a dear soul—when she was sober—but not a beauty."

"I don't think she trusted men."

"Well, who does?"

"They were after her money."

"Who wasn't?"

"Did you see her recently?"

"I visited her in Santa Fe six months ago. She didn't look well then."

"She meant well, but she was so headstrong, so opinionated."

"It was the drinking."

"Awful, just awful, poor dear."

"I was told she had been sober for the last years."

"In the end, I heard that her liver and kidneys gave out—ruined from the drinking. Such a painful death. Such a bad way to go."

"Terrible."

"Painful. Trust me, before I married my husband, the doctor, I was a nurse. I should know."

And so the gossip went, gathering boldness, but laced with deference for the deceased. Reminded of their own mortality, people were careful not to exceed the boundaries of social protocol. And so Santa Barbara's society mingled, mixed, shook hands, embraced, exchanged pleasantries—and sometimes gossiped, always speaking in muted funereal tones, an unintended street-level social requiem for Caprice Jordan Taylor. And as they did so, they carefully assessed each other's appearance: shoes, hairdos, cosmetic surgeries, designer clothes, jewelry, and spouses. After all, life must go on.

Father Brantingham presided over the Mass. Everyone thought it was beautiful, if perhaps a bit long. When it was done, everyone left hurriedly.

Before he left, John Butler shook hands with Peter Stern and Father Brantingham and said his goodbyes to a few friends. Then he escorted Clarissa to his car. All the while he could not stop thinking about Caprice Jordan Taylor's last will and testament, and the scandal it would cause.

3

The Reading of the Will

IN ITS DAY, twenty million dollars constituted a sizable estate. And for that kind of money Caprice Jordan Taylor's will was remarkably straightforward.

Her charitable interests were few, and not publicly known. Her interests had been art, botanical gardens, animals and, of course, her hospital. Pueblo Hospital was expected to be the biggest beneficiary of her will, because Caprice had been admitted on so many occasions to dry out from her alcoholic episodes.

On September 15, 1977, at 10:00 A.M., the legatees and their lawyers gathered for the reading of the will of Caprice Jordan Taylor at the Santa Barbara offices of Winslow, Cabrillo, & Hollister, where John Butler was an associate. Butler had invited four charities to attend: Pueblo Hospital, the Art Museum, the Fleischmann Museum of Natural History, and the Botanical Gardens. The only private individual invited was Clarissa Crane, as there were no other individual heirs. The participants arrived promptly, expectantly, all of them exercising their best manners, like winners in an Olympic Games awards ceremony. Conviviality filled the room. After all, today was a day during which a lot of money would pass to the charities. Everyone expected that.

There were two unknowns: first, none of them knew whether there were other legatees. Second, no legatee knew how much each might receive. This added a note of competitiveness to the legatees' expectations.

John Butler knew those things. He also knew that one sentence in the will would upset everyone. Over the years he had drafted and amended Mrs. Taylor's last will and testament many times, but he had never discussed it with anyone. He was professionally bound to privacy, and he had a reputation for keeping confidences; and Caprice had insisted. Thus the reading of the will was much anticipated.

The boardroom of Butler's law firm provided an appropriate stage for the reading. The spacious room covered at least a thousand square feet. Oak walls lined with bookshelves formed the west and east sides of the room. The ceiling was high and barrel vaulted. Tall vaulted windows faced south. The north wall was entirely windowed and draped with beige curtains. An expensive Persian rug covered most of the room's dark hardwood floor. A fabulous sixteenth-century chandelier hung over the center of the board table. It had formerly hung in an ancient, now-demolished Catholic church outside Madrid, Spain. How the church had ever approved its sale and removal was a mystery. Some dealer in relics must have somehow purchased it and resold it surreptitiously. Now it was in Santa Barbara, California.

Two paintings, one by Joan Miró, the other by Georges Braque, both gifts from Caprice to the law firm's now deceased founder, hung on the east and west walls. A valuable Sir Henry Moore sculpture stood in a corner, out of the way but where everyone could plainly see it. It was in the shape of a heart, sculpted from black marble, and titled *Banker's Heart*. It was a smaller version of the original *Banker's Heart* located in the plaza of Bank of America in San Francisco. Caprice had loved it and its motif.

Eighteen leather chairs were placed around the room's stunning table. The table, called the Partners' Table, fashioned from a single magnificent piece of African Chacate Preto, occupied most of the length and center of the room. Light flooded down from pot lamps inset in the ceiling, illuminating the table's colors: dark, nearly black-brown, with lighter honey brown longitudinal streaks. Name cards marked the assigned places of each of the participants. English Wedgewood cups and saucers were placed at each table setting, and waiters stood ready to pour water, coffee, or tea. It was magnificent theater.

Although the beneficiaries were few in number, their legal retainers were numerous. More in fees would be charged than originally imagined. Where there is honey, there too are bees.

Representing Pueblo Hospital was Dr. Wendy Sprott, Director, and Guy Bray, their lead counsel. Two lawyers represented the

Art Museum: Jack Orso and his assistant, who provided counsel on charitable gifts. Then there was Miranda White, Director of the Fleischmann Museum of Natural History, and Bill Bass representing that institution. Bass brought along a junior lawyer to assist him. Last was Dick Lambert, representing the Botanical Gardens. Peter Stern of the Jordan Family Trust attended as a guest, although John Butler was aware that his goal was to buy up as many of the legatees' shares of Jordan Oil as possible.

Butler's firm's partner emeritus, Edward Winslow, was also a guest, moving around the room, acknowledging guests, and generally hobnobbing as the participants arrived. Butler had asked him to attend because he was a heavyweight in Santa Barbara law, society, and politics both statewide and national, outranking everyone else in the room. His law degree was from Harvard, and his pedigree traced back to Plymouth Colony. Gossip was that one of his ancestors had been the colony's financier and its third governor. Santa Barbara's social set bowed to the same idols as did socialites in most cities. It was important where you came from and whom you knew, and Winslow knew everyone worth knowing. He had been Attorney General for Governor Earl Warren. Later, when Warren was appointed Chief Justice of the United States Supreme Court, Winslow had followed him to Washington, D.C.

Further, Winslow's age added a patina to the setting. Butler had invited him to the reading of the will to provide caution and a steadying influence, if those should become necessary, and Winslow had been fully briefed by Butler about certain surprises that were contained in the will.

"Mr. Stern, good morning," Butler said, interrupting a conversation between Stern and Winslow. "If you would be kind enough to sit to the right of Mr. Winslow. A placard has your name on it." Stern happily moved to the right side of Winslow. Beaming, he thanked Butler warmly, all the while holding Winslow's arm, monopolizing him. Being seated next to this social icon made him anticipate a glorious day.

"Edward," Peter effused as the two took their seats, "it's great to see you this morning. I didn't think you'd bother attending this little meeting."

"Mrs. Taylor was most cherished by us," Winslow lied. "A woman

I regarded highly—so sad. She will be missed by her family, and especially by me and the firm."

Winslow had just lied twice. He had given Caprice's account to John Butler years ago, so that he wouldn't have to deal with her troubles.

"Clarissa—er, Miss Crane, excuse my informality," Butler said, regretting that he had exposed their familiarity in such formal surroundings. "Please sit here beside me—here on my right."

Clarissa acknowledged him with a polite smile and wordlessly took the seat he proffered.

Butler was nervous, but he didn't think it showed. This was not your ordinary estate proceeding. But he knew how he would handle the reading itself: slowly, deliberately, point by point, professionally. In fact, the night before he had rehearsed in his mind every possible scenario that might arise. John Butler consistently presented a good impression.

Buckling to the task, Butler pressed on and helped the rest of the participants to their seats, then took his own seat at the center of one side of the large conference table, and asked for everyone's attention and quiet. The attendees' response was courteous and immediate. They were attentive, alert, listening.

Butler began the reading.

"For the record, I have instructed my secretary, Ms. Copeland here, to note the date, time, place, and those present. Starting with you, Mr. Stern, for the record please state your full name and, if you have representative counsel, the full name of counsel and counsel's firm." He turned and nodded to Ms. Copeland, who had seated herself immediately behind him, as one by one the participants gave their names and affiliation.

"Good," John concluded after everyone had been named and identified.

Then the solemnity and weight of the reading descended upon the meeting. Like well-trained, dutiful adults who understand the charity process, all eyes turned to the moment's authority, John Butler. Not a word was spoken. Everyone waited, curious, uncertain, wondering what charitable prizes would be revealed.

Butler looked down at Caprice Jordan Taylor's will, put on his glasses, and cleared his throat so that he would speak firmly and authoritatively. He would make a good impression for Edward Winslow. He found himself inexplicably wishing Caprice were present to witness the distribution of her estate. For a moment it seemed strange, dividing large assets into small pieces and distributing those pieces to strangers. An enormous estate was being broken up. He had long been impressed at how well Caprice had taken care of her portion of the Jordan family's wealth. But now it would be bequeathed, to be spent or squandered as the recipients wished, gone from his influence and care.

He had decided in advance that he would read the will in its entirety without stopping. This was for several reasons. First, the estate was large and important, which in itself seemed of compelling interest to those unfamiliar with such distributions. Second, it was simply interesting to read; it was well framed and skillfully written, even if he said so himself. Third, it declared Caprice's last wishes and testament. And, last, the legatees' reactions would be a point of interest.

Butler began to read, slowly and carefully.

"'I, Caprice Jordan Taylor, a resident of Santa Barbara, County of Santa Barbara, and State of California, do make, publish, and declare this my last will and testament, hereby revoking all former wills and codicils by me at any time made.

"'Article I. I direct that my funeral expenses and the costs of settling my estate be paid promptly.

"'Article II. I give and bequeath, net of settlement fees and all other fees, taxes, and other levies owing, all my investment property and all other similar tangible investment property in the following manner. Let it be known that my investment portfolio shall be that portfolio named as such and administered by the law firm of Winslow, Cabrillo, and Hollister, and invested by and managed by Suisse Paribas.'"

Butler looked up, pausing for effect. When would he get to settle an estate like this one again?

He continued.

"'1. To my beloved companion, Miss Clarissa Crane, I bequeath my free title home in Santa Fe plus two million dollars cash.'"

All eyes shifted to Clarissa who, though surprised, showed no reaction whatsoever to the generous gift. Except for Peter Stern's furrowed eyebrows, no reactions were betrayed. Butler was pleased by

Clarissa's self-control, because he knew she had no idea of the size of her inheritance. That was a lot of money for her. At the time he was instructed to prepare the will, this clause had pleased him immensely. After all, it was Clarissa who had done the hard work.

He continued reading.

"'2. Conditionally, to the Museum of Art, twenty percent of my holdings of Jordan Oil stock, less fees and expenses of this distribution.'"

Peter Stern frowned, confused by that word "conditionally," and he turned and stared quizzically at Jack Orso, the museum's counsel. But he decided to wait politely until the entire will had been read. He would ask questions later.

"'3. Conditionally, to the Botanical Gardens, ten percent of my holdings of Jordan Oil stock, less legal fees and expenses of this distribution.

"'4. Conditionally, to the Museum of Natural History, ten percent of my holdings of Jordan Oil stock, less legal fees and expenses of this distribution;

"'5. Conditionally, to Pueblo Hospital, sixty percent of my holdings of Jordan Oil stock, less legal fees and expenses of the estate's distribution.'"

Everyone looked at Peter Stern. Not a word was spoken. Butler read on.

"'6. Conditionally, to the Humane Society of Santa Barbara one hundred thousand dollars.'"

Caprice had loved animals. But this paragraph was barely heard by the legatees, who by this time were wondering what the word *conditionally* actually meant.

Butler braced himself, and read on calmly and firmly.

"'With the exception of my immediate gift to Miss Clarissa Crane, all of the above shall be deferred conditionally until the following stipulation is honored.

"'7. For my beloved husband, Dante Montepulciano, if he shall survive me, the estate shall be held whole and undivided, and it shall provide and distribute all of its income as and when earned to his sole benefit until his death. Only upon his death, or upon an amount to be settled on him, as my legatees shall negotiate, shall the above conditional distributions of my estate be settled.'"

Butler had hardly gotten out those last words before an open hand loudly slammed down on the table, rattling water glasses, coffee cups, saucers, and spoons. Everyone was startled. All eyes jerked toward Peter Stern.

Stern jumped to his feet and marched around the Chacate Preto table bellowing, "This is an outrage! I say we find and kill that bastard Monte-whatever, *now*. Husband? Caprice never remarried—not after Mr. Taylor, the suicide. The Jordan family will sue the son-of-a-bitch for everything he has coming. Her husband, my ass! What a travesty— a *travesty*, that's what this is!"

Everyone was transfixed, stunned, paralyzed by Stern's venomous tirade. Butler had expected a reaction to this bombshell, and probably from Peter Stern. But he, too, was aghast at Stern's crude outburst. He had never seen Stern behave so badly.

"Husband!" Peter growled. "She never remarried!" He swung around and glared at Butler, his face contorted by anger. "What do you know about this, counselor?"

Butler ignored him.

"What are you hiding?"

Butler kept his eyes on the papers before him and did not reply.

"You knew about this all along. You shylock!"

Winslow was the first to snap out of his stunned silence. "Mr. Stern, *stop*. Stop immediately. Right now. I won't tolerate that kind of language under my roof."

Stern leaned over into Butler's face and, out of deference to Winslow's presence, lowered his voice to a whisper. "You've known this all along," he hissed. "Yet you've kept this little secret to yourself." The veins in his neck throbbed. "Okay, Butler, have it your way. But you're not going to delay the settlement of this money. You're *not* going to distribute a *dime* from Caprice Jordan Taylor's estate to some goddamn money-grubbing gigolo no one has ever heard of!"

"Sit down, Peter," Butler said calmly, without looking up.

"This is not going to happen! Jordan Oil intends to buy *all* of its shares from the beneficiaries. *All of them!*"

Butler stole a look at Winslow. Winslow looked sick.

"You've let Mrs. Caprice Taylor *fuck* us," Stern spat.

At this Winslow stood up and pushed the apoplectic Stern down into his leather chair. "Peter, you are *not* a beneficiary of this estate, so pipe down. Just shut the hell up, or I'll ask you to leave this minute. Do you understand?"

"Yes, sir," said Stern, in an abashed but no less angry tone. "Goddamn right I understand. But I remind everyone that the Jordans want to purchase Mrs. Taylor's shares of Jordan Oil—at market price. Understand? So this is the way you legal beagles managed Mrs. Taylor's money and collected fees? Right. Goddamn right."

Spent, Stern slouched down in his chair. "Shit," he whispered, exhausted. "That alcoholic head case really did it. Husband, my ass! She never remarried. Don't you understand, Mr. Winslow? She never remarried. She died a *spinster.* It's bogus. She tricked you, Butler."

Butler felt like slapping Stern, but he kept his grip on the papers.

Winslow interceded. "John, have you finished reading the will?"

"No, there's more."

"Then I suggest you finish the reading."

"Isn't the money all gone by now to an unknown husband?" Stern grumbled through an angry smirk.

"Peter Stern, I said restrain yourself," Winslow ordered.

But Stern continued, keeping his voice to a conversational level. "It's very clear, Winslow. This falling-down drunken sot meets some jerk-off in one of her alcoholic blackouts, he sees a lottery ticket wagging at him, tags it, and now we owe him millions—maybe even the whole estate."

"You're being illogical, Peter," Winslow said.

"Please don't tell me I'm being illogical, goddamn it," Stern shot back, his raspy voice trailing off as he wound down.

Then Stern focused on Clarissa Crane. "How about you, Ms. Crane? What do you know about this?"

Clarissa looked at him for a long time before replying quietly and with dignity. "Mrs. Taylor neither disclosed nor discussed her will with me, Mr. Stern." Clarissa knew a lot of Caprice's secrets, but they had never discussed the will. Besides, Clarissa loathed Peter Stern, and she had no desire to assist him in any way.

Stern groaned and put his hands over his forehead.

Butler soldiered on. "Gentlemen, ladies, allow me to complete the reading, and then I suggest we come back and discuss the ramifications and alternatives."

Winslow agreed. "Yes, Mr. Butler, please finish the reading."

"Husband, my ass," Stern said again. He stared sullenly at the table in front of him.

Butler continued reading.

"'8. If my husband does not survive me, I give, devise, and bequeath all my personal art and property and household effects of every kind and all other similar tangible personal property to any cousins and nieces who may survive me, to be divided equally among them, and such division shall be administered by my Executor, Mr. John Butler, whose determination shall be conclusive upon all persons having an interest in my estate.'"

"Shit."

Everyone again turned and looked at Peter Stern, disgusted with him, his language, and his representation of the Jordan estate.

"Paragraph nine follows," John said.

"'9. I give, devise, and bequeath my furniture and my car, not otherwise effectively disposed of in this my last will and testament, whether or not heretofore mentioned, to my companion, Clarissa Crane, if she shall survive me. If she shall not survive me, I give, devise, and bequeath this portion of my estate to The Salvation Army.'"

Stern interrupted again, oblivious to Clarissa's feelings. "Goddamn it, if it's not the phantom husband, it's Ms. Clarissa Crane. Next thing we know nothing will be left."

All of the charity lawyers were upset by Stern's unnecessary personal remark. Bill Bass apologized for the remark and assured Clarissa they were grateful for all of her contributions to Mrs. Taylor.

Butler continued, ignoring Stern's interruptions.

"'10a. I nominate, constitute, and appoint my lawyer, John Butler, as the Executor of this my last will and testament. If John Butler shall predecease me or fail to qualify or act as Executor hereunder or for any reason cease to act as such, then I nominate, constitute, and appoint Edward Winslow of Santa Barbara, California, the successor Executor under this my last will and testament.

"'10b. Any individual at any time acting hereunder as Executor shall be compensated for such services.

"'11. All powers of my Executor, whether conferred by this my last will and testament or by law, may be exercised without authorization of any court and except as otherwise specifically provided in this my last will and testament shall be exercisable:

"'(a) by the Executor and by any successor or substitute for the time being acting;

"'(b) and shall remain exercisable until actual final distribution.'"

Butler concluded:

"'In witness whereof, I, Caprice Jordan Taylor, sign, seal, publish, and declare this as my last will and testament, in the presence of the persons witnessing it at my request, this twenty-first day of November, nineteen sixty-seven.'"

Butler noted that the will had been signed in Basel, Switzerland, and sworn by a notary of the public on November 21, 1967.

Finished at last, Butler looked up and after a pause added, careful not to smile, which would have ignited Stern again, "None of the above can occur until Mrs. Taylor's husband is dealt with."

"Husband?" Stern shouted again.

"There may be something to it," Butler said. "I've met this Dante Montepulciano. He's Italian. But I have no idea where he is, or whether he is even still alive."

Stern crumpled, as though a vampire had just bitten his jugular vein and drained all his life juices. "Unbelievable! An Italian—a 'goodfella,' I suppose," he muttered to himself, spent, dazed.

Winslow protested his slur on Italians, and Stern apologized sullenly.

"Mr. Butler," Winslow said, "does *anybody* knows of the—uh, husband's whereabouts?"

"Not to my knowledge," Butler said. "But we do know a few things. We've done some research on this since Mrs. Taylor's death. We may know who he is, but we don't know whether he was actually Mrs. Taylor's legal husband. As for his whereabouts, we suspect he may be somewhere in or near Milan, or perhaps Lake Como, which is north of Milan. I'm still inquiring."

"So we don't know where he lives?" Stern asked, adding, "Or even *if* the guy is still alive?"

"That's correct."

"Montepulciano," Stern said, emphasizing *"ciano."*

Everyone else ignored Stern and lapsed into thoughtfulness.

"Could he conceivably get all the money?" Guy Bray asked

"Yes, conceivably," Butler said, "but that's unlikely. Mrs. Taylor clearly stipulated the importance of the charities—"

"Then we'll fight him to the death," Stern broke in. "I'd like to have a little talk with counsels for these charities—in private, if you don't mind."

"Certainly," said Butler. "There's a free room next door."

Stern and the lawyers left the conference table and adjourned to the next room. Twenty minutes passed before they returned.

Guy Bray, the hospital's representative, spoke for the charities' lawyers. "Mr. Butler, Mr. Winslow, we've decided to meet together tomorrow morning to discuss this situation further. I've been elected to head that effort. I'll be in touch with you tomorrow. Okay?"

"Yes, I understand," Butler said. "Call me when you're ready to proceed."

"Do we each have a copy of Mrs. Taylor's will?" Bray asked, looking in turn at each of the parties.

Everyone did.

"Anything else?"

"Remember," cautioned Butler, "this is not yet a public document, so all of you must observe the protocols of privacy and confidentiality."

"I understand," said Bray.

With that, Butler called an end to the meeting and promised to deal with each beneficiary privately later, one on one.

After the meeting broke up, John Butler slowly paced back and forth in his office, pondering what to do next. No one among the charities was happy. They wanted action—quickly. How could he begin to find Caprice Taylor's supposed husband, Mr. Montepulciano? He didn't want to hire a detective agency. He was certain he could find the man on his own. But what would be the best first step? He decided to begin with Clarissa Crane.

Just at that moment, his office phone rang. It was none other than Clarissa herself.

"Clarissa! I was just going to phone you."

"John, I have something to tell you. I didn't think the reading of Caprice's will was the right time to speak out on what I know."

"What can you tell me? Is it about Caprice's 'husband?'"

"Yes."

"Please tell me."

"John, I know who Dante Montepulciano is, but I never knew he was her husband—I mean in the legal sense."

Clarissa explained that she didn't know where Dante lived exactly, but she thought Butler was right about Milan or the Italian lake district—probably Milan, she thought. She thought he had lived in a small walkup apartment before resigning from his job as a physical education teacher at a small parochial school in north Milan to join Caprice. But she wasn't sure of anything—her information was based on few and distant memories, because Caprice had refused to talk about Dante for the last eight or nine years of her life.

She also told Butler that Caprice and Dante had once shared a house in Rifle, Colorado, but she didn't know who owned the house. She had assumed Caprice owned it, because Dante never had any money—Caprice paid for everything. In fact, he appeared to care very little about money, or the material side of life in general. So she thought the house must have belonged to Caprice, but that was just a guess.

"She never talked much about money," Clarissa explained. "She kept that to herself, which was fine. It was her money."

This was not news. Butler had known Dante Montepulciano as Caprice's lover, but not her husband. Still, he only now realized how little he actually knew about Caprice's private life. With her money, any number of men would have eagerly married her.

But Rifle, Colorado, was news. Here was a thread Butler could pull. His next step, he decided, would be to hire Jeff Kennedy, a private detective he had worked with successfully before. A quick phone call to Guy Bray gave him the approval of the charities. By the end of that day, Kennedy was on the case.

Kennedy's assignment was clear: Go to Rifle, Colorado, and find whatever documentation there might be, if there was any, of Mrs. Caprice Jordan Taylor and Dante Montepulciano. Had they really lived together in Rifle? For how long? Had they owned a house there? Had they married?

Kennedy told Butler that he expected the assignment to take three days, plus a day to write a report for Butler and the charity lawyers, who were under pressure from their clients regarding the disposition of the estate. Costs would include his fees and transportation.

Detective Work

JEFF KENNEDY FROWNED. Rifle, Colorado, wasn't his grandest assignment.

His first stop, however, was in Denver, where he searched marriage records for Taylors, Jordans, and Montepulcianos. He found nothing.

But in searching property records, he found a prize: a microfiche copy of a deed to a house in Rifle, bearing two signatures: Caprice Montepulciano, and Dante Montepulciano—the woman's name first, which struck him as unusual. It was a copy, but the place of filing was specified as Rifle. He'd need the original, but now he knew where to find it.

Buoyed by this success, Kennedy took a commuter turboprop over the mountains to Rifle, arriving at sunset. As he deplaned on the tarmac, he marveled at the sun setting opposite the tall, snow-capped peaks of the Rockies, turning them into shades of deep red, mauve, and gray shadows.

He rented a car at the airport and drove into town to his hotel. The hotel's Western decor gave it an old-fashioned air. At the reception desk he was greeted by a clerk who looked as old as the hotel.

"I have a reservation for two nights—Jeff Kennedy."

"Yes, sir. We have several empty rooms," the clerk said. "Would you have any preferences?"

"I like quiet. I just need a place to sleep and work."

"Well, sir, I have just the room for you. Sign here, please. Will that be cash or check?"

"Cash."

"One hundred dollars, please," said the clerk. "It's fifty dollars a night."

Kennedy gave him two fifty-dollar bills. "Does that include taxes?"

"Yes, sir."

Kennedy thanked him and picked up his suitcase and briefcase, but before starting up the stairs to his room he stopped and asked, "Where's a good place to eat dinner?"

"What kind of food do you like?"

"Italian."

"As you go out the main door, turn right," said the clerk. "It's only a few stores down. It's called Luigi's—it's real Italian."

Kennedy thanked him and set off for his room. The room was at the back of the hotel on the second floor. After throwing his bags on the bed and freshening up, he went back downstairs and walked down the street to Luigi's.

He immediately liked the restaurant. The host greeted him warmly.

"Good evening, sir! Welcome."

"A table for one," said Kennedy. "Are you Luigi?"

"I am! Follow me, please," said the Luigi, showing him to a table in a corner.

"Would you like a nice bottle of wine? Maybe a good Amarone della Valpolicella?"

"I have to work this evening—sorry," Kennedy said. "But that sounds like a very nice wine. Do you have an Italian red by the glass?"

"Of course. Montepulciano d'Abruzzo."

Kennedy laughed and said, "Well I'll be damned, Montepulciano. Yeah, sure, I'll have a glass of that. Looks like Montepulciano has found me before I could find him!"

"Excuse me?"

"Nothing, it's a private joke," Kennedy said.

"I'll bring it right away."

Luigi hurried away and returned quickly bearing a carafe of Montepulciano d'Abruzzo, and poured a glass for Kennedy. Kennedy took a sip and swished it in his mouth, and looked up at his host and smiled. "That's a good wine," he said.

"*Grazie.* And what can I bring you to eat?"

"I'd like a small plate of linguine *aglio e olio,* and then a steak medium rare, please."

Luigi hurried away and gave Jeff's order to the kitchen. Then he returned, but cautiously because he didn't want to bother his guest. From a polite distance he observed his customer reading what looked like some official papers.

Kennedy looked up and beckoned the man over. "How long has your restaurant been here?" he asked.

"More than twenty years."

"I'm trying to find information about a man named Montepulciano—like the name of this wine," Kennedy said. "Dante Montepulciano, and a Mrs. Caprice Jordan Taylor. I understand they used to live in Rifle. Do you remember a couple by those names?"

"Why, yes—that is, I knew a Dante and Caprice Montepulciano," Luigi replied. "It was years ago—more than ten years. They came here often. He was Italian—we spoke Italian only. In fact, she spoke good Italian too. And, yes, they lived in town."

"I see," Kennedy said. "They were married, then?"

"I assumed so. Of course, you never know. I never asked—that would have been rude. But they were definitely in love! And the rumor was that Mrs. Montepulciano was a woman of great wealth. I never knew that for sure, but it was always she who paid. We all loved Dante. He was such a wonderful man. But she was another story."

"What do you mean?"

Luigi paused and shook his head, "It's difficult to talk about. I don't want to offend anyone. After all, you may be family."

"I'm not family," Kennedy said, presenting his business card. "Mrs. Montepulciano died recently, and I'm trying to contact Mr. Montepulciano with regard to her estate."

"Holy Mother of Jesus! I'm sorry to hear that. It's even more difficult to talk about the dead."

"Yes, I understand," Kennedy said. "But I already know she could be a somewhat difficult person."

Their conversation was interrupted by the entrance of other diners, and Luigi had to attend to them. Another waiter brought Kennedy's meal—the pasta perfectly al dente, the steak tender and pink. When he had finished and paid, Kennedy paused at the door to thank his host. "You've been a great help to me. And you have a fine restaurant here. I'll be back. Thank you."

"*Grazie, signore.*"

Now that Kennedy had the deed to the house and Luigi's confirmation, it was time to contact John Butler. He dialed Butler's home phone from his hotel.

"John Butler speaking."

"John, it's Jeff Kennedy. Sorry to phone you at this late hour."

"It's okay. Where are you?"

"Rifle, Colorado. Do you have a minute?"

"Of course. How's it going?"

"The trail is hot. I spent most of the day in Denver, cozying up to clerks and getting them to dig through some records that are supposed to be off limits, I don't know why. They found no wedding certificate, so if they were married, they must have gotten hitched before they moved to Colorado."

"Or after?" Butler suggested.

"Nope. Before. Listen to this. My last search in Denver was real estate records. Glory be, they have the whole state's historical records on microfiche and, long story short, there was a copy of the deed to the house in Rifle, in the names of Caprice and Dante *Montepulciano*—signed that way by both of them. And the original was filed here in Rifle."

"Wow!" said Butler. "This is excellent."

"There's more. I just finished having dinner at a restaurant called Luigi's, and learned that Caprice and Dante were known in the community. The owner of the restaurant remembers them. They went around town acting like they were a couple, like a husband and wife. She was known as Mrs. Montepulciano."

"Good investigating, Jeff," said Butler.

"Thanks. But as you know, joint ownership can be tricky. I suggest you find out everything you can about common-law marriage in the state of Colorado."

"So you think it was common-law?"

"Right now, that's my hunch."

"Okay. Keep me posted, Jeff."

"Will do. I'll phone again tomorrow."

And with that Kennedy hung up, determined to obtain the best evidence he could.

First thing the next morning, Jeff Kennedy went downstairs to talk to the desk clerk.

"Excuse me, I wonder if you might help me."

"If I can, sir."

"I'm trying to locate some people: a man by the name of Montepulciano, Dante Montepulciano, an Italian; and a woman, Caprice Montepulciano, or maybe Caprice Jordan Taylor. Do those names ring a bell? I'm wondering whether perhaps they stayed at this hotel nine or ten years ago?"

The clerk looked away, scratched his head, and thought. "That's a long time ago, son. I'm not sure I can remember. Ah, wait! Come to think of it, I do recall something." He leaned across the desk and continued in confidential tones. "They did stay here on and off. The woman, Mrs. Montepulciano, she was cantankerous as all hell. She would only stay in room thirty-three. I'm surprised I still remember that! Her husband was Italian and seemed to take care of her. Had a terrible scar on his head. Something was wrong with her, but he was a perfectly decent type, always trying to make her happy. They stopped coming after a while, but I saw them around town once or twice. I think they bought a house or something. But like I said, that was years ago. I guess they must have moved away. It was a long time ago, Mr. Kennedy."

Kennedy thanked him with a twenty-dollar tip, and left.

Looking for breakfast, Kennedy spotted a coffee shop almost directly opposite Luigi's, so he went in.

"Howdy. How can I hep you, honey?" said a waitress wearing a mid-thigh pink dress with dancer's black stockings.

Kennedy almost laughed at the greeting. The waitress was at least sixty, but dressed like a woman a third that age.

"How about two eggs over easy, bacon crisp, rye toast," he said, taking a stool at the counter. "Coffee first."

"You betcha."

The waitress quickly poured a cup of steaming American coffee and placed it before him, along with a small pitcher of cream. She wrote up his order and gave it to the kitchen, then returned to the counter. Kennedy was the only customer in the place, and she obviously wanted to talk.

"You're not from these parts are you, hon?"

"How can you tell?" Kennedy said, laughing.

"That suit you're wearin' is a dead giveaway. You look like a banker or sumpin' worse, maybe a undertaker."

"I'm a private investigator," he said, laughing again.

"Oh, no! I ain't done nothin' wrong, honey," she said, chuckling to herself, "though I wish I had."

A bell dinged at the kitchen window. Kennedy's order was up, and the waitress went and brought back a plate of eggs, bacon, and toast.

"Don't worry," Kennedy said, "I'm not investigating you."

"Well then, who are you investigatin'?"

"A couple who used to live here, about ten or twelve years ago."

"Did they do sumpin' bad?"

"Absolutely not. They're nice people, as far as I know. In fact, maybe you know them."

"I still got a purty good memory, Mr. Investigator-man. Try me."

"Were this restaurant and you around here then?"

"Damn betcha!"

"Well, it's a Dante Montepulciano, and a Caprice Montepulciano, or maybe Caprice Jordan Taylor. They lived here in Rifle for a few years. He was Italian, but she was American. Ring any bells?"

"Did she have red hair?" said the waitress.

"Yes, flaming red. She would have been thirty-something, maybe forty."

"You betcha, honey. I remember them real well. The Italian was a sweetie. But the woman could be a real b— Well, she had a temper. Never knew their names. Yessiree, he was a sweet guy—spoke beautiful English, broken, but real pretty sounding. I remember he had a big ol' scar acrost his head—from the war, he said. Used to ask me for aspirins, said he got real bad headaches all the time. Why you askin'?"

"I'm trying to establish whether they were married or not," Kennedy said, trying his best not to look too interested.

"We all thought they were married. They lived over on the north edge of town. Good citizens, as far I could tell, 'cept maybe for that temper."

Kennedy mopped up the last of his eggs with a crust of toast. "Thank you, ma'am," he said, leaving a ten-dollar tip on the counter. His next stop would be the public records office.

Kennedy stepped into the Rifle branch of the Garfield County public records office and went to a service window that looked like a bank teller's cage. He explained that he wanted to search property records, and was directed to a room down a hallway. He walked down the hall and stopped at the third door on his left. It was marked PROPERTY RECORDS, so he entered.

"Can I help you?" an overweight woman behind the counter said.

"Yes. My name is Jeff Kennedy, and I'm a private investigator from Santa Barbara, California—here's my card. I'm looking for the original deed to a house here in Rifle under the name of Montepulciano. Here's the address."

"I can look it up for you right now."

"It was ten or twelve years ago."

The woman went over to rows of filing cabinets, pulled open a drawer, and began to search. A few minutes later she returned holding a thin sheaf of papers.

"Here it is," she said. "Mrs. Caprice Montepulciano and Mr. Dante Montepulciano. Her name comes first. Funny."

"Well, I'll be damned," said Kennedy, feigning surprise. "Can I take a look at that?"

Kennedy felt a jolt of adrenalin surge through him as he held the actual deed in his hand. He'd seen the microfiche in Denver, but this was the real thing. And it was indeed signed "Caprice Montepulciano" and "Dante Montepulciano," joint owners.

"Can I get copy of this?" he asked.

"Of course," the clerk said. She disappeared into the next room, and returned a few moments later with the copy.

"Thank you, thank you very much," Kennedy said. "Do you also keep marriage certificates here?"

"Yes, for marriages that take place in Rifle. But those would be in a different department, down the hall. Second door on your right."

Kennedy thanked the woman again, and moved on.

In an office marked personal records, Kennedy asked a clerk to search from 1961 through 1964 for the name Montepulciano. After a long wait, the clerk returned empty handed. "I'm sorry, sir. I can't find anything. I looked twice. I'm sorry."

That was a disappointment. A marriage certificate would have enabled him to give John Butler a report all tied up with a bow.

But he did have the deed to the house, and that would please Butler. He walked across town to the address listed on the deed and took pictures of the house. Clients always appreciated pictures. The house was nothing special: rather small, clapboard exterior, surrounded by a picket fence. Still occupied. Kennedy took pictures of the exterior and neighborhood then headed back to the hotel.

In his room, Kennedy made notes on the information he'd received from Luigi, the hotel owner, and the waitress. There was no question that Caprice and Dante had jointly owned the house together, and that they and the community had considered them husband and wife—their signatures on the deed showed that plainly. But other questions popped into Kennedy's mind. Had Caprice put up all the money? Had she acted freely? How long had they lived in Colorado?

The next day, Jeff Kennedy flew back to Santa Barbara. He finished his report on the plane, and went straight to John Butler's office and turned it in. Butler especially appreciated the copy of the deed; the recollections of the locals weren't solid evidence of anything, but they were welcome in confirming what was on paper in black and white.

As soon as Kennedy left, Butler pressed the intercom button for his secretary. "Ms. Copeland, book me two seats, business class, to Milan, Italy, for next Thursday. It will be me and Guy Bray from Pueblo Hospital."

"Will that be on United Airlines, Mr. Butler?"

"Yes, to New York; then book us on Alitalia, please, to Milan."

"Yes, sir."

"Thank you, Ms. Copeland. I'll phone Bray and let him know."

II: Milan

5

Flying to Milan

TO CELEBRATE THEIR upgrade from business class to first class, they each ordered a single malt scotch, The Macallan. They clinked their glasses.

Then Bray recounted the charity lawyers' meeting. He started by complimenting Butler's communication of his discoveries as they were made. It made Bray's job as lead counsel for the charities easier. He agreed with Butler's actions, conclusions, and recommendations. He thought Butler was doing a good job handling Caprice's estate.

On the plane to Milan, Butler showed Bray the subpoena he had obtained from a California court, ordering Dante Montepulciano to attend a deposition to be held in the city of Milan, at the offices of the law firm of Galileo & Rossi, the firm that had represented Dante in the past. As the plane approached the city, they studied a map of Milan and traced the route to Galileo & Rossi.

"Did Peter Stern attend the charities' meeting?" Butler asked. "I hope to God he's not coming to Milan."

—⚏—

I WAS SITTING, relaxing. I felt tired from a soccer class for 14 year olds. They are good boys and I enjoyed teaching their physical education class.

The phone rang. It was my brother, Guido.

"NO, Peter Stern was not allowed to attend," Bray said. "After the previous day's antics, he was *persona non grata*. Jack Orso from the art museum volunteered to meet with him and tell him the truth—he was disruptive and unwelcome. And as far as Orso is concerned, it's the lawyers' work, not Peter's. Nothing good could come from his attending the meeting. So Peter had to acquiesce, but only after whining about how much Caprice hated him and conspired to not sell any of her shares of Jordan Oil back to her father.

"What have you found out about the husband?" Bray asked.

Butler looked Bray fully in the eyes.

"That bad?" said Bray, expecting to be disappointed.

"Mr. Montepulciano," Butler said, "is the common law husband of Mrs. Caprice Taylor under Colorado law."

"Really."

"Damn, we're in a hard spot, John," Bray said wondering what actions to take. "Do you have much information on him? Like where lives? His current circumstances?"

—∭—

I ANSWERED the phone.

"Mr. John Butler is flying to Milan to see you," Guido said.

"Yes, we all like him, Dante."

"Do you think something is wrong with Caprice"?

"Your lawyer, Mr. Rossi, says the American lawyers have not told him anything," Guido said. "Don't jump to such conclusions. It may just be another estate quarrel. It wouldn't be the first time."

"Are other lawyers coming?" I said.

"Rossi did not say."

I hung up the telephone and left my apartment. I needed to walk. I found the call disturbing. All of my old emotions were beginning to surface and I felt sad and I did not know why.

"NOT much," said Butler. "We're not sure where Dante lives. We do know that his lawyer is a partner in a good firm in Milan. And for years—nine, I think—Dante sent one postcard per year, which Caprice kept. Each postcard arrived before her birthday, wishing her a happy birthday and each is signed 'Love, Dante.'"

"What makes Orso think that Caprice and Dante were married?" said Bray.

"Orso is a sharp lawyer," Butler said. "A legal spouse could take the whole inheritance. We still don't know if they were really married. But Jeff Kennedy couldn't find any documentation indicating Mrs. Taylor was married—to anybody."

"Can we rely on that?"

Butler laughed, spilling some scotch.

"Hardly," he said. "Kennedy is an ethical investigator. We can trust him to work hard and tell the truth. But he doesn't know the whole truth. Nobody does, except for Mrs. Taylor, and she's no longer available to tell us."

"This guy Montepulciano sounds like trouble to me," said Bray.

Butler tapped Bray's wrist. "Wrong, Guy," John said. "Mr. Montepulciano is an amazing and honest man."

"That's no help," said Bray smiling.

"Everything is a surprise with Montepulciano."

"I hope there's room to maneuver."

"You'll find a way."

—∿—

BY THE TIME I finished my walk, I was worrying that gangsters might kill me. American Mafia! So I telephoned Guido.

"Yes?" said Guido.

"I'm afraid that the American Mafia might kill me."

"Dante, I was told by your lawyer that Mr. Butler wanted to meet with you. So don't drive yourself crazy. Just wait and meet with Butler. You know that ever since your war wound, things like this upset you too much. Right? Mr. Butler is your friend and you went to America and visited him at his home Andrew met his wife and children. Please recall you had a very good time. You can trust Mr. Butler."

"SO, what course of action did you recommend the charities take?" Butler asked.

"It's hard to know what to do, John. We don't know whether or not they were married, or if it was by common-law. We don't know what state or country they might have been married in, so we don't know what legal jurisdiction we're dealing with. We don't know whether we're dealing with American law, or Italian. We are in total ignorance."

"So how did the meeting go?"

"Each lawyer was given a copy of the will, with a face sheet summarizing the beneficiaries' portions of the estate. I reminded them that, with the exception of Clarissa Crane's gift of two million dollars and the house, all other gifts are *conditional*—subject to a settlement with Mrs. Taylor's supposed husband.

"The charity lawyers were very upset," Bray continued. "Who wouldn't be upset? They're asking for a deposition. They want to question this husband—if he ever existed and if he's still alive—and see if they can get him out of the will."

"Guy, I've already explained to them—"reported" is a better term—that they are facing a Colorado common law husband and wife issue,"" said Butler, using a bit of a whine in his voice, which he hated.

"I get it, John," Bray said, "it's just that they don't. Once they understand that Montepulciano is on firm territory, they'll be careful."

"I hope so," said John.

"The deposition is the road to take," Bray said.

"Isn't the stock moving up?"

"Over 40 million now."

———❧———

"YES, I sometimes exaggerate, that's true. But I have a feeling something is wrong. Rossi's telephone call bothers me."

"I don't understand you. All Rossi said was that Butler is coming to Milan.

"I still think the American Mafia is coming to kill me."

"That's rubbish, Dante."

"SKIP to the conclusion, Guy. What course of action did they decide on?" said Butler.

"Two things," Bray said. "First, find Dante Montepulciano, if he exists, and find out if he can document that he and Mrs. Taylor were indeed married. If so, since he has a claim on the estate, we would need to negotiate a settlement and quitclaim with the guy."

"How much are the charities willing to settle on Montepulciano if he doesn't have documents of a marriage?"

"They thought a flat five hundred thousand dollars," Guy said. "It's generous, but we're guessing it would get him out of the picture."

"It's at least a twenty-five-million-dollar estate," said Butler. "They're low-balling him. What if he *is* a real husband?" Butler added.

"If he is the husband, we'll agree to settle—say for five percent of the estate. In return, the charity lawyers will want him to sign a quitclaim giving up any future rights to the estate. You know, the usual. And they'd want him to agree that the State of California is the jurisdiction governing any and all agreements—not Italy."

"If his lawyers take it to the state of Colorado, he might win. Do the charity lawyers understand that?"

—⟁—

IN the moment, I regretted ever knowing Caprice.

I never sought her wealth.

Caprice believed me—it was a foundation of her trust in me. Most other people gravitated to her because of her wealth. Like it or not, she was always the uncomfortable center of social attention.

The daily gossip press hounded her. She fled the gossip, hating the mostly made-up or exaggerated stories. Yet they were right about her alcoholism and self-destructive ways.

IS that it, Guy?" Butler said.

Bray nodded. "Yes. That's it."

"Warn them against doing something stupid," Butler said, wagging his empty drink glass.

They ordered a second round, and talked about other things.

—w—

AFTER hanging up from Guido, I sat staring at the phone.

I was unhappy and felt morose.

Something wasn't right. I remembered that the last time Caprice and I were together, she was not well—thus the Golden Pact, which by itself upset me.

The Mafia was surely coming to threaten me, at least hurt me— maybe even kill me.

I decided to go for a walk in the public park beside my small apartment.

6

Sightings

BUTLER AND BRAY arrived the next morning in Milan, five months to the day after the reading of the will. They planned to stay two weeks, hoping to find and meet Dante. Earlier, they had again contacted Dante's Italian attorney, Adam Rossi, but his news was disappointing. He hadn't done much. In fact, his hunt for Dante amounted to a phone chat with Dante's brother Guido, and not much more. There was a lot of work to do.

—∞—

I MOVED in with my brother Guido and told no one. Guido was exasperated with me, but he and his wife allowed me to stay.

I also told the administrators of my school of the possible threat of the American Mafia. That upset them. They wondered what I'd done to deserve such a threat. I had never mentioned Caprice Taylor to them. For the first time in my years of teaching, they began to wonder about my past.

I'm not sure when I began worrying about the Mafia. I think it was when caprice and I were staying in Colorado. She told me about how much money she was worth. I was stunned and worried. I assured her that I did not want money but that I love her and simply enjoyed her company. Actually, that was one of the reasons why she trusted me. She took me at her word and we seldom talked about the problem of having great wealth. We lived simply.

ROSSI'S inaction was a serious problem, because Butler's investigator had discovered evidence in Colorado, which, if confirmed, could cause the entire estate to go to Dante. Bray was alarmed—as were the charities' other lawyers.

So, with Butler and Bray now in Milan, things changed dramatically at the law firm of Galileo & Rossi. First, Adam Rossi got busy tracing Dante's whereabouts—with the understanding that his firm would represent Dante's interests. They would charge handsomely, too—top rates—for this was a high-stakes game.

It helped that Rossi was bilingual in Italian and English. Together, he and the two American lawyers paid a visit the government records office in Milan, and found the Montepulciano family records, including Dante's birth certificate.

As Rossi explained to the Americans, in Italy a birth certificate is much more than the simple document it is in the United States. It can be updated throughout one's life, noting such milestones as marriage.

And so, to the Americans' surprise, on Dante's birth certificate, alongside his name, in the column for spouses, was written *nessuna,* "no one," meaning that he was not married.

But that wasn't necessarily conclusive. As Rossi further explained, marriage records were not always kept here in the central registry, but were more often kept by local parishes. And that introduced another issue: the number of parishes in the city of Milan was enormous, well into the hundreds.

—⁓—

I TOOK a bus across town and telephoned Mr. Rossi from a pay phone. He immediately demanded to know where I was, saying Butler was in his office. Would I like to speak to him?

I dropped the phone and ran for the bus. I fled back to my brother's house.

I was certain the American Mafia was now in Milan.

Dear Caprice, what is happening? I haven't wanted your money. Why are these people here and what do they want with me?

BUTLER looked at Adam Rossi in disbelief. "He just phoned you, and then hung up?"

"Don't worry, we'll find him."

"Let's find his marriage certificate," Butler said. "First things first." Bray agreed.

After thinking a moment, Rossi said, "For starters, let's try a church not far from us, San Giorgio al Palazzo. 'Palazzo' because a cardinal used to use it as his home. I understand Dante and Caprice attended services there from time to time. Maybe there's some history there."

Butler grinned at Bray, and both agreed.

So the three lawyers drove through Milan's rain-washed streets to San Giorgio al Palazzo to search its parish records.

—〰—

I WONDERED whether John Butler might have written to me about Caprice and his trip to Milan. So I went to the post office to check my mail. So as not to be observed by the Mafia, I dressed differently than usual, and wore dark glasses.

In the past, Caprice would have protected me. She wouldn't have wanted this trouble for me. She knew that when I was anxious, my thinking and actions were often illogical—like the time we visited the Grand Canyon in Arizona. I couldn't approach the rim. I was afraid of heights. I froze and then ran back to the car and got back in, shaking. Caprice laughed and laughed, but it wasn't funny—only then did she realize my fear was real, and she apologized.

ON the way, Rossi explained to the two Americans that the church had been built to preserve the Catholic name of St. George, and been built in the time of the early Roman emperors. The Cardinal's namesake palace no longer existed; only the church itself remained. It was relatively small, but its baroque façade stood out, even in the small crowded streets of this district of Milan. With much difficulty they found a parking space, walked back several blocks, and entered.

Rossi approached one of the priests and spoke to him in Italian. "Excuse me, Father, but we would like to look at your parish's marriage records."

"And who are you?" said the priest, also in Italian.

"Excuse me; please forgive my lack of manners. My name is Adam Rossi, and I'm with a law firm here in Milan called Galileo and Rossi. These are two American lawyers from Santa Barbara, California." He drew a business card from his pocket and politely offered it to the priest.

—⁘—

I LOOKED around the cavernous interior of the post office for American Mafia. I saw no suspicious characters. Posters of Sophia Loren were pasted on the walls.

I cautiously went to my mailbox, unlocked it, and looked inside.

Nothing. If anything was wrong with Caprice, I was sure Mr. John Butler would have written to me. Caprice had depended upon Mr. Butler for estate matters—even for guidance on our Golden Pact, our *Atto Solenne.*

But still the Mafia might be looking for me. I left quickly. I stayed in the cover of crowds wherever possible. I took buses and sat in the rear on the way back to Guido's house.

"I SEE," said the priest, examining the card. "Galileo? That's a famous name."

"We are looking for a marriage record for a Mr. Dante Valentino Caesar Montepulciano and an American lady named Caprice Jordan Taylor. May we look at your marriage records?

"What does this concern?"

"The estate of Ms. Taylor, or Mrs. Montepulciano, if they were married. She passed away recently. We think they might have been married in a church here in Milan."

"I'm so sorry. The records are downstairs in a vault. Someone there will help you."

The three lawyers thanked the priest and went downstairs, where they met another priest, and Rossi explained their mission again. "May we have a look?" he asked.

"Yes, but for what year?" asked the priest.

"We think they may have married sometime between nineteen sixty-four and nineteen sixty-eight. We would like to search those years."

They spent most of the afternoon poring over old church records written by hand, but all to no avail.

—m—

FOR the next few days I asked Madam Rosa, my housekeeper and friend, to fetch my mail. She did so, and reported that three men appeared to be lingering by my post box—and two of them looked like Americans! She couldn't be certain because of the distance they kept from her, and she could not describe them well.

Three men! Terrible! The American Mafia had sent three men.

When Guido returned that night, I told him Madam Rosa's story.

"Guido, I was right all along! The American Mafiosi have arrived, and they're looking for me."

"Dante, calm down. I still don't believe you."

BUTLER, Bray, and Rossi found nothing at San Giorgio. They found nothing anywhere. For days they went from one parish church to another. It was the same routine over and over. A dozen parishes later, and with scores more all over the city, the three lawyers realized the futility of their approach.

But they had another lead. In Caprice's accounting records Butler had found a post office box address for Dante: Box 356, Milano Centrale. From Galileo & Rossi they sent a letter requesting that Dante contact Adam Rossi.

Then the three lawyers staked out the post office, waiting for Dante to show up. Instead, a woman who looked like a housekeeper checked the box one afternoon. Could they have the wrong address? Perhaps Dante had given up the box, and it had a new owner? The trio were stumped.

On their last day in Milan, Butler and Bray were bidding goodbye to Adam Rossi when Rossi's phone rang. Rossi answered, listened, and began gesturing wildly to Butler and Bray. It was Dante!

"People are out to kill me," Dante whispered into the phone. "I hear there are three American Mafia assassins."

"No, no!" Rossi shouted into the phone. "They are here to *help* you! Listen to me. I'm sorry to tell you this over the telephone. Mrs. Taylor has passed away. We are trying to reach you in order to settle her estate. Mr. Montepulciano? Are you still there? Hello?"

A long, loud wail came from the receiver. Even Butler and Bray heard it.

"Mr. Montepulciano, are you still there? Hello? Hello?"

—⚌—

I DROPPED the phone and screamed with pain at that news.

Oh my God, Caprice was dead! Guilt overwhelmed me, because in all of the years since we parted I still loved her—deeply—and yet I had not seen her in all these years.

My knees buckled, and I collapsed onto the floor.

THE GOLDEN PACT

ROSSI hung up the phone. He told Butler and Bray that he would talk with Dante later and get back to them.

He also told them that the day before he had located a man named Guido Montepulciano, who turned out to be Dante's brother. Guido also lived in Milan. Rossi would try to enlist Guido in their cause.

"After you two leave for Santa Barbara, I will meet with Guido. I was told that he is approachable."

"That's good," said Butler, "but we still need to have someone authorized under California law to serve a subpoena on Dante to appear at a deposition. That was the purpose of this trip. We'll have to come back. I'll let you know when. Until then, let's stay in touch."

As events unfolded, Adam Rossi learned that Dante was working as a soccer coach and teaching philosophy at a Catholic school in Milan. Guido agreed to set up a meeting between Butler, Bray, and Dante. Guido warned Rossi that Dante feared being assassinated by the Mafia, and that he thought the Americans were Mafiosi.

—◊◊—

MY heart was broken. I had failed to deliver on my part of the Golden Pact made privately between Caprice and me.

And now Caprice was gone.

TRUE to his word, with Guido's help Rossi had arranged a face-to-face meeting between himself, Dante, and Guido.

But the meeting never took place. At the last minute, Dante cancelled, with no explanation.

—✺—

MY health has been deteriorating for years, and I wasn't feeling good. I just wanted to sleep. My head ached terribly.

But I kept recalling the pact I made with Caprice, and I was depressed by her death. Had she died alone? Or had her companion Clarissa been with her? Did Caprice die suddenly, or had she suffered a long illness? Perhaps that's why she never returned my postcards—she had a chronic illness. So many questions with no answers.

Miserable, I got into bed and pulled the covers over me and fell asleep, grateful that at least my brother Guido was always nearby.

I awoke several hours later determined to call Adam Rossi and find out what was happening.

Mr. Rossi invited me to visit him at his office. He asked me bring Guido too. I agreed. I trusted Rossi when he told me that one of the Americans was John Butler, because whenever Caprice made changes to her will (which was fairly often), Butler had helped her. At first she had worked with Mr. Winslow, but he later handed her account to Mr. Butler.

I never understood why Caprice included me in such meetings—I was penniless, and she knew that I didn't want her money. She said it was because I was her husband. I said I was happy being her husband, but I wanted no part of her family or her wealth.

She always told me not to worry. She said she intended to give her money to a hospital, an art museum, a botanic garden, and a museum of natural history.

Caprice's explanation always settled me down.

THE GOLDEN PACT

The Chase

ONE MONTH LATER, Butler and Bray were back in Milan. They had obtained a subpoena requiring Dante to appear for a deposition at the offices of Galileo & Rossi.

Butler asked Rossi to bring them up to date regarding Dante.

"After you left Milan on your last visit," Rossi said, "I phoned Guido, Dante's brother, and asked if I could come and visit with Dante. He agreed. When we met, I apologized to Dante for telling him about Caprice's death over the telephone. At that time I was able to have a constructive short meeting with him and I explained the legal process to him. For some reason he brought up the American Mafia."

Rossi learned from Guido where Dante was teaching. Now, with no date, time, or place for a rescheduled meeting, Butler and Bray decided to go to the school and find Dante there, and serve the subpoena. Rossi agreed to join them.

WHEREVER the Americans went, my neighborhood friends informed me. These people loved me. The black Mercedes sedan the Americans drove was conspicuous to everyone in our modest neighborhood. The entire district gossiped about it. Definitely a Mafia car! In my ghetto of Milan, people walked, took buses, rode bicycles, or drove motor scooters and compact little Fiats, not "black Marias." The trattoria owners alerted me when they saw the car; my postman told me the Americans had been seen outside the post office; even the local police alerted me.

ROSSI told the two American lawyers that their plan was all wrong. It went against Italian protocol. It was sure to frighten Dante. They ignored him.

The black Mercedes sedan skidded to a neck-snapping halt on the wet cobblestones before the entrance to Villa Massini, a decayed old Romanesque ruin of former wealth, splendor, and ecclesiastical power. Some four hundred years earlier, it had belonged to a Cardinal Massini—then a powerful figure in the Catholic Church in Milan. Some people still called the old estate Villa Massini. Now it belonged to the state, and it was used as a public school. And it was here that Dante Montepulciano taught philosophy and physical education, as Guido had told Rossi.

As he unbuckled his seat belt, John Butler rubbed the back of his neck and ruefully wondered why Italians insisted on driving as though they were contestants in a grand prix. What an insane national habit. He was convinced that he would die in a ghastly accident before he could get back to Santa Barbara, where the major threat of injury came from forgetful senior citizens running stoplights. Santa Barbara's worst traffic problems paled in comparison to Italian every-day driving habits.

Once outside the limousine, Rossi stretched, looked around, and cheerily announced in Italian, "Mr. Butler, we have arrived—at the school where I am told the Professor teaches. Follow me."

—⟋⟍—

I HEARD car tires squeal on the wet cobblestones.

I sat very still in my office, and listened. But there were no sounds of footsteps in the ancient corridor. If I heard footsteps—and the old flooring groaned and squeaked no matter how lightly one walked—I was prepared to slip out the back and escape.

ROSSI recounted the school building's history to his American colleagues. He loved Italian history.

"It was built in the fifteenth century," he said. "There's a small church over there, next to the main building, the villa. The wealthy would build chapels right on their own lands—to buy their way into Purgatory, so to speak. Of course, the aristocrats were corrupt and the Church itself was corrupt. It still is," he grumbled. "If Christ himself returned, he would be angry—like when he cast the moneylenders from the temple. More than just the Cardinal Massini would dance in Hell! The entire bureaucracy would be cast into the flames." He mused and laughed.

"Anyway, Cardinal Massini is long dead, and today the villa is a school for working class children. I have to admit, the Church has some of the best schools in the country, so not all is lost. At least something worthwhile has come of this place."

Rossi opened a large black umbrella against the light rain, and escorted the two American lawyers to the entrance. He ushered them through the massive, weathered, wooden front door and into a cavernous, high-ceilinged hallway that felt damp and cold and smelled of mildew.

Rossi went to the directory in a glass case along the wall. "The administrative offices are on the third floor. I don't see an elevator, and there probably isn't one. We'll have to take the stairs."

—✠—

I KEPT still, listening for footsteps in the corridor.

I watched my fingers turn white as they gripped the edge of the desk. My heart was beating fast, and I could hear myself breathe. I don't remember ever being this tense, not even in North Africa.

BUTLER wasn't too surprised by the lack of an elevator, but he wondered if the building even had central heating as he squinted up into the dank and chilly darkness of the stone stairwell. Worn steps climbed steeply up in a narrow spiral. "I wonder why administration isn't on the first floor," he said aloud. He couldn't imagine a sixty-year-old man like Dante having to climb the steep, narrow stairs several times every day. Butler was years younger, and fairly fit, but even he felt the exertion.

All of them arrived at the second floor out of breath. Rossi leaned against the stairwell wall, drew a handkerchief from his jacket, and wiped his brow. He was out of wind and perspiring despite the hall's chill dankness. "My god," he said. His voice echoed against the stone walls. "One more step and I would have had to wave you by." He again mopped his forehead with his handkerchief. "Montepulciano had better be here, or my widow will sue him for causing my death. How in hell does a wounded war veteran climb these stairs every day?"

"I'm winded too," Butler confessed, "and I jog regularly. I don't know how he does it. I'm impressed. He must be fit."

"Exactly."

—⁓—

DEAR Caprice, I prayed in Italian, *if you can hear me, save me!*

I do not want her money, but I do want the recipients of her money to honor her gifts. So far none of the lawyers had mentioned that the charities were going to honor her name.

I must stand up for Caprice, my heart, my love.

In truth I was still grieving. Even confused.

Although I was a battle-tested soldier, I was finding these circumstances—and Mrs. Taylor's death—emotional, especially the thought that these visitors might be American Mafia people in disguise.

A FEW yards down the corridor a dim light could be seen coming from the nearly opaque windows of a large room, which proved to be the administrative office. The room was cluttered with old worn desks and chairs and rows of oak filing cabinets. File folders and papers were stacked everywhere. Nothing was modern, including the thin middle-aged woman behind the counter. She wore a shapeless woolen sweater to protect her from the damp chill, and she stood there reading some papers and smoking a cigarette. The smoke hung around her like fog in a valley. She ignored the three lawyers and continued to read, seemingly absorbed by the documents.

After a long, silent wait, Rossi coughed. The sound echoed around the room, announcing his impatience and irritation at being kept waiting by a mere clerk. But the woman just kept reading.

"Madam, excuse me," he said finally.

She ignored him.

Several seconds passed. Rossi coughed again.

"I'm busy," she said sternly, not looking up. "Can't you see that?"

"Excuse me," Rossi said, feeling like a disciplined youngster. He controlled his urge to shout at her. They would need her cooperation, not obdurate enmity.

But the woman just kept on reading.

Rossi turned to Butler and whispered, saying, "Goddamn bureaucrat."

"She's perfect," Butler grinned. "Successfully holding off three lawyers who have no scheduled appointment."

"She's definitely the boss," Bray said with a twinkle in his eyes.

WHAT was taking them so long? I shuffled the folders on my desk, stacking them differently each time. I listened for footsteps coming down the corridor.

I had told our Deputy Administrator to sound the warning button under my desk. That would give me a head start.

We also discussed what I would do.

I simply said I would flee.

SHE ignored them for what seemed an eternity, puffing nonchalantly on her cigarette. Finally she dropped the papers on top of a desk and looked up at Rossi, acknowledging his presence.

"Yes, sir, what do you want?"

"Madam, my name is Rossi. Adam Rossi. We would like to visit with a teacher named Mr. Montepulciano."

"Montepulciano?" she said, waving a thin, pale hand. The tone of her voice indicated that Montepulciano might be an alien from another planet, someone she didn't know.

"Yes, Mr. Montepulciano."

Silence.

This had gone far enough. Rossi decided it was time to use some authority. He explained that he was a lawyer living and practicing law in Milan. He introduced the two American lawyers. Finally, he explained that he had talked with her District Administrator, who had arranged for them to come to the school to meet with Montepulciano. "Your District Administrator told me he worked here and gave permission to visit," Rossi said. "Has the District Administrator called you and explained this?"

"Oh, you must be referring to *Professor* Montepulciano," she said while inspecting the well-dressed lawyer from Milan.

"Excuse me. *Professor* Montepulciano," Rossi agreed.

"So you're the one who called the District Administrator?" she said in a reprimanding tone, making clear her annoyance at Rossi for going over her head.

—m—

I STOOD up and put on my coat so that I would be ready to escape and evade them.

"NO, excuse me, please, Madam Deputy Administrator, but someone in my firm called. I myself did not—"

"You don't dial your own calls? Never mind, it isn't important," she said. A bony right hand with cigarette-stained fingers fluttered in a tired gesture, dismissing his transgression, tossing Rossi's ignorance of her importance into an overfull psychological dustbin of discourtesies, slights, and other misdemeanors committed by countless other ignorant, thoughtless citizens. She was used to it, and his was just another.

"Please excuse me, Madam Deputy Director. I had no intention to be rude."

"And I am an *assistant* administrator—not a deputy administrator."

She ignored his attempt to pacify her. She didn't believe him.

"And the Americans?" she said, interrupting, pointing specifically at John Butler.

"Yes, we are together. They have come all the way from America to meet Mr.—*Professor* Montepulciano, and—

"Do you have identification, sirs?" she said, reaching out her hand, demanding cooperation, wiggling her long, thin, tobacco-stained, fingers that badly needed a manicure. "We must protect our school and its children."

Butler and Bray quickly produced their passports and handed them to her. Rossi presented his business card.

—⚭—

I SAT back down, but this time while I waited I sipped on a cup of espresso that I had made a little while ago. It was still warm.

A buzzer sounded from the administrator's office. I jumped, partly in dread. It was our prearranged signal that the Americans were in her office.

"MADAM Assistant Administrator," Rossi said, "is the Professor in?"

"Is he in any trouble?" she asked.

"No."

"Then, if there is no trouble, may I enquire as to the nature of this unusual visit? After all, isn't it unusual for a professor to be disturbed during working hours? You could have arranged a meeting after school hours. Right?"

Rossi smiled politely. This woman was the best bureaucrat he had ever met, and twice as irritable. He began to admire her.

"Madam," he said, "my firm has been employed by Mr. Butler to find Professor Montepulciano and arrange a meeting with him. It concerns the execution of a will, the settlement of an American estate. That is the nature of our visit."

"I see," said the woman. "Then why didn't you say so at the beginning?"

Rossi was exasperated, but he said nothing. Behind his back, Butler grinned, admiring this amazing little Italian misanthrope.

She let several moments of silence pass.

"Professor Montepulciano is not an easy man to meet," said Butler. "Every time we have tried to meet him, he's been unavailable."

"That's unfortunate," said the Assistant Administrator, thinking their approach to Mr. Montepulciano was not tasteful.

"Yes," said Butler, speaking Italian, "we hope to meet him here at your school. At least we can reacquaint ourselves."

Not if I have anything to do with it, thought Angela to herself.

"May we see him?" Rossi said. "Now."

The administrator needed to delay to give Montepulciano more time.

ANGELA'S buzzer sounded again in my office—two buzzes close together—announcing that visitors soon would be coming down to my basement office—or some similar intrusion.

I decided to leave as soon as I heard footsteps on the stairs.

I would go out through the back door of the gymnasium, which led to a small soccer field and to a back alley behind a row of shops. My idea was to become lost in the shopping traffic.

"OH, you speak Italian," the Assistant Administrator said to Butler, noting his excellent use of her language. He spoke Italian with almost no trace of an American accent. "You speak good Italian, sir."

"Thank you."

"You're welcome," she said, examining his American looks through a veil of exhaled smoke: the short hair, scrubbed features, and the cuffs of his slacks. *They're all the same*, she decided, smiling to herself.

"Where did you learn to speak our language?" said Angela.

"At university in northern California," Butler said.

"Well, you speak like you were raised in Italy," she said warming up.

John appreciated her comments.

"I mean what I say, sir."

"Thank you."

Rossi decided to get on with things. It was important to get their meeting with Montepulciano under way.

"Madam, if you would be so kind. My senior partner, Mr. Galileo himself, phoned the District Administrator. We were instructed to come here to the school and to introduce ourselves to you. I'm told that you will let us meet with the professor."

"I see."

"Did the Administrator phone you?"

"Yes, yes, of course he called," she answered with a scowl.

"We are here to meet the Professor," Rossi said again, producing a letter from the Administrator. The woman read it.

The woman returned the Americans' passports, saying, "You have my permission to meet him. His office is near the gymnasium, which is in the basement. He is there now. He is in every day at this hour, preparing for tomorrow's classes."

—m—

I OPENED the door enough to peek down the long corridor that the men would have to walk. I left my coffee and closed the door as quietly as possible. I started my escape.

"THANK you, Madam," said Rossi. "How do we get to his office?

"Excuse me, gentlemen. Of course, you do not know the way. Come with me. I will show you where to find him."

They followed her to the stairs. She pointed downward and said, "Professor Montepulciano's office is in the basement. You can't miss it. The only way to it is by these stairs. Just open that door—it's not locked—and walk down. His office is number nine-B," She tightly wrapped her woolen sweater around her and shivered with the chill.

—⁊⁊⁊—

CAPRICE would have loved this scene. Always paranoid, she could make wonderful fun of herself. In fact, she must have been part Italian—she loved farce. Both of us loved farce. She would love this and howl with laughter.

Not me. I hoped the American Mafia wouldn't catch me. To be captured would be an inglorious ending for an Italian officer. I must live up to the medal for valor my country gave me. How inglorious to be murdered by American Mafia thugs.

Having made my way to the Gymnasium, I peeked back out of its door and listened for footsteps descending. I heard voices but they were too far away to understand. Then things began to change rapidly.

Suddenly I heard steps—many steps, approaching in a hurry. I ran down the hall into the empty gymnasium, crossed the basketball court, and quickly opened the back door to the soccer field, and stepped out into the rain. The grass was wet.

WHEN the three lawyers reached the basement they found themselves in a maze of hallways and corridors. Rossi looked at Butler and Bray, shrugged, and said, "Okay, fellows, let's see if we can find our wealthy gym teacher—the one who may or may not have been the husband of Caprice Jordan Taylor."

"That shouldn't be much trouble," Bray said. "Dante's office number is nine-B. And the doors are clearly numbered"

"So they are," Butler observed, "but there seems to be no order to them."

Somewhere down the corridor a door slammed shut. The lawyers looked at each other.

"That was a door," Rossi said. "Did that goddamn woman phone ahead and warn him?"

"Follow that noise!" Butler said. "That's our only clue."

The chase was on.

"This client is driving me crazy," said Rossi, cursing as he ran.

"He must be in damn good physical condition," Butler said.

"I hope not," Rossi grumbled. "But we'll soon see. Look there, that must be his office. That one at the end of this hall. That's nine-B. Let's go!"

"Are you sure?" Bray asked.

"No, but I'm sure I'll give up if it's not."

They stopped in front of an office door numbered 9B. Underneath the number was a sign holder containing a yellowed nameplate: PROFESSOR DANTE V. S. MONTEPULCIANO. The door was closed.

—⚏—

I STARTED running on the edge of the soccer pitch. The soccer pitch itself was asphalt—shameful. The grass was slippery because of the rain, and I was afraid I might fall and hurt myself, but I ran as fast as I could. I wanted to escape into one of the nearby cafés close to the school.

I turned and looked back. Nobody yet.

NO one answered our first knock. Rossi knocked again, more loudly this time. "Mr. Montepulciano! It's me, Adam Rossi. May I speak with you—for only a moment? Mr. Montepulciano?"

Silence.

Rossi pushed open the door and peered cautiously into the small, cluttered office. No one was in.

"Dammit, that *was* him—he's escaped outside!" Rossi shouted.

"Quickly! We can't lose him," Butler yelled, starting down the hall and opening the door to the gym. He crossed the gym and opened a door that led out to a soccer pitch. "There, over there—by the edge of the soccer pitch."

Rossi began to run.

Butler moved ahead and was already on the soccer pitch.

Bray wished he spoke Italian.

Butler ran, the sudden daylight making him blink. Halfway across the edge of the pitch he saw Dante moving quickly, as though his very life depended on it.

They moved carefully down the stone steps, avoiding slips and falls.

"Be careful," said Rossi, "these stone steps are worn as smooth as a baby's bottom. This is an old building."

"I'm watching my step, Roberto," Butler said. "My problem is the dim light. It would be easy to break a leg down here. How are you doing Bray? Your height might be an impediment—all 6'6" of you."

"I'm fine," said Bray laughing.

"I think we're in a horror movie," Rossi said.

"I hope we find Mr. Montepulciano," Bray said.

MY heart couldn't stand much more of this.

I'd break my neck if I fell.

I looked back and saw one of the Americans closing our distance. My legs were getting wobbly. I wasn't going to make it.

"Caprice!" I screamed, not knowing why I did so. My brain was in one of its commotions, unable to be logical. I was frightened out of my wits. Again I shouted, "Caprice! Save me!"

I looked back and saw three men chasing me. The Mafia!

"MR. Montepulciano, stop!" Rossi shouted. "We only want to speak with you."

Butler ran with balance and speed, almost catching up with Dante.

"That is for certain our millionaire," Rossi panted, falling behind. He felt ungainly. "He's too shy. I'm beginning to tire of this game of cat and mouse. I'm too out of condition for this."

"Good God," Bray shouted, "what's taken hold of him? Surely he doesn't think we intend to harm him!"

"I don't know," Butler shouted back, "but I'm going after him. This nonsense has to stop." He raced away athletically, across the soccer pitch in full pursuit.

"Go, get him," Rossi shouted. "Stop him. If we don't get him this time, we may never get him."

—m—

AGAIN I looked back and saw the American Mafioso gaining on me. I couldn't see his features, because the mobster was wearing a baseball cap.

"God, help me!" I pleaded, more fearfully than at any time during the fighting in North Africa during World War II. "Caprice, save me from these bad people! I've done nothing bad. I've never done anything bad to you!"

I was a running out of strength. My lungs hurt, my legs were getting weak, and my head was beginning to ache.

This was certainly my end. How inglorious!

I hoped the schoolchildren weren't watching from the windows. They would see their teacher's humiliation. Awful!

I was out of breath. Done.

BUTLER had almost caught up with Dante, who seemed to be having difficulty keeping his footing.

Rossi too was beginning to flag. His hair was streaming, and he sputtered in Italian as he ran. He fell behind the two Americans, slackening to a pace his bulk could maintain. He was no athlete, and his awkward running gait showed it. "Damn her! Damn, damn!"

"Mr. Montepulciano, don't run!" Butler shouted ahead. "Stop! You might fall! You'll hurt yourself! We only want to ask you some questions. Stop, stop!"

Bray was close behind Butler. He said, "I'm afraid our witness is going to fall, John. This not going to end well."

"Oh my God," Butler said looking at Montepulciano ahead of them, coat flying, a man totally out of control.

"Try and get him to stop running," shouted Rossi.

Butler was not certain that Montepulciano could avoid a disaster. Bray with his long frame was running beside Butler.

But Dante heard nothing. He was in a full-blown amygdala hijack. Then suddenly he lurched, his arms flailing, his balance gone.

"Mr. Montepulciano!" Butler shouted again, wincing at the thought of Dante falling and hurting himself. In the same instant, he realized the old man wasn't going to make it. "Good God," he muttered, "He's going to fall!"

Dante lurched to the left. He glanced back behind him, his eyes wide with fear. Wildly he worked to maintain his footing, but his feet splayed out in front of him and he fell heavily to the wet grass. He groaned aloud with pain. He tried to regain his feet, desperate to resume his escape, but the his worn shoes could find no foothold in the wet grass, and he just flopped helplessly like a landed fish.

I GAVE up all hope. I was out of control.

Completely out of breath.

I was down.

Actually, I found it all humorous. I just lay there flopping around like a fish on land, feeling ridiculous, alone, and wanting to cry. But I was too proud to cry. Then a great anger welled up and took over.

"MR. Montepulciano!" Butler shouted as he got closer to the fallen man. "Oh my god, are you all right? Don't get up. Here, let me help you. Sorry, sorry—oh my god!"

The closer the American got, the greater Dante's fear. He held up his hands as if to ward off a blow.

"Don't kill me, don't kill me!" he screamed, out of breath. "I'm only a soccer coach! I haven't done anything wrong! Please, please!" He was convinced that these were his last moments of life.

Butler didn't hear his hysterical pleading. Everything was moving too fast, and his Italian couldn't keep up with Dante's panicked frenzy. He could only try to lift the old man to his feet, which caused another hysterical outburst.

Butler tried to calm their witness.

"Dante, it's me, John Butler."

Montepulciano jerked away.

"Dante, it's me, John Butler," John said in a hopefully soothing voice, but Montepulciano's eyes showed only great fear.

Guy Bray moved near Butler and tried also to lift Montepulciano.

"Sirs, no, no! Don't kill me! I am only a poor old man, not worth killing! Just a school teacher! I want nothing—no money. Please, I beg you, don't kill me!" Dante struggled to get up off the muddy wet grass and free himself from the grip of the American Mafioso.

I WATCHED the American reach inside his overcoat. I was sure he was going to take out a gun. Instead he had an envelope in his hand—an envelope, not a gun—and he was handing it to me.

An envelope? What was happening?

Then, everything changed. All of a sudden, I thought I knew this gangster. I struggled against the incoherent commotion inside my head.

The American kept saying, "Mr. Montepulciano, it's me, John Butler! You know me. We're friends. I handle Mrs. Taylor's estate."

John? John Butler? Mrs. Taylor's estate?

Then I think I momentarily fainted.

WHEN Adam Rossi caught up to Butler and the fallen school-teacher, he spoke in Italian in soft tones, and tried to comfort Dante.

"What have you done?" Rossi said to Butler.

Exasperated, Butler let go of Dante. "What in the hell is going on here?" he shot back. "I only tried to help. He fell on his ass, and I'm just trying to help him stand up. Christ, everybody in this country is a goddamned operatic drama diva." He threw up his hands in disgust.

Bray laughed at the dramatic scene. Then he asked Rossi to explain to Dante why they were here.

"Mr. Montepulciano, are you hurt?" asked Rossi.

Dante was trying to catch his breath.

"Are you hurt? Shall I call a doctor?" Rossi repeated.

Dante's eyes flicked back to Butler. "Don't let that American gangster kill me!" he blurted.

"What?" Rossi said. "What are you talking about?"

"Him, both of them, the American Mafiosi," Dante said, wagging a muddy finger between Butler and Bray.

"Sir, I see you are Italian." Dante said, gasping. "You are a countryman. I am a decorated officer of the Italian Army. I have done nothing wrong. I am only a poorly paid school teacher. Don't let the Americans kill me."

"What?" said Adam Rossi. For the first time he realized that Dante hadn't recognized them. Well, to be fair, it had been years since last they met.

Rossi began to laugh, and pointed at John Butler and Guy Bray. "These harmless gentlemen?"

—⚏—

MY lungs hurt.

I begged for my life.

I had hit the mud hard. I hurt all over, but especially the back of my head, and I was wet all over. I felt like a fool and shouted, Caprice!

"MAFIA?" Rossi was thunderstruck.

"Yes. People in town say you are American Mafiosi," Dante said, pointing at them. Oddly, though, he thought he knew the American.

Now Rossi doubled over in laughter. "So that's it. You think our American friends are Mafia and they want to kill you." He looked at Butler, laughing even more loudly. "This is a splendid farce! Professor Montepulciano thinks you are Mafia and that you are going to kill him."

Butler shook his head and frowned.

Rossi turned to Dante. "My friend, he is not Mafia. He does not want to kill you. He is a lawyer—Caprice's lawyer, John Butler. You know him, or at least you used to."

"A lawyer? Not Mafia?" The fear slowly ebbed from Dante's face. "Is this true?"

"Yes, Dante, it's true."

Now rising anger swept over Dante. "What are you all doing, scaring an old man out of his wits like this? You have no right. Look at me! I've fallen. I could have broken something. Maybe I have."

"We do not want to humiliate, Mr. Montepulciano," Bray said looking quizzically at Butler.

"I don't know what in the world he's talking about," said Butler.

Bray threw up his hands saying, "Now I've heard it all: Mafia, humiliation, and God knows what else."

Rossi asked for everyone to calm down and to let him handle matters.

SUDDENLY I remembered John Butler. Yes, the American was the lawyer Caprice used whenever she changed her will.

Now what?

I decided to play my humiliating role. Yes, this was most embarrassing.

"Mr. Butler, please forgive me. I apologize. I remember you now. Caprice thought highly of you. She trusted you."

I hadn't seen Butler since Caprice and I met with him in Basel, Switzerland—at least ten years ago.

Then I recognized Adam Rossi.

ROSSI smiled reassuringly. "Yes, Professor Montepulciano, this is all a dreadful mistake. You've taken a serious fall. I hope you haven't hurt yourself. That was a bad fall, but you didn't have to run—"

"This is not a good thing," said Dante. "I hope my students didn't see my disgrace."

"No, I don't think they saw this," Bray said. "I think they're in their classes and—"

"Who are you?" said Dante, pointing at Bray. Again he blushed at his own humiliation in front of these two Americans, and possibly in front of the entire student body as well—perhaps even the school superintendent. He imagined them all watching from the school windows.

Rossi, Butler, and Bray helped the old man to his feet, wiping mud and grass off his ruined overcoat. His pride wounded, Dante struggled to his feet and moved away from them. Then he furiously brushed and wiped at his dirty clothes.

"Leave me alone," he muttered. "I can take care of myself. It's fortunate that I'm still alive—such a scare—goddamn Americans anyway. You have no manners."

Rossi laughed again.

"What's so funny?" Dante shouted. "You didn't fall on your ass. *I* fell on my ass. Not you. Fortunately I didn't break a hip—at my age. This is awful. You have humiliated me."

—꩜—

THOUGH Rossi was Caprice's Italian estate lawyer, and though I did remember John Butler from my days with Caprice, I decided an operatic response was called for.

What did I have to lose? I had already acted like a complete fool. Here goes.

ROSSI stopped laughing and offered a face-saving remedy.

"Yes, Mr. Montepulciano," he said. "This is an embarrassing state of affairs. We apologize profoundly for chasing you. This is terrible. It is frightful that you fell. You could have seriously hurt yourself—and I trust you are not badly hurt, sir. I will pay to have your clothes cleaned. Actually, since your clothes are ruined, we will buy you new clothes—and we will replace your overcoat—immediately."

Rossi opened his wallet and counted out several large-denomination Italian lira notes, more than enough to replace the school teacher's ruined clothes. "Your health and safety are very important to us, Mr. Montepulciano. Please forgive us. We didn't intend to frighten you, or anyone else."

With a growing sense of confidence, Dante got control of himself and began to take charge of the situation. "What are you two American lawyers doing here? Everyone in town is gossiping that the Americans here are Mafiosi and intend to kill me—something about money."

Rossi stepped in to explain. "These men are my respected friends—American lawyers—Mr. John Butler, whom you know from years ago, and Mr. Guy Bray, also an estate lawyer, who represents a hospital in Santa Barbara. If you will, Mr. Montepulciano, they have asked me to represent you."

—◊◊◊—

I RECALLED who John Butler was now, but I didn't know the other American—the hospital guy. Still, since Rossi was being so polite and solicitous, I decided to continue this little farce.

I was truly feeling foolish about all of this.

I desperately hoped none of my students had witnessed this inglorious scene. I would have damaged my relationship with them as a teacher and coach. And who knows whether some of the townspeople saw me run and fall and get muddied up.

It was time to redeem myself.

"EXACTLY, yes, sir, a lawyer, a charity lawyer," said Bray.

"Not a Mafia mobster?" Dante asked, leaning toward Butler in order to get a better view of the American who had just chased him across the soccer field.

"On my word—as an Italian, sir," Rossi said.

"I was talking to Mr. Butler," Dante said pointing to the American lawyer."

"Mr. Butler?" said Rossi looking at John Butler.

Butler made sure that his eyes met Dante's. "On my word, Mr. Montepulciano, none of us are Mafia."

Montepulciano looked as though both descriptions were difficult to distinguish.

Rossi laughed.

Dante mumbled something inaudible and carefully appraised Butler. "Yes, I see—I remember him. His eyes look too nice to kill anyone—even a wounded veteran like me." Dante grinned.

Rossi guffawed. "Now, now, Mr. Montepulciano, believe me, John Butler is a very nice young man, and a man you will come to trust."

"And you're sure the other one's a lawyer too?" Dante said, indicating Guy Bray, dragging the game out a little longer.

"Yes."

"Is he a good one?"

"Yes, a very good one. He represents a very fine hospital."

"Truly?

"Yes, truly. Very famous where he comes from," Rossi said, embellishing the truth just enough to impress Dante. Actually, Rossi doubted that many people knew Bray at all. Few estate lawyers are celebrities—even Dante knew that. But Rossi's client Mrs. Caprice Jordan Taylor had certainly been famous, so Dante accepted that Rossi was close to the truth.

I SUSPECTED Bray was an enemy as soon as Rossi said that he represented a hospital. In my bones I knew he was my enemy.

Those charity lawyers would seek to discredit me. Dishonor me. Shame me. The American charities' lawyers would make our marriage a scandal.

"WHERE in Santa Barbara do you live?" Dante asked Butler.

Butler paused, reached into his suit jacket, and found a business card. He presented it to Dante with a formal air, speaking Italian. "In Montecito. You and Mrs. Taylor came to my office in Santa Barbara a few times."

Dante took off his overcoat—it was such a mess. All three lawyers immediately offered their overcoats to him. Dante almost laughed at the comedy of it—pure Italian farce. He took Rossi's overcoat, because it was Italian.

Not yet willing to forgive Caprice's young American lawyer, Dante spoke gruffly, "Mr. Winslow was a friend. I could trust him."

"I know," John Butler said. "He is our senior partner."

"Do you also scare the shit out of old men in California?" Dante said, looking at the Americans, relaxing a little, wanting to tease them a bit.

Rossi changed the direction of their conversation.

"I have a suggestion, Mr. Montepulciano. Let's all go to lunch and discuss this awkward situation over a glass of wine and some good food. Lunch is on me!"

"I am a teacher, sir," Dante said, "and I must do my lesson plans."

"Of course, sir," said Rossi putting an arm around Dante's shoulders, "but at least let me buy you a new coat. Emilio, my driver will come tomorrow with slacks, a white shirt, and a blazer to replace your ruined one."

"But…"

"No "buts". Let's go to lunch. You can meet Mr. Bray and renew your friendship with Mr. Butler."

Well…," said Dante"

"Mr. Montepulciano," Butler said, "this is a good idea."

AT the moment, I didn't give a damn about the lesson plans, but I instinctively knew I had to play hard to get.

Still, I wondered what they wanted. What did Caprice do that sent Butler and Bray to Milan?

And why was Rossi being so solicitous?

DANTE nodded. "Okay. But I must let Miss Angela Zilli know where I'm going."

"Pardon?" Rossi and Butler said simultaneously.

"The Assistant Administrator...."

"Oh, yes, her," Rossi said glumly. "Here, use my phone."

"My students need me, and it would not be correct to conduct afternoon classes after drinking wine. I have my responsibilities, you know," Dante said, taking a tough attitude. "We must arrange for a substitute instructor."

Rossi suggested that Dante arrange whatever was required, and offered to help him while Butler and Bray waited with the car.

Dante at last agreed.

"I apologize, Mr. Montepulciano," Rossi said. "Your fall was terrible. We did not plan on such a bad thing happening."

I STRAIGHTENED up, feeling unsure.

My clothes were a mess. I tried to wipe off the mud, but only spread it around further, ruining my clothes.

Rossi told me he had a spare overcoat in his car. Until he bought me a new one, I could wear that.

Finally, I agreed.

Oh, my back, I yelled. I think it's broken.

The lawyers looked at me in unison, eyes wide, stricken with fright.

They placed me carefully back on the wet grass.

I allowed Butler to support me because of my unsteadiness and, in fact, I did feel fairly scrambled by my inglorious fall. Butler asked me about my brother, Gino. I told him how well Gino was doing. I even told Butler I was staying at his house.

My shoes squished as I moved my feet. The holes in my shoes' soles had let in quite a bit of water.

Rossi noticed and promised to get a new pair of shoes and socks.

I went and explained things to Angela, my Administrator.

Actually, the Administrator gladly excused me for the rest of then day. She even looked at me with more respect. It must have been at my prospects of possibly inheriting some money.

AFTER a short time Dante Montepulciano descended the school's front steps and walked over to the car.

"You didn't tell me you had a limousine," Dante said to Rossi.

"It's a company car. It's not mine," Rossi lied.

"Everyone in town will notice," Dante said. "Now all my friends will ask to borrow money from me—this car creates a bad impression for me."

"Never mind," Rossi said opening the back seat door.

"It's black, like a Mafia car," Dante said.

Rossi sighed. "I told you, we're lawyers."

Once he was inside the limousine, Rossi apologized again for Dante's fall. "You must be hurt. I hope you haven't broken anything, or pulled a muscle. Should we stop at a doctor's office?"

Dante knew how to play to the gallery, and when to stop. "No, no. I'm okay. Even though I'm older than you two spring chickens, I've always been strong. No, it's over. It's my pride that was damaged the most. I was embarrassed by the fall."

"Sir, you are remarkable. A lesser man would be in the hospital," Rossi agreed.

—⚬—

NONE of these people wrere intent on killing me. So I felt comfortable going to lunch with them.

Still, I didn't trust the American lawyer named Bray.

Caprice and I had liked John Butler. She had trusted him with her will. That was good enough for me.

"THAT'S right," said Dante, his confidence surging. "Since you Americans are not going to kill me, and because you, Mr. Rossi, are Italian and look like a man of integrity, I accept your offer of lunch."

Rossi patted Dante on the back, complimenting him effusively. Since it was still early, he suggested they drive to Tremezzo, on the shore of Lake Como, for lunch at a restaurant called Red and White.

—⁓—

I EXPECTED Rossi to pick up the tab. Surely he knew that I was too poor to afford a restaurant in Tremezzo.

I remembered when Caprice and I frequented the grand restaurants of the world. How happy and in love we were! Of course she always paid, because I was poor.

Then I felt sad because she was gone forever from my life.

8

Red and White

EARLIER, ADAM ROSSI had instructed his driver, Emilio, that if Mr. Montepulciano accepted a ride to lunch with the lawyers at the restaurant called Red and White in Tremezzo, Emilio was to treat the old man as an *aristocrat*. Therefore, as soon as Dante stepped into the limousine, Emilio could not do enough: he donned his chauffeur's hat, and used respectful language.

"Mr. Montepulciano," Emilio said looking at him in the limousine's rearview mirror, "How are you feeling, sir?"

"Thank you, I'm recovering, Emilio."

"Excellent, very good, sir," Emilio said. "The car has a phone in the back seat. Please feel free if you need to use it—you know, to call your home. Or your banker or the Prime Minister—whomever," said Emilio, winking at Dante in the rearview mirror."

"Just drive the goddamn car, Emilio," said Rossi gruffly.

I IMMEDIATELY liked Rossi's chauffeur, Emilio. Of course he knew I didn't know the Italian Prime Minister, and we both knew I didn't have a banker. He knew I was a mud-spattered, underpaid schoolteacher. But Emilio was poor too, and the poor have respect for each other. And he knew I lived in a slum.

I knew they wanted something—perhaps I was in a stronger position than I realized. Time would tell.

Rossi and I would have to talk privately, again.

My brother Guido could help me.

AFTER Dante had settled comfortably into the leather back seat and the car door was shut, Rossi got into the front seat. He leaned over and hissed into Emilio's ear, "For Christ's sake, don't overplay it. You never treat me with such deference." Emilio smiled to himself. He liked the old man in the back seat, and felt he had much in common with him. The two Americans joined Dante in the back seat.

Horn blaring, the large black Mercedes merged into traffic. The oncoming traffic blared back, drivers gesturing profanely at Emilio's abrupt maneuver, which had caused several cars to brake. Butler shut his eyes, swearing under his breath at Italian drivers in general.

Dante reached over put his hand on Butler's shoulder. "Excuse me, Sir, but aren't you the American that Caprice and I met in Switzerland?"

"Yes."

"So you are that lawyer?"

"Yes," Butler said repeating himself. "I was Mrs. Taylor's estate lawyer. Her account was given to me by my law firm's senior partner."

"Ah, yes," said Dante.

"Although it's been over twelve or thirteen years," John Butler said, 'I've handled her estate. Dante, we know each other. You have been to my house in Santa Barbara."

"Yes it's coming back to me—I must have hit my head in my fall back there."

"And you've met my wife and two boys."

"Correct. Yes, yes, it's all come back to me, Mr. Butler," said Dante grasping Butler's right hand, shaking it in a welcoming way.

Butler smiled back at Dante and said, "Good."

—∞—

THEN it all came back to me—clearly.

John Butler was the lawyer who approved the agreement that Caprice and I called the Golden Pact or *Atto Solenne*. He had traveled from Santa Barbara to Bern, where Caprice and I were staying at the time.

Just because I fell on my ass trying to escape them wasn't reason enough to drive all the way to Tremezzo and Red & White.

"YES, I gave you my card. Here's another one." Butler handed Dante another business card. Dante took it, turned it over, and looked at it thoughtfully.

It was a more than an hour's drive to Tremezzo. On the way they engaged in small talk about the weather and the scenery. Dante grew more and more puzzled about what they wanted from him.

In Tremezzo, the car stopped abruptly, tires screeching, pitching the occupants forward, and then pitching them back against their seats. This time, even Rossi complained. "Emilio, be careful. We have guests, and one is a wounded veteran!"

Emilio apologized, his eyes looking back in the rear view mirror. He winked at Dante.

Emilio parked the limousine on the side of the road that fronted Lake Como. They would have to walk across the street to get to the restaurant. He sprang from the driver's seat to the curbside back door, opened it with a flourish, and helped his new charge step out. Butler, Bray, and Rossi managed their own exits, Butler still cursing silently to himself.

Tremezzo is a medieval town with narrow cobblestone streets, so they had only a short walk to the canvas awnings of the Red & White. Already Dante was getting stiff from his fall.

—⚒—

I HAD visited here before. Caprice and I had stayed at the Grand Hotel Tremezzo, which was just a short walk north of the restaurant. As you walk, you can see the stunning snow-capped Alps. The Grand Hotel is a luxurious five-star hotel. Caprice always enjoyed the good life.

I turned to Butler and explained that I remembered all of this. He seemed happy that my memory had cleared up.

I told him that my body was beginning to feel sore. He told that news to Rossi and Bray, who both said they were sorry to hear this.

Rossi said we would some wine as soon we sat down in the Red & White Restaurant to help me relax.

AFTER seating his guests, the owner of the Red & White asked Rossi what wine they wanted. Rossi explained in a torrent of Italian that the old man had fallen and could use something to clear his head and settle his spirits. The owner returned with a sparkling white wine and a tumbler of cold water. Already Dante felt better.

Rossi took control of the lunch. An observant, well trained host, he quickly introduced the reason for their lunch meeting.

"Mr. Montepulciano, again I apologize for disturbing you. Neither Mr. Butler nor Mr. Bray nor I intended in any way to scare you. If you have injured yourself, my firm will pay your medical expenses. Please be assured. I was horrified when I saw you take that bad fall."

"It's nothing. I am quite all right," said Dante. "I'm very strong for my age. I still coach the boys' soccer teams, you know."

THE restaurant owner hurried over to me and pointed at the small rolled ribbon decoration for bravery in war, which I always wear in my lapel.

"Sir, only a few Italians have been awarded that honor."

"Yes."

"Where were you wounded?"

"I was wounded in North Africa during the Rommel campaigns."

"Sir, I am proud to give you wine and lunch free."

I tried to object, but he insisted.

"No sir, your lunch is free—on the house. I won't hear another word about it."

"Thank you, sir."

"No, thank *you*, sir. My wife and I remember you when you and your wife, Mrs. Caprice Montepulciano, dined here years ago.

I thanked him very much, and looked at Mr. Bray who showed a slight irritation at Red & White's owner's recollection.

"Our pleasure."

The Red & White restaurant is famous in this part of Lake Como. Caprice and I ate at this restaurant every time we visited Tremezzo. The Restaurant was small and run by a congenial husband and wife. He used to to hug Caprice, but I doubted that he would remember me.

"YES," Rossi chimed in, "we all salute your service. But you are also a famous soccer coach, are you not? Anyone in Milan who loves the game of soccer knows the name of Dante Montepulciano. After all, you were one of the coaches of Italy's national soccer team. That's quite an accomplishment. Very few men in the entire world have ever coached a national soccer team."

"Yes, it was a great privilege," Dante remarked. "But it was a long time ago. Almost twenty years. Our countrymen remember some of our teams, but not the coaches so much."

Dante appreciated the acknowledgement, and his smile became noticeably relaxed once he decided that at least the Italian lawyer could be trusted.

MORE details came back to me. Bern, Caprice, Mr. Butler, the Golden Pact by which I agreed to take care of her. By then she was ill and desperate.

"Sir, my best wine for you," said Red & White's owner as he approached our table wearing a big smile and bearing a big bottle beaded with sweat. An Amarone della Valpolicella, a very nice wine indeed. We had hardly touched the sparkling white wine he had given us when we first sat down.

I tasted the Amarone. It was good. "I thank you very much."

"It's the least I can do for a recipient of the Italian Medal of Valor."

ROSSI and the two Americans watched the special attention shown to Dante. It was clear from the puzzled looks on the Americans' faces that they didn't know the significance of Dante's war decoration.

The owner was happy to explain, with Rossi translating. "That medal, my friends, is worn by only a few Italians. It honors conspicuous bravery in battle."

Rossi interrupted. "Okay, my new friends, before we talk any business, it is only appropriate that first we order. Then we can talk— that is, if you will permit it. Professor Montepulciano, we must salute you and your bravery."

—⁓—

I WONDERED what Rossi and the Americans were up to.

The American called Bray told me in the limousine that he represented Santa Barbara's largest hospital and that on this trip he also represented other charity lawyers receiving gifts from Mrs. Taylor.

I had no idea what "this trip" meant. I had never met Bray, although he seemed perfectly reasonable and he had good manners.

It seemed I was having lunch with estate lawyers.

"Gentlemen," said the owner, after pouring everyone at our table a glass of Amarone, "I salute a brave man."

Everyone saluted me, and nearby guests cheered. I was more than flattered, but I felt sad for all of the dead soldiers on both sides.

Despite his gushing sincerity, I hoped the owner would drop his attention to my war honors. So many other good Italians lost their lives in Rommel's North African campaigns. I find the subject of war depressing. War should never be considered as a solution to mankind's endless quarrels.

Caprice had liked my lapel ribbon. She realized how bad my head wound was and understood my limitations and frequent bouts of dreadful headaches.

"Thank you for this lunch. Thank you, everyone," I said.

THE four diners silently scanned their menus. A lively discussion broke out between Rossi and Dante concerning the attributes of each dish. Dante, like so many Italians, had a passionate interest in food and wines.

Dante pointed to several items, always soliciting Rossi's opinion. "Did you say, Mr. Rossi, that you are from Rome? If you come from Rome and have the wallet of a big Milan lawyer, you must have a very cosmopolitan palate. Rome is famous for fish with rich sauces and heavy desserts, no?"

"Ah, of course you would know Rome—"

"Of course, I coached soccer in Rome," said Dante.

"In Rome? I thought you were from here."

"Sirs, I was a coach for the Italian national soccer team," Dante said in English, smiling shyly. "We placed fourth in the nineteen sixty Olympics."

"Mamma mia," said Rossi, knocking his head. "How could I forget? How stupid. Forgive me. What a terrible oversight! After all, fourth place is very honorable—"

"Yes, Mr. Rossi, it was an honor."

—⁂—

I LOVED that time coaching our national soccer team.

Even the Americans today seemed genuinely happy.

"Mr. Butler, do your boys play soccer?"

"Yes, my oldest does," said Butler.

"Is he a good player?"

"I think so," Butler answered, "speaking as a father."

I smiled at Butler. Good father.

ROSSI reached across the table, grabbed Dante's right hand, and pumped it as he said, "That was a great time for all Italians. You brought our little country some great games. For once we challenged Europe and America—Americans can't play soccer anyway—Argentina, all of them. For a brief moment we had them by the balls—and we squeezed a little, eh?" He pantomimed squeezing imaginary balls in his right hand, laughing and stamping his feet. He looked over at the American. "Sorry, Mr. Butler, but we Italians take our pleasures gladly. And it's true, you Americans are no good at soccer. You can invent atomic bombs and shoot rockets to the moon, but you can't shoot a ball into a soccer net." He and Dante laughed deliriously.

Approving of his host's passion, irreverence, and good manners, Dante relaxed. He was glad now that he had lost his balance and fallen. He smiled to himself: had he not fallen, he wondered whether he would be at lunch with these three lawyers celebrating 1960.

Bray perked up and said, "Yes, what an honor, Mr. Montepulciano. I also played soccer—at Cambridge—in England."

"What position?" Dante asked.

"Goalie," said Bray, smiling. "But we were not a national team—let alone an Olympic one."

Dante looked around their table and said, "Goalie is a tough position."

THE restaurant owner came to the table loaded with dishes full of salads and vegetables. He smiled at me.

"How are you now, Mr. Montepulciano?"

"Happy," I said. I smiled back.

He announced to all of his diners, "Ladies and gentlemen, meet one of the coaches of Italy's national soccer team! Dante Montepulciano!"

Everyone in the room began to shout. "Bravo, Mr. Montepulciano!"

Then turning to Rossi, the owner said, "Everybody gets a free dessert!"

"Bravo!" shouted the diners.

Even Emilio outside was jumping up and down by the black Mercedes sedan.

ROSSI went out and brought Emilio back to the table, but not before asking the chauffeur to leave his hat in the car.

"So, Mr. Rossi," the restaurant owner said, "here in this small village on the western shores of Lake Como we are very good at cooking game: deer, rabbit, birds. You must try the rabbit! But not before you try a hearty country soup. And before that we must order more of this fine Amarone. Do you like the Amarone?"

Rossi turned to Dante. "Mr. Olympic coach, please order more of this excellent wine," he said. "But only under one condition."

"What is that?" Dante asked.

"You must allow me to pay—for everything."

Dante leaned back in his chair and pretended to be contemplating Rossi's proposal. Then he sat upright and said, "I allow you to pay. Besides it's no secret: you all know I am only a poorly paid teacher who could not pay for such a meal in the first place." He moved his face closer to Rossi's face. "It is only proper that a wealthy lawyer from Milano pick up the bill. Sir, I permit you. The National Teachers' Union permits you. I accept your kind offer."

"Then it is settled," roared Rossi, laughing, holding his guest's right arm. "Thank you for permitting me."

"Permission granted."

"Forgive me, gentlemen," the restaurant owner said, "but I must remind you that there will be no bill. This meal—and the wine—are on the house!"

—m—

I LIKED and trusted this Milanese lawyer.

"Is it your intention to represent me?"

"Yes sir," said Rossi, shaking my hand gleefully.

"And you will honor Mrs. Caprice Jordan Taylor?"

"On my word of honor."

"Then I will trust you."

"Please do."

AT Rossi's insistence Dante ordered two more bottles of Romano Dal Forno Amarone della Valpolicella. "On my teaching salary I would never be able to order such a wine."

"Now that that's settled, you must help us order our lunch," Rossi said.

"Will you try the rabbit?" said the owner.

"Of course," replied Rossi. "Mr. Butler? Mr. Bray?"

"Yes, it sounds delicious," they said in unison.

"Excellent! But you must start with the soup," said the owner. "It is flavored with our local herbs—especially good on a cold, wet day like today—and I will bring a nice country bread to go with it."

Dante turned to Rossi. "You will get your money's worth—and *I* will get your money's worth!" They both broke into laughter, enjoying their new camaraderie.

—⚉—

I ASKED John Butler, "What was that paper you put into my coat pocket at the school?"

"A subpoena from California. I'm sorry, but I had to do that."

I turned to Rossi and asked, "What is a subpoena?"

"A court order to appear and answer questions."

"About what?"

"Not 'what.' 'Whom.' It's about Caprice Taylor"

"What kind of questions?"

"Questions about whether or not she was married to you."

"We were husband and wife."

"Yes, I know. We all know. But we must have your sworn statement."

"Why?"

"In order for Mrs. Taylor's estate to be distributed."

"They understand we were husband and wife?"

"Of course, but first they need to settle with you."

"Really?" I said. "So a negotiation is called for?"

"Yes."

I looked at everyone and smiled at them.

ROSSI made certain his two American guests ordered what they wanted. After they ordered, Dante decided to volunteer some information about himself.

"Did I tell you that my name—*Montepulciano*—has every vowel in the alphabet?" he said, adding, *"a-e-i-o-u,"* for emphasis. "Every vowel."

Rossi and Butler laughed and acknowledged this fact.

"My last name has only two of the five vowels: *o* and *i*," Rossi said.

Butler grinned and added his vowel count: "Two only: *e* and *u*."

"Then I win," said Dante. "I have all five vowels: *a-e-i-o-u*."

Rossi proposed a toast to Dante's five-vowel last name. Dante stood up, grinned, and bowed.

After Rossi's toast and everyone was seated, Dante began thinking about the coming deposition.

"What is this coming deposition?" I asked addressing Bray.

Rossi interrupted Bray and said not to worry. He insisted everyone was gathered for a happy lunch.

"We can talk later, coach," Rossi said. "No need to worry."

Dante quieted down and the lunch continued.

—∞—

I BEGAN worrying about the deposition. What happens at one?

I knew that Bray and the charities he represented would try to deny my marriage to Caprice. They would attack my character—all lawyers do that. That made me unhappy.

I turned to Rossi and said, "Will the charity lawyers try to prove I was not Caprice's husband?"

"Yes."

"Then I will not attend the deposition."

"You shouldn't worry."

"Why not?"

"Because the facts are on your side."

"Are you certain?"

"Yes—don't worry."

"I HAVE never had such a fine red wine," said Dante.

"Nor have I, to tell you the truth," said Rossi.

"We must salute the restaurant owner's taste in wine. And I hope you have the good sense to ship some of this Amarone to Mr. Butler's home in Santa Barbara. *Salute!*"

"*Salute!*" they all shouted.

Their lunch dishes arrived with a flourish. Throughout the meal Dante entertained them with memories of his Italian soccer team's feats in the Rome Olympics. Rossi and Butler were entranced by Dante's continuous stream of humorous stories and his animated style of telling them.

"So we had no choice," he said. "No choice except to win! Of course, we were under tremendous pressure. It's a very difficult thing to compete in the Olympics when you're the home team. I now know this is true." Dante smiled ruefully, remembering the razor's edge on which he had once lived. "But we placed in the Final Four, and that made all the difference in my life."

Rossi rejoiced. "Yes, you are a famous Italian—a celebrity, my dear friend."

—ɯ—

I STILL didn't feel comfortable about this deposition. I worry too much. As we say in Italy, *coo che dio fa e ben fatto*. Each day brings its own bread.

Although everyone was encouraging and cheerful, my life lessons had taught me to not expect much. For one thing I did not feel like a celebrity.

War taught me that victory was won only through terrible suffering. Mussolini taught me that despots are to be avoided. Caprice taught that excessive drinking also destroyed people. I was wary about lawyers.

I remembered my mother's warning: A king's favor is no inheritance.

Ah, poor Caprice.

In her death I only hope that all will be well.

DANTE smiled again, and exhaled a puff of air dismissively as he dropped his eyes to the table.

"I never knew you were a decorated war veteran," Rossi said interested in this amazing Italian man.

"Remember, Sir, I had to have a shell explode over my head."

"I am proud to know you," said Rossi.

"I am not hero, Mr. Rossi. The people who died are the heroes."

"No, no. You can't deny it. Presidents and prime ministers and businessmen have sought you out."

"For a while, Mr. Rossi. But it all passed eventually, and now I'm just an ordinary man reveling in the past. I am no longer a celebrity. Just a teacher living on a beginning teacher's insufficient wages."

"I don't understand—beginning? You have many years—"

Dante interrupted by placing his right hand on Rossi's arm. "You see, I refused to sign an oath to Italy. Therefore I cannot qualify for tenure and the salary of a full professor."

"No. We must change the subject."

Dante laughed. "Tell me, finally, since you have not come here to kill me, why have you come here and started all the townspeople gossiping that you are the American Mafia? Just to hold a deposition?"

—⁂—

I SAID, "I think this deposition will very bad for me, Mr. Rossi."

"It's something we have to do, Dante."

"How many American lawyers will attend the deposition?"

"In all, perhaps six—maybe only four."

"Six!"

"Probably only four."

"Including Mr. Butler and Mr. Bray?"

"Yes. And Mr. Murray—you've met him. He was Mrs. Taylor's Los Angeles lawyer."

Rossi's answer frightened me—two against four, or six! Not fair!

"Dante, you mustn't worry. I'll be there to help you, and so will my partner, Mr. Galileo."

NOW Rossi turned serious and introduced his reason for meeting.

"Mr. Montepulciano, I thank you for having lunch with us, and we are grateful for the chance to get to know you better. You are a gentleman. And I like you, sir. It is an honor to share wine and a meal together. You remind me how much I miss the countryside outside Milano. But there is another reason this meeting is important."

Concern filled Dante's eyes, and he tensed.

"No, no," assured Rossi, "it is nothing threatening. I have news— yes, sad news—about Mrs. Taylor, whom you knew. A long time ago."

Dante looked at John Butler. "Is this about my wife?" he asked quietly, his voice hushed, respectful, apprehensive of the unknown.

"Pardon me?" John said, not expecting his question.

"Is this about Caprice's death?"

"Yes, Dante," Butler said. "We're sorry to have to bring this up again."

"Is it about her will?"

"Yes."

"So this is about the death of Mrs. Taylor—and her will, and the California deposition to be held in Milano?" said Dante putting it all together.

"Yes."

"Why not just sit down with me and tell me what my wife wanted?"

""It's the way California law works, Mr. Montepulciano," said Bray interjecting and wanting to end the conversation.

Dante looked at Rossi and threw up his hands, saying, "So be it."

—⟋⟍—

I HAD no real idea what a deposition was, but I was sure it wasn't good. It felt foreboding. The saying, "The more law, the less justice" came to my mind. Caprice, too, had liked that Italian proverb.

When Caprice and I were together, we had no legal entanglements. John Butler took care of that. Because he was present now, I felt comfortable. Caprice trusted him. He had also accepted me without any difficulty.

"WHEN did she die? How long ago?" Dante asked.

"A little more than a year ago—June twenty-third 1977, to be exact," said. Butler. He reached for Dante's arm and held it gently. "Again, we all offer our condolences."

"How did she die?"

"From the complications of alcohol."

"Where?"

"At her home in Santa Fe. In New Mexico."

"Where is New Mexico?" Dante said asking in a quizzical tone.

"Mr. Bray, why don't you answer him?" said Rossi.

"Sure," said Bray. "Mr. Montepulciano, New Mexico is located beneath Colorado, east of Arizona, and it touches Texas."

"Don't forget that even Oklahoma touches New Mexico," Butler said.

"So Caprice died because of alcohol?"

"Yes, Dante," Rossi said reaffirming his previous information.

No one spoke for a while.

"I see," Dante said softly, moved by what he already suspected. Caprice was not in good health when he left.

"And Clarissa was there with her at the end?" Dante said. Rossi had said so on the phone, but Dante wanted to be sure.

"That's right," Butler said.

Dante smiled sadly. "Clarissa was her great and longtime friend. I am glad to hear Caprice was not alone."

"Yes, I was glad too."

—m—

I WAS beginning to figure it out. If this was about Caprice's will, our marriage would have to be an obstacle to any other heirs. But I knew nothing about American law.

I whispered to Rossi, "I was her husband, yes. But I am not interested in Caprice's money—and she knew that too."

"Please don't bring this up today," Rossi replied.

But now I knew I was in a strong position. I would enjoy lunch and just be curious.

DANTE smiled, but he was worried.

As Rossi spoke, Dante looked down at the table. His shoulders sagged. He looked frail and alone. For a long moment he remained quiet, twisting his hands and fingers. Then he looked up at Rossi. His magnificent black eyes were flooded with tears.

Butler reached out sympathetically and rested a hand on Dante's shoulder. Dante reached for a handkerchief and wiped his eyes. He then rose awkwardly from the table.

"I'd like to go outside and walk around a bit," Dante said. "Please, don't get up. Have a cappuccino. I'll be back soon. Please allow me. I just need to get some fresh air." He walked out onto the sidewalk and turned left.

—⚏—

I WALKED up the street to the Grand Hotel Tremezzo.

I was dumbstruck to think that Caprice would have left me anything. She knew I wasn't interested in her wealth. Never! I loved her for herself, not her oil fortune. Most people would befriend her wealth, but not me. That was the foundation of our relationship.

Wealth would change my life, and I did not welcome that. I was poor, but I could get along. I was a schoolteacher and a volunteer who helped other poor people. That's who I was. I didn't want to become someone else.

My head began to ache a bit. I hoped I could make it back to the Red & White restaurant. Whenever I feel stress, I get headaches, bad ones sometimes.

I decided to completely trust Mr. Rossi. Once again, I had no choice but to win.

I felt I could trust Butler, Caprice's estate lawyer. Bray was a different matter. My understanding was that he represented the hospital in Santa Barbara and, at the same time, was the managing lawyer for Mrs. Taylor's charitable gifts. To me America seemed one huge collection of lawyers.

I shook my head and had a good laugh.

WHEN Dante left, Rossi ordered a round of cappuccinos for himself and the two American lawyers. Emilio went back out to the Mercedes and waited for the luncheon to end. The three lawyers talked quietly among themselves. Rossi explained that it might not be appropriate to pursue matters much further. He was confident that Dante would show up for the deposition, despite what he might have said earlier. For now, it would be best if they simply took him home and arranged to meet again later.

"By the way, Bray, do you know which lawyers are attending the deposition," Butler asked wondering which charities would be represented.

"Me for the hospital."

"And—"

"Bass for the botanical gardens."

"That might be trouble," said Butler.

"Mr. Orso for the art museum."

"And probably Lambert for the museum of natural history."

"Good," said Butler.

"Let me know who for sure is coming, John," Rossi said.

"Of course," Butler said assuring him.

Dante was gone for about twenty minutes. He came back in a more settled state of mind. He sat down slowly, expelling his breath in a labored sigh.

"It's all right. I am okay. Even though Mr. Rossi already told me Caprice had passed, I was not emotionally prepared. One is never prepared—"

Adam interrupted, "We understand, Dante."

"Did you know Caprice?" Dante asked Guy Bray.

"No, I didn't. But the hospital I represent did. She was always very generous to the hospital."

———※———

MR. Bray was sympathetic now, but I was certain that when push came to shove, he would be my enemy. That's the way it works, and I have to accept this. Rossi had explained this to me.

"IT'S all right," Dante said. "You seem like a nice person. But the townspeople in my part of Milan think you are Mafia—"

"Please understand—"

"Yes, yes, I understand fully," said Dante, slowly waving his right hand to calm Bray.

"We understand you were Mrs. Taylor's husband," Butler said, wanting to hear Dante's confirmation, and hoping for an explanation where his own investigations had failed. He was careful not to hurry Dante. He didn't want to be insensitive. But Dante abruptly solved his curiosity.

"Mr. Butler, according to Colorado law, Caprice was my lawful *wife.*"

"But you haven't heard from her in several years, have you?" Butler pressed. "That surprised me." At the same time, he thought to himself, *At least I've confirmed that Dante regards himself as her husband. That fact alone joins the issue of her estate and her will.*

"No," said Dante, "I haven't heard from Caprice since I left Basel, Switzerland years ago. I sent her a birthday card every year, but she never acknowledged them. I don't know why. It's all very sad."

The birthday postcards were another piece of evidence. Butler was becoming more and more convinced that Dante could prove that he was, in fact and, indeed, Caprice's lawful husband.

—m—

I KNEW by their conversation and body language that Rossi and Butler got along. They probably had a good professional relationship. That was good, because I would need their mutual support. Also, Butler knew about the Golden Pact. It was Butler who had approved it and included it in Mrs. Taylor's will.

I remember that after Caprice and I had drawn up our *Atto Solenne* (the Golden Pact), Mr. Butler came to Basel, Switzerland, and approved our agreement.

That's when he realized how sick Caprice was.

That's when he advised me to get in touch with Clarissa.

"PLEASE tell me what will happen in my deposition," Dante asked Butler.

Butler decided to give him a short, truthful explanation. "It's the process of giving sworn testimony."

"What kind of testimony?"

"Testimony that you are Mrs. Taylor's lawful husband."

"Who else will attend?

"I'd like to invite your brother Guido. He suggested we also invite your brother-in-law Giuseppe Lassa, Guido's wife's brother. Mr. Rossi and his law partner, Mr. Roberto Galileo, will be with you for legal counsel, as he said earlier."

"Then who will you represent?"

"I'll represent the estate itself."

"Anyone else?"

"Mr. Bray, who as you know represents Pueblo Hospital," Butler said. "And a Mr. Jack Orso, who represents the Santa Barbara Art Museum, and a Mr. Bill Bass, who represents the Fleischmann Museum of Natural History. Also a Mr. Dick Lambert, representing the Botanical Gardens."

"That's a lot of lawyers," Dante observed.

"Those are the four charities to whom Mrs. Taylor has gifted money."

"I understand, Mr. Butler."

"That's what this is all about, Dante."

—◊—

STILL, I knew the deposition would be mostly an attack on my character. That did not sit well with me. Nor did I want to be in the media and misinterpreted—as Caprice had been most of her life.

I hoped it would not be a long deposition.

My brother Guido hinted it might go four days.

I still hoped it would not take four days. In my view, one day was more than enough. I was certain that four—maybe more than six—would cost the estate a lot of money.

BUTLER continued, "Because I'm handling Mrs. Taylor's estate I've been asked to discuss certain matters with you."

"What matters?" Dante asked.

"Money matters, Dante. You are named as an heir, and—"

"I was never interested in Caprice's money," Dante insisted.

"Nevertheless, she has named you in her will, as well as those four charities. But the charities can't receive their gifts until they settle with you. As Caprice's husband, you are first in line."

Dante repeated, "It doesn't matter. I don't want the money."

"But Dante, it's quite a lot of money."

"I don't want it."

"I am authorized to offer you—"

"No, you cannot tempt me."

"Five hundred thousand dollars, U.S."

—⚬—

THAT puny amount was insulting. Something was wrong.

I knew Caprice's estate was large. She and I owned certain properties together, despite our breakup many years ago.

Insulting.

I decided to address them all.

"I took care of Caprice—my wife—for years. At least four years. I did so because I was in love with her. And now you offer me just five hundred thousand dollars. It is an insult to me that you even say that number! My lawyer's fees are probably five hundred dollars.

"You have said nothing about honoring her. All you talk about is money. I'm not stupid. I know Jordan Oil stock has been rising. Caprice's estate must be worth tens of millions of dollars. And your offer of a settlement to me is half a million? Caprice would be very angry. And so am I!"

THE GOLDEN PACT

DANTE looked across the table at the American lawyers and said, in English, "Mr. Butler, I like you and I already trust you—not the law, you. I know that my wife was wealthy. It would be better if you didn't mention this money. I tell you again: I don't want the money. None of it."

Butler blushed, embarrassed by his mistake of prematurely broaching the subject of money. He had only done so because the charities had insisted on it. Dante was bright. He had seen through the estate's bribe in an instant. Butler wanted the old man to get the money that was due him, not a stingy payoff.

Rossi interrupted, speaking Italian. "You are right, Dante. This is not the time or place to discuss your wife's estate. We've scheduled the deposition for October twenty-fourth at my office—it's in the letter we sent to your post office box, and it's on the subpoena. It's very important that you be there. The Superior Court of the County of Santa Barbara has ordered us to—"

"Do I have to go?"

"Yes, you do. And I will be there as your lawyer to answer some questions too—if you'll permit me."

"Yes. Of course."

"Including The Golden Pact?" Dante said speaking in Italian.

"Yes," Butler said in Italian.

Bray said politely interrupting, "Gentlemen, if you speak in English I will be able to understand."

"Dante just asked whether our visit had to do with Caprice's will," said Butler. "I affirmed it and also affirmed that their Golden Pact would be a subject of the deposition."

Bray thanked John Butler.

—⚍—

MY head began to ache terribly. I felt sick.

"Mr. Rossi?"

"Yes, Dante?"

"I feel sick. Can we go?"

"Certainly. We'll take you home immediately."

DANTE turned again to the American lawyers.

"Okay. I will attend your deposition."

"Thank you, Dante," said Guy Bray.

"But you said the subpoena comes from the Santa Barbara court?"

"Yes, that's right," said Butler.

"But this is Italy. Since when does California have jurisdiction here?" Dante asked.

"That's not the point," Rossi said, putting a hand on Dante's arm. "The estate is being settled in California, but they've specified Milan for your deposition out of deference to you."

"How is that?"

"If they wanted to, they could have ordered you to appear at the Superior Court in Santa Barbara—"

"I would refuse to go," Dante said.

"You couldn't refuse," Rossi explained, using his most persuasive manner. "They could order you to appear, and ask the Italian police to escort you to California."

"This is stupid!"

"Dante, stop for a moment and look at the effort they've made to make this easy for you," Rossi said. "They have agreed to come to you. The California court has agreed to let your deposition take place here. Without any threats, they have arranged for your every convenience. Don't you see?"

—⚍—

I DIDN'T see anything. I just wanted to go home.

I needed rest and my medicine.

I needed to end this.

DANTE thought it over for several seconds. Then he said to Rossi, speaking in rapid Italian, "Why are they being so kind? It's not like lawyers to be kind. They want to discredit and cheat me—they want Caprice's money."

"The estate must formally establish that you are her husband," Rossi explained patiently, as though he were talking to a child.

"I see."

"Good, then you agree?"

"As long as you promise to protect Caprice's honor."

"Yes, I will, with all of my ability—with the help of Mr. Butler too."

"And you will not let them damage my reputation either?"

"I will uphold your integrity."

IT seemed quite strange to me that Italy would allow an American legal proceeding to take place on Italian soil. Perhaps it all went back to Italy's losing World War II.

I decided that as soon as I got home I would call Guido ask him to visit me and swear to help me.

Money is a great divider. When Caprice fully realized that her money did not interest me, she was doubtful and surprised. Then she began to wonder just how damaged I was from my head wound. Later we would both laugh about it and make jokes about me being crazy, but we always ended up laughing and she relaxed and realized I was serious. And she became a serious lover and companion.

My headache was getting worse. I was starting to see blue halos around everything. A migraine was coming on.

I turned to Rossi. "I must get home. I'm feeling terrible."

"What about school?" said Rossi

"Please phone the administrator for me and explain that I'm ill. I will return to work tomorrow."

"OKAY," Dante said, in English, after a long silence. "Since I must consent—unhappy about it as I am—I will attend your American deposition in Italy. But you and Mr. Butler must do a good job representing me."

Butler agreed.

Also, my brother, Guido and I had discussed this thing called a deposition," said Dante. "Guido had a constructive view."

"Look at it this way Dante," he said, "Caprice was an oil heiress—a wealthy woman, and her family is influential. She was used to great wealth and insincerity. Lot's of people envied her and spoke unpleasant gossip, deserved or not. You were not like that. She had will and in it she gave her money away"

I agreed with him.

"And because you were married to her, you are a threat."

I understood Guido. I was a threat

Rossi and Butler nodded at each other. "I've already said I will," Rossi told Dante. "I give you my word of honor."

"So do I," said Butler, reaching across the table to offer Dante his hand. "I'll do all I can to protect your reputation."

Dante shook hands with Butler, and then with Rossi. "I must get home now," he said.

Rossi gave the restaurant owner a credit card. Before leaving, Dante agreed to meet with Rossi two weeks before the deposition to rehearse his testimony. Lastly, Rossi proposed a final toast to Dante.

Emilio drove them back to Milan. Butler dreaded the drive, knowing that Emilio was just waiting to scare the hell out of him. He didn't think he would ever understand how Italy worked.

—◊—

WHEN I got home, I went to bed immediately. I was exhausted.

God, save me, I prayed.

Caprice, watch over me.

III: The Deposition

9

En Route

JOHN BUTLER TESTED the door handle to his hotel room, making sure the door had locked behind him, and walked along the carpeted corridor toward the elevators. Unsatisfied, he went back and double-checked the lock. Then he hurried back down the hallway. When he reached the elevator, he pressed the down arrow and waited.

—⁂—

I ASKED my brother Guido what I should wear to the deposition.

"Dress poorly, Dante," he told me, "as you usually do. Be yourself."

I laughed. "But Guido, I'm a retired military officer."

"Look at what that got you, dear brother—a broken head."

"I'll wear what I wear as a teacher. Then I'll be myself."

"That's good, my dear brother. You'll look just fine."

"No, I'll look like a poor physical education teacher. But at least my outfit will reflect who I really am."

Guido sighed.

"Guido, don't worry. I know what I'm doing."

Again Guido sighed.

"Even Caprice liked my casual clothes," I said, defending myself. "Although when I wore my officer's uniform, she went pretty crazy and the sex was pretty exciting."

BUTLER examined his reflection in the polished metal elevator doors and decided he was dressed appropriately, like any Italian lawyer of his stature on his way to a deposition. No American styling. He wore a white shirt, a deep blue Italian-cut evening business suit with trousers hemmed in the European way, without cuffs and with the pant legs touching each shoe's heel. His shoes were Italian, expensive, and deeply shined. A designer wine-red silk tie and a matching hand-kerchief in the breast pocket completed the ensemble.

Dress mattered to Butler. He was here to represent a sizeable estate, and he need to look the part. John Butler was in his ele-ment. So much of his estate work was routine, keeping up with tax codes, reasonably non-quarrelsome clients, trying to establish a good reputation, trying to become a partner—the same thing others in his firm hoped for. Estate law was a good part of the law but pretty rou-tine. Then Caprice Jordan Taylor died and his life suddenly became thought-provoking and motivating.

The elevator doors opened without warning, catching him off guard inspecting himself. Fortunately, the elevator was empty. He entered and pushed the lobby button.

He looked at his watch: 8:19 P.M.

The elevator descended directly to the lobby without stopping. Butler stepped out into the lobby and looked around, searching for Emilio, Adam Rossi's limousine driver, who would drive him to the deposition.

I PUT on a worn pair of slacks and an old blazer. My shoes had holes in the soles. How times had changed! Caprice always bought my clothes, because she wanted me to look handsome.

Guido arrived to pick me up. He was dressed properly: an Armani suit, a white shirt, and a modern tie. He was a top executive for an Italian company that managed ports and their marine assets. I was proud of my younger brother. Caprice had liked Guido too. She trusted him.

THE GOLDEN PACT

"EXCUSE me, Mr. Butler—over here!"

Butler recognized the limousine driver's voice and turned that way. Emilio was dressed in his black chauffeur's uniform. He could have passed for a banking executive, except for his chauffeur's cap, which was tucked under his left arm. Emilio was proud of his job. The law firm of Galileo & Rossi was one of Milan's most prestigious small firms. He hurried over to greet Butler.

"Mr. Butler, good evening, sir."

"Good evening," said Butler, returning the driver's greeting in Italian. "I won't say 'good night,'" he added with a smile, to show the driver that he knew the difference.

—⚏—

GUIDO looked great. His clothing complemented his good looks and lean physique. I depended on him in many ways.

My war wound left me with a long scar across the left side of my head, ending halfway across my brow. It didn't help my looks. Moreover, though I was intellectually bright, I suffered agonizing headaches that usually left me feeling commotion in my brain.

Anyway back to Guido. He always owned outstanding sports cars.

His current car was a 1967 Ferrari 275 GTB by Scaglietti. It was a Ferrari berlinetta coupe with a four cam V-12 engine. It was a dark blue with dark blue leather seating. (A combination of Blue Sera over Pelle Bleu.) I loved the sound of the car's throbbing engine.

Sometimes, in the summers, he would take me on roads leading up to the Italian Alps behind Lake Como. Exciting, quite special.

This evening we headed into central Milan for the first day of depositions.

EMILIO ignored the American's display of his language skills. He already knew Butler spoke fluent Italian. While they shook hands, he took note of the American's trim figure and expensive clothes. He was taller than Butler. He took Butler's leather briefcase, turned, and walked out of the hotel, beckoning Butler to the black Mercedes sedan.

Rain was drenching the hotel driveway. The hotel's doorman hurried behind Butler with a small umbrella. Emilio positioned himself next to the black sedan, which was double-parked near the entrance to the hotel, and opened the rear passenger door.

While he waited for Butler to get into the back seat, Emilio thanked and dismissed the doorman, and held his own umbrella over the open car door. Butler hurried inside and sat.

As Emilio drove slowly out of the driveway, Butler glanced back through the rear window at the hotel that was his residence while he stayed in Milan. He already knew Emilio's driving from their recent trip to Tremezzo, and he hoped he wasn't in for another harrowing ride.

—⁂—

"DANTE," Guido said, "your wonderful, eccentric personality will get you through this just fine."

"These are lawyers, Guido."

"So?"

"So! These Americans don't want me to be Caprice's husband."

"So what?" said Guido, "You are in fact her husband. Or were."

"Lawyers and their twisted logic can make people think black is white. And you are a philosopher—you too can turn black into white and vice-versa."

Yes, my younger brother was an engineer and deep-sea diver and I admired him and all of his accomplishments. Our cousin Lessa felt the same way.

I was so glad that Guido was protected from the war. He was lucky.

He was whole, not like me: damaged goods.

I wasn't gloomy. Quite the opposite—I was a coach and a teacher and I loved what I did.

THE Sheraton Palace Hotel was located three long blocks from the Stazione Centrale, Milan's central train station, off the Piazza della Republica, opposite a small, untidy public park orphaned by a funds-starved municipal civil service. Italians called the hotel Palazzo Sempione. It had been one of the city's more elegant older hotels, but it had recently been purchased by Sheraton, a less-than-luxurious American hotel chain. Sheraton was hardly the Ritz-Carlton, but in Italy it boasted several attractive properties. This was one of them.

Those travelers who want privacy, or those doing business in this part of Milan, often chose the Palace Hotel, which is why John Butler was billeted there. It was a suitable home away from home for the key lawyer in the settlement of a grand estate.

And that estate was also the most lucrative piece of current business of the Milanese firm of Galileo & Rossi. It was they who had registered Butler and his American colleagues at the Palazzo Sempione. It was fairly expensive, but the Italian team felt it was necessary to make a good impression on these American lawyers and their firms.

—◆—

"DON'T be anxious, dear brother."

"But I don't trust lawyers. They destroy a person's reputation."

"You have a good reputation," Guido said.

I did not need Guido talking about my reputation. I knew well what probably lay in front of us—a no fun four days, days of lawyers running me down, insulting my past, and discrediting my marriage to Caprice.

So I stopped our conversation.

"Really, Dante," Guido said, as the two brothers drove on in silence to the law offices of Galileo & Rossi.

"Eventually they will all treat you well."

"I doubt that," I said laughing.

BUTLER was an estate lawyer. He had graduated *summa cum laude* from the USC Gould School of Law. His résumé inspired confidence. For their immediate purposes, Galileo & Rossi valued two of Butler's attributes in particular: first, he controlled the settlement of Caprice Jordan Taylor's estate; second, he was fluent in Italian. Galileo & Rossi's client, Dante Montepulciano, needed both attributes.

In fact the Italians felt fortunate in having an American counselor who could bridge the language and cultural barriers between Italian and American English. And they knew their client, a true Italian, admired Butler's linguistic abilities and Italian sensitivities.

None of the other American lawyers spoke Italian. As far as Galileo & Rossi knew, none of them had ever visited Italy. One lawyer, Orso, had a connection--his father had immigrated from the city of Bologna, but the son spoke no Italian.

—ɯ—

GUIDO and I got into Guido's Ferrari and started the drive through Milan's wet, winding streets.

I loved riding in my brother's car.

"Don't go too fast. No point arriving early."

"Okay."

So Guido slowed down by 2,000 RPMs.

I relaxed and thought about the coming deposition. Guido's car made me feel good. Finally, I felt that I could do something good for Caprice.

THE GOLDEN PACT

THE involvement of Galileo & Rossi had begun several months earlier. A letter addressed to both Roberto Galileo and Adam Rossi, from a John Butler, Esq., in Santa Barbara had arrived at their offices. It notified them of the death of an American, Mrs. Caprice Jordan Taylor. Before this letter, Galileo had known nothing of Caprice Jordan Taylor, nor of John Butler. He had no idea of the coming legal tangles.

Galileo had just left his office and was walking down the corridor toward the lift, on his way to the Duomo to attend morning Mass, when his partner, Adam Rossi, opened the letter, read it, and chased after him. Rossi handed him the letter.

"Roberto, this letter just arrived from California, and I think it means big business for us." He handed Galileo an envelope postmarked Santa Barbara, California, USA. Leaning against the hallway wall, Galileo opened it.

Looking up at Rossi, he nodded and said, "You're right. We must reply and accept this American's—John Butler's—request for assistance. This could mean good money for us."

First, however, Galileo asked Rossi to look up Butler's firm in the international directory of law firms, and then to telephone Donald Murray, a Los Angeles-based associate, and enquire about Butler's firm, and write up a short summary of his findings.

THE Ferrari's engine growled as Guido shifted gears. Guido was proud of his 101 Pininfarina-designed sports car.

"You love your Ferrari," I said laughing at Guido's enjoyment.

"Yes," he said, "I get a big high driving this car. I'm like a little boy playing with his tricycle.

We both laughed, remembering our youths.

"Life was simpler back then."

GALILEO buttoned his overcoat, threw a scarf around his neck, and headed out into Milan's winter chill. He walked more lightly than usual. He thought nothing more of the letter, only about which route he would take to the Duomo. He would walk up Corso Matteotti, take a left on Via Mazzini, and go straight to the Piazza del Duomo—less than eight blocks all together.

Months passed after that letter until John Butler first visited Milan. In that interval, a flurry of correspondence passed between the two law firms. When the American did visit, Galileo & Rossi put him up in a suite at the Palace Hotel, which would serve as both his home away from home and his office. It had both a telephone for local calls, and a fax machine for overseas communication. It was expensive, but that didn't matter, because the cost would ultimately be billed to Mrs. Taylor's estate.

—◇—

"YOU'RE still driving too fast!"

"Okay, okay!" Guido reduced his speed.

"Tonight will give me a chance to set the record straight."

"I hope you follow Rossi's advice: Listen first, then speak carefully."

"I will, I will."

"Promise?"

"I promise."

"What did I say?" Guido said, asking in a stern voice.

"Listen first, then speak carefully."

"Excellent!"

"Despite my war wound, I'm not a complete imbecile."

"Well..." Guido laughed.

I punched his arm, causing him to swerve.

"Ouch, that hurt," said Guido. "Be careful or we'll crash."

You never crash, young brother.

EMILIO turned the limousine in the direction of Corso Matteotti, the street where Galileo & Rossi's offices were located, where the deposition would be held. In no time they were caught up in Milan's congested traffic.

The streets glistened, reflecting car head- and taillights along with a kaleidoscope of flickering neon lights in all colors. The car's single large center-positioned windshield wiper silently swiped the pouring rain off the windshield. Despite the late hour—8:27 P.M.—horns blared and drivers gestured. Even at that hour the traffic was slow, congested, pulsating with frequent stops and starts. Milan's traffic was one of the main reasons for Butler's love–hate relationship with the city.

Knowing it would take a while to get to Galileo & Rossi, Butler leaned back in the comfortable black leather seat and pondered the events that had led up to this.

In Butler's mind, it had been a long and fascinating winding road. His dream had come true: an important estate settlement, intrigue, controversy, and, above all, uncertainty. No one yet knew whether the Santa Barbara–based charities could strike a deal with the surprise Italian heir, Dante Montepulciano. That would follow the deposition, which would take place over the next four evenings, October 24 through 27.

—⧟—

"YOU still drove too fast."

"We've arrived," Guido said. "Now we just have to enter the courtyard and park."

"I hope you don't find any parking. Then I won't have to attend," said Dante sullenly.

"You have to attend. You promised."

"I did, and now I wish I hadn't."

"You'll do just great—just like you did at coaching."

"Yes. I was a good coach."

10

Day 1: The Deposition Begins

IT WAS 9:07 P.M., and everyone was arriving at the same time. Dante and Guido had just pulled into the interior courtyard of Galileo & Rossi in Milan's Corso District, two blocks south of Via Montenapoleone, an important commercial street. Rain was pelting down. Guido parked his car, making tight turns, skidding, brakes squealing, car doors opening and slamming shut. Their brother-in-law, Giuseppe Lessa, came right behind them.

—⚏—

AS the cars arrived, I watched with interest at the lawyers clutching briefcases and running across the inner courtyard to the safety of the building. I spoke to Guido.

"It's good it's raining. Everyone will hate an evening deposition."

"Yes, they will not like either the rain or working in the evening."

I laughed.

Guido laughed back.

"I think they won't like your agenda changes."

"That's okay. We have our duty and they have theirs."

I thought how Caprice would enjoy all of this. With her money she did not suffer lawyers lightly, but she approved of John Butler— from the moment they first met.

"Time to get going, brother," Guido said.

"I'm with you. Let's go."

LIMOUSINES jostled for the remaining parking spots. Men shouted confusing orders at each other. Dante and Guido hurried to the building's entrance to get out of the cold, wet night and the traffic melee in the courtyard. They pushed through the door, eager to get inside.

Adam Rossi met them at the door. Dante embraced Rossi, kissed him on both cheeks, and growled about the dirty weather and the deposition. Rossi greeted the others in the same way as they hurried in out of the rain, with practiced Milanese civility. All the important characters in this courtroom drama were finally meeting each other.

"Good evening, gentlemen. Come in, come in! Mr. Butler will be here any minute. My driver, Emilio, is bringing him here from the Palazzo Sempione," Rossi explained. Although the deposition was scheduled for 10:30, Dante's party had agreed to meet earlier, at 9:00, for a brief strategy session. The Montepulciano brothers and their brother-in-law, Mr. Lessa, had just finished dinner, and everyone appeared in good spirits.

—⚏—

THE absence of John Butler made me anxious. I found it difficult to talk about Caprice. Our relationship was private, and I already knew that her family history had painted her in dark colors—colors I seldom saw. I did not want her demeaned. I had told this to Adam Rossi beforehand, and he had promised to stop any such talk. But despite his good intentions I didn't believe he could. I knew that at some point the deposition would become confrontational.

AS the Montepulciano clan entered, they saw Donald Murray, Caprice's Los Angeles attorney, standing behind Rossi. He had met Dante, Guido, and Giuseppe earlier in the week. They had discussed deposition strategies, and Murray had answered Dante's questions—especially about Dante's suspicion that the American lawyers were out to trick him or humiliate him. Guido had advised Dante to take some of his anxiety medication.

Also present was a stranger whom Adam Rossi introduced as James Nelson, the official court reporter of the Santa Barbara Superior Court. Rossi explained that Nelson's job would be to administer whatever oaths or affirmations were required, as well as to tape record and simultaneously make a written transcript of the proceedings.

Adam Rossi moved everybody into a tastefully decorated private office hung with oil paintings by Carlo Canevari on three of the walls. Rossi collected modern Italian art, mostly oils, and Canevari was a favorite.

"Please, make yourselves at home," Rossi said in his most hospitable manner, taking their wet raincoats. "Thank you for coming early. It's best that we review this evening's agenda before the deposition starts. Come with me. We'll use Galileo's office. The others should be here around ten, but no later than ten-thirty. Emilio and Mr. Galileo have gone to fetch them."

—*m*—

AS I looked at Mr. Murray, I slowly began to remember. Caprice brought me with her when she visited him, and he always seemed hospitable. He had something to do with her family's foundation. If am correct, he represented her in the affairs of the Jordan family. Not an easy task. We didn't see much of him, but he appeared to watch out for her interests.

MURRAY smiled at Dante and followed behind as Rossi led them into Galileo's office. As soon as they sat down, Dante voiced his recurring fear.

"Mr. Rossi, I'm worried," he said.

"Yes?"

"I'm worried that the American lawyers will accuse me of being—how can I say it—illegitimate. That's the word."

Rossi smiled and nodded. "Yes, illegitimate. That is the right word."

"They will say I am nothing but a fortune hunter. They will insist I am just trying to cash in on my past relationship with Caprice."

Rossi shrugged his shoulders and waved his hands with palms open, and said in his most reassuring tone of voice, "Yes, I know, but that's their job, Mr. Montepulciano. Anyway," he continued, smiling wryly, "we all know you are a fortune-hunter. And what's wrong with that, my friend?"

"No, Mr. Rossi, don't joke. This is not the right time. Don't treat this lightly. I worry. My reputation and integrity are important to me, and I don't want any lawyers, especially those Americans, questioning my legitimacy. They are like hounds ready to tear apart the fox. You know this is true."

"That's a pretty callous charge, Dante," Rossi said. "I am here in part to stop a hounds and fox scenario, and I'm here to help you make your case, sir. Please have more trust in me."

Dante went over to Rossi and embraced him. "Apologies, Mr. Rossi. I'm just nervous."

"We all are, Dante."

"Yes, we probably are—all of us."

"Just tell me whenever you want a break, a pause."

"Many pauses," said Dante, feeling better.

The two men laughed together.

—⁂—

IT'S true: A lawyer with a briefcase can steal more money than the man with a gun. What a predicament I was in!

THE GOLDEN PACT

EVERYONE in the room, including Guido and Giuseppe, turned their eyes to the frail, weathered teacher. They understood the pressure on him. They sympathized with him, as they had all along.

Rossi had told them that Caprice's estate was now worth about fifty million U.S. dollars, the stock price of Jordan Oil having skyrocketed in the two years since Caprice's death. That was large enough to worry the charity beneficiaries and their lawyers severely. The charities had become greedy. If the courts ruled that Dante was indeed Caprice's legitimate husband, he could claim at least fifty percent of the estate—perhaps even all of it. Dante understood all of this, and his stress showed on his face.

But Butler, Rossi, and Murray had expressed confidence that Dante's claim was legitimate. Dante just needed to calm down. Rossi decided he had better settle Dante's jangled nerves.

"Dante, my dear friend, don't worry. You are the most legitimate man I have ever met." Guido nodded his agreement and repeated his allegiance to Dante, assuring him of his own total belief and support.

But Dante would have none of it, and dismissed them, waving his arms and fingers.

"No," he said, refusing to be pacified, "I'm being realistic. This is war, and they are the aggressors—and they have the weapons. They will use American law to deny me. I have been in war. And I have been wounded. I know what it is like to lose."

—⚉—

A MEMORY of romantic happiness with Caprice crossed my mind. And all of sudden I knew my mission: Honor Caprice.

I changed, and I smiled.

I was ready for battle.

"THAT'S just it," Dante said, exasperated, his voice rising. "We should never have told Caprice's estate that I was her husband. *I don't want the money.* These conniving American lawyers wouldn't be coming to Milan to tear me apart. Don't deny it. They want to make me look like a vulture eating some dead animal lying on the ground."

"Stop it, Mr. Montepulciano," Donald Murray said.

Dante's attention jerked from himself to Murray. "Pardon?"

"I said stop it," Murray ordered, looking at Rossi. "You are demeaning yourself. It is your right to receive money from her estate. You are Mrs. Taylor's husband. She put you in her will. Therefore it is your duty to prove that you deserve it, to respect her wishes and to uphold your own good name," He grabbed Dante by the shoulder and gently shook him to add emphasis.

"I hear you," Dante said.

"Even though you were husband and wife by Colorado common law, you were still husband and wife."

"That's true, Mr. Murray."

"Dante, the charity lawyers' clients expect them to give you a difficult time. That's just the way it works."

"Of course, Mr. Murray. I will have more confidence."

DESPITE my befuddled and anxious brain, I knew that Mr. Murray was right.

I was the husband of Caprice. And she was my wife. If she wanted to leave money to me, I should accept it. But she didn't—she only said I should "settle" with the charities. What did that mean?

But there was still the matter of my solemn oath to her—our *Atto Solenne*, the Golden Pact. No one but the two of us knew about it. It was a secret oath.

I turned and addressed both Rossi and Murray. "No, I cannot accept the money—no matter how much it may amount to."

"We'll see," said Rossi.

THE GOLDEN PACT

A KNOCK on the door interrupted them. Rossi called to whoever it was to enter. Emilio entered with John Butler in tow.

"Mr. Rossi, Mr. Butler is here," Emilio announced, gesturing to John Butler, who stood behind him. "We are late because of the rain and the traffic." Rossi jumped up and greeted Butler. Dante's mood changed instantly as he went over to greet him.

Emilio backed out of the office, saying, "Mr. Rossi, the other lawyers—the Americans—have arrived. They're waiting in the reception area."

Rossi excused himself and left the meeting room to go and greet the American charities' lawyers.

It was now 10:24 P.M., but only two American lawyers had arrived. Roberto Galileo had brought Jack Orso of the art museum and Bill Bass of the natural history museum. Bass was a litigator known for his brawling skills. Orso, on the other hand, was regarded as a specialized estate lawyer with a gentle demeanor and professional manners. Guy Bray had brought the combative—and often profane—Bass into it for his negotiating abilities, in case they were needed. Rossi escorted the two Americans into the conference room, and asked Galileo to keep them company them there until the others arrived.

—m—

SEEING the opposition lawyers didn't help me calm down.

THE remaining two American lawyers didn't arrive until after 10:30—10:47 to be exact. Their car, driven by a hired driver, had taken a wrong turn. At long last, however, in walked a rain-soaked Dick Lambert, of the botanical garden, and Guy Bray, of Pueblo Hospital.

The others had no choice but to wait for them, for it was Bray who had been ordered by the Santa Barbara Superior Court to conduct the deposition. When he did finally arrive, he made apologies to everyone, with particular effort to ingratiate himself with Dante, whom he liked personally. Nevertheless, Bray knew full well his client was Pueblo Hospital. And Bray stood to earn a very large fee. After all, his client was to receive sixty percent of the estate, as much as thirty-three million dollars.

—ɯ—

WE went into the conference room and everyone sat down, my team with me on one side, the charity lawyers all grouped facing me.

A nightmare, I said to myself.

"You and the rest of my team better be damn good," I whispered to Rossi and Butler.

"We *are* damn good," said Butler in Italian, smiling at me. Somehow his assurance helped lift my spirits.

I looked at Guido and smiled. He knew I would be careful.

I looked at my cousin Lessa. Lessa looked assured. He would stand up for me.

I looked back at Butler and said, "Here we go, Mr. Butler. Caprice will be proud of us."

Rossi agreed.

WITH everyone now assembled, Guy Bray quickly called the deposition to order. He stated its purpose. and noted that although it was being held in Milan, it was nonetheless being conducted under the California Code of Civil Procedure, in accordance with a California court order. In fact, he admitted, it would have been difficult or impossible to hold the deposition in California, because an Italian citizen resident in Italy could not be required to appear in California for a civil action. Therefore the deposition was being held in Milan, with the acquiescence of Dante Montepulciano. He urged that this point not be forgotten.

Nevertheless, Bray also noted that the deposition would be conducted in English, and he apologized for his lack of Italian. "Mr. Nelson will be making a transcript of the proceedings. We could make it available to you as we go along, if it would help," Bray said to Rossi.

"No, it's okay. If you speak slowly, I can translate as we go along," Rossi said.

"Fine. Let the record reflect it is ten fifty P.M. on the twenty-fourth day of October, nineteen seventy-nine. We are here assembled in the law offices of Galileo and Rossi. The address is…" He paused.

"Corso Matteotti, number forty," Galileo said.

"…in Milan, Italy. This meeting is for the purpose of taking the deposition of Mr. Dante Montepulciano, an Italian citizen. It is being held under California law, with Mr. Montepulciano's agreement."

—m—

AND so it began.

I still didn't understand how a California legal proceeding could occur in Italy. But, so it began.

"FOR the record, let us each introduce ourselves," Bray continued. "My name is Guy Bray, and I am legal counsel for Santa Barbara Pueblo Hospital." He looked over to Bill Bass.

"I'm Bill Bass. I represent the Fleischmann Museum of Natural History." Bass looked rumpled and tired. The trip from Santa Barbara had been long, interrupted by a long delay at Heathrow Airport. He had been unhappy about their 10:30 P.M. deposition meeting time, and it was now nearly 11:00.

The Americans continued in turn around the room clockwise.

"Jack Orso, representing the Art Museum." Orso was even more unhappy with the deposition's timing. But being of Italian heritage, he better understood things Italian, including late-night work sessions.

"Dick Lambert, representing the Botanic Gardens." Lambert had almost missed his flight, and still seemed only half-present.

"John Butler. I represent the estate of Caprice Jordan Taylor."

For the record, Guy Bray noted the others present. "Also present are Adam Rossi, representing Mr. Montepulciano." Rossi pointed to his law partner, and introduced Roberto Galileo.

—ɱ—

I LIKED Orso because of his Italian background and his warmth. But he didn't speak Italian, which seemed strange to me. But then I remembered meeting many Italians in America who didn't speak Italian.

I didn't like Bass, the rumpled, tired American lawyer.

I did like Bray, but I couldn't read him. His stoic countenance hid his thoughts; however his polite manners appeared sincere. If it wasn't for the fact that he represented Pueblo Hospital's charity, I thought he'd be more trustworthy concerning my relationship with Caprice.

Mr. Lambert seemed unengaged.

Jack Orso, the son of an Italian immigrant, puzzled me. I thought he would speak and understand Italian.

ROBERTO Galileo then introduced Dante's brother, Guido Montepulciano, and their brother-in-law, Giuseppe Lessa.

"Mr. Lessa has been invited by Dante Montepulciano to act as a character witness," Galileo told his American colleagues. "So we have two brothers," he remarked, waving at Dante and his support team. Everyone appreciated his levity. Then he added, "You may discover that Dante Montepulciano is quite learned and still teaches and coaches soccer."

The charity lawyers didn't appear to care.

Dante touched Rossi's arm and whispered something to him in Italian.

Rossi raised a hand to ask for attention.

Bray was not amused.

Dante's hand shot up.

"Yes, Mr. Montepulciano," said Bray.

"Excuse me, sir."

"Yes, Mr. Montepulciano, you may speak," said Bray, wondering what had alarmed Dante.

"Thank you, thank you, sir."

—◊◊◊—

IN KEEPING with my plan (after first getting Rossi's cautious approval), I decided to try to divert the American lawyers' plan to quickly nail me to the cross of illegitimacy. Rossi cautioned me to be careful and not overdo it.

I watched everyone's response to my interruption.

Mr. Lambert, of the botanic gardens, seemed to be the most reluctant to listen. In fact, he seemed disrespectful of us. But I had to be careful of them all, because Rossi had told me that Caprice's estate had nearly doubled in value.

Christ on the cross, right? I was Christ.

"EXCUSE me," Dante said, with Rossi translating. "But when you stated that these proceedings are being held under California law, I was reminded of California's flag. Shouldn't it be present here?"

Everyone turned to Dante and Rossi. Dante whispered to Rossi again for a few seconds, gesticulating animatedly in his Italian way. Then Rossi looked up, smiling, amused, admiring his eccentric client.

"My client is concerned that the flag of California is missing. He feels a small replica of it should be on the center of our meeting room table—to note that California jurisdiction has been transported to us here in Milan."

Dead silence. The Americans looked at each other, puzzled. Annoyed, they questioned the relevancy of the California flag.

—⁓—

PERFECT. Now I controlled the time and the subject. I knew it wouldn't last, but for the moment the fox was outsmarting the hounds.

I asked Rossi and Guido and Lessa to gather around me.

"Mr. Rossi," I said, "do you have a flag of California?"

"Of course not."

"Does Mr. Galileo?"

"No, of course not."

"Then I think this deposition is unlawful," I said, looking at Rossi. " I think we should present this position to the California charity lawyers."

Rossi told Butler about my position. Then Rossi told Bray who discussed it with the other charity lawyers. All of them said bullshit and insisted on continuing. Bass said he was tired and to just get the first day's foundation work finished.

"We insist on continuing," Bray announced.

I complained.

Bray insisted and Rossi agreed.

"WE'LL need to have a translator present, since Mr. Montepulciano's native tongue is Italian," Bray said. He turned to Adam Rossi. "Because you've previously acted as attorney for this estate, and because you're fluent in both Italian and English, we would be comfortable to have you act as translator. Is that okay with you, Mr. Rossi?"

"Certainly," Rossi said.

Dante, who understood eighty percent of spoken English, listened and smiled to himself. He tugged at Rossi's sleeve and spoke rapidly in Italian.

"Tell them that I speak Greek and French and Spanish. See if we can use a language other than English." He winked and continued, "We must make them understand that I am a man of letters, not just the high school physical education teacher they're going to try to portray me as. I am an educated man."

Rossi understood his client's wish. Dante Montepulciano was a proud man: a war hero, a famous coach, and a respected teacher.

—⁂—

I THOUGHT the Americans looked tired and annoyed, particularly Bass, who had flown all night to get to Milan. But it was Bray I wanted most to annoy, since he was the main lawyer for the charities.

Unfortunately, Adam Rossi did not share my intention. Even John Butler cautioned me about annoying the Americans.

"Okay, okay, I'll behave," I promised them.

Caprice was adept with this kind of thing: good at reading people, she was a good listener, and excellent at guiding conversations away from sensitive topics. In fact, she was masterful.

She would have managed the charity lawyers.

I had no money—big disadvantage. But my advantage was that I didn't want money. Money would change my life and I was comfortable being poor.

ADAM Rossi apparently changed his mind when he asked, "Do any of you—Bray, Orso, Bass, Murray, Lambert—speak Greek?"

A chorus of *no*s echoed through the room. Bass added *Jesus* to his answer.

"Spanish? *Español?*"

Another chorus of *no*s and one *Jesus*.

"Then how about French? *Française?*" Rossi asked, looking at Dante.

Lambert said he had studied French in college. The others just shook their heads, more negatives with one *Jesus*, one *shit*, and one *goddammit*.

The Italians ignored the Americans' swear words.

"Isn't English the business language of the world?" said Orso.

Dante smiled at Rossi and in silent Italian mouthed the words, *"Magnificent, excellent."*

It flashed through Bray's mind that this definitely was not going to be a routine deposition. In keeping with John Butler's earlier cautions, Dante Montepulciano marched to a different drummer. He would not be intimidated by the American lawyers.

—◇—

ROSSI warned me again to be careful and not to annoy them any further. Everyone was tired and on edge already.

Mr. Bray looked at me and said, "Mr. Montepulciano, we're holding this first round of deposition in the evening at your request. I would appreciate it, as head of this disposition, if you would be kind enough to let me chair the meeting. Can we agree on this?"

"Of course, Sir," I answered.

"You don't have to address me as Sir," said Bray.

I was happy we had gotten off to this start. At least they understood I would stand up for myself.

Adam Rossi patted my arm approvingly.

GUY Bray smiled to himself. The old man was no pushover. Already in the first few minutes, things threatened to spin out of Bray's control. The Americans had had to address the California flag, and confess their ignorance of foreign languages. He understood why Butler deeply liked, trusted, and respected the aging Italian. In fact, he regretted that his own role was confined to defeating Montepulciano and denying his claim to the Taylor estate. He deserved better. Not to worry, he thought, Butler would protect Montepulciano.

"All right, then," Bray continued. "We'll conduct the deposition in English, and Mr. Rossi will translate. All agreed?"

Rossi translated Bray's suggestion to Dante. Replying in Italian, Dante said the arrangement was okay with him. But he advised Rossi not to let on that he, Dante, could understand most of what was said in English. Rossi agreed.

Rossi, of course, understood and smiled his own acknowledgment. Butler too understood every word spoken in both languages.

—〜〜—

COMPARED to the American lawyers, I was casually dressed, which did not embarrass me. Caprice had always approved of the way I dress: mostly khaki slacks, casual shirts and shoes.

One thing I liked about Caprice was her inclination to dress comfortably—casually—despite her wealth.

I grabbed Rossi's arm and said, "Remember, don't let them know I know English. After all I spent at least three years in Colorado."

Rossi assured me he would do as instructed. Suddenly Bass interrupted.

"Mr. Rossi, what did Mr. Montepulciano just say?"

I definitely did not like Bass.

"Mr. Bass, he just wanted to clear the translation matter."

"Mr. Montepulciano needs to understand our role here," Bass said using an annoying tone.

No, Bass had to understand my marriage to Caprice.

"YOU understand that you will translate English into Italian and Italian into English," Bray further explained in a demanding way. "And that we will accept the translation as accurate unless clarifications are made at any time during the period of the deposition by Mr. Galileo, who also speaks English and Italian."

Then he added, "Mr. Galileo, if Mr. Rossi misspeaks, please let us know immediately."

"I certainly will," Galileo said, startled by the rudeness of Guy Bray's tone. He hoped that was unintentional; everyone was getting a little tense. He knew his law partner Rossi would feel the same way.

"The correct word is 'supervise,'" Dante insisted, not wanting his Italian lawyers to lose control of the deposition.

"Supervise is a good word," Rossi said. "Also, don't forget that Mr. Butler is present, and he too speaks fluent Italian."

"Ah, yes, Mr. Butler speaks very good Italian!" Dante exclaimed.

"The tape recorder will be running, of course," Bray quickly added, "but please remember that the official record of this deposition will be the written transcript made by the court reporter, Mr. Nelson. Are these stipulations acceptable to you, Mr. Murray? You're Mr. Montepulciano's California counsel."

"Yes," Donald Murray replied.

"All right, then," Bray said. "Let's begin."

Mr. Orso interrupted, saying, "Excuse me, Mr. Bray, would you please explicitly put on the tapped recording of this disposition the names of the Americans in this room who do not speak Italian?"

"Yes."

"Thank you."

"Mr. Bray, Mr. Bass, Mr. Orso, Mr. Lambert, and Mr. Murray do not speak Italian."

"Thank you, let's proceed," said Orso.

—m—

I PRAYED to Caprice for guidance.

She knew I would not betray her.

I had never loved a woman as much as I loved her.

"THE only question I have," Murray said, "is whether Mr. Montepulciano's deposition will be valid without his reading and signing it. Can we send a registered copy to him and if, after thirty days of it arriving here in Mr. Galileo's office, it hasn't been signed, we can deem it signed by default? That gives him thirty days to review it. Mr. Montepulciano, is that—"

"Wait a minute," Rossi interrupted. "Mr. Montepulciano didn't understand that. He has to agree—"

"No problem for me," Dante said in English.

"Hold on a minute, Mr. Montepulciano," Rossi said. Then he addressed Bray.

"My client will want to review the transcript carefully. He is concerned about inadvertently making incorrect statements—names and dates, things like that. He wants to be as honest and accurate as possible. That's always a concern."

"Won't thirty days be enough for him to do so?" Bray asked.

—ɯ—

"I UNDERSTAND, I understand," I said.

I turned to Mr. Rossi and suggested ninety days, and he agreed.

But Guido wasn't convinced. "You and Caprice left documents over half of Europe—and Colorado. Will even ninety days be enough?"

"Yes, I have copies of everything here in Milan."

"You do?" said Guido.

"My head may bear a terrible scar, but I am not careless," I said.

ROSSI wasn't finished. "Earlier—before you arrived—Mr. Montepulciano asked me what would happen if he has to refer to a document that we don't have here. Suppose it is elsewhere: in California, Colorado, Switzerland, or France. That would present a problem, right?"

"Probably," Bray thought aloud.

"What I would like you to do," Rossi insisted, "is make clear to Mr. Montepulciano that for the purposes of this deposition what counts is his words, and if he knows something to be true, he need only affirm it. Okay?"

"That's right," said Bray. "What's important now is what we say on the record."

Rossi continued, "You all must understand that Dante's position is this: He will declare only what he is sure he can demonstrate. Do you understand us clearly, Mr. Bray?"

"That's all that is required of him—his personal knowledge, nothing else. That's all we ask."

Mr. Murray, the Los Angeles lawyer, chimed in. "I'm confused. Did we agree that thirty days is enough time for Dante to review the deposition, or not?"

"Time? Giving deadlines to Mr. Montepulciano is always a problem," Rossi asserted. "If you give him thirty days, he will ask for forty. If you give him forty, he will ask for fifty, and so on."

A chuckle went around the room.

—✷—

I LAUGHED too. Things were getting silly.

And that was okay with me. In farce lies truth. One of Italy's great gifts to the world is farce, especially where the purpose of comedy is simply to make the audience laugh.

It was good that everyone was having a good laugh at my expense.

As I said farce in Italy is soul cleansing. First, farce uses an improbable situation like me being the husband of Caprice. Next, my war wound that controls too much of my character. Third and last, the fact I exaggerate and am given to humorous horseplay. I know how to make people laugh.

"ASK him to do it in one day; but we will give him thirty to get it done," Guy Bray joked.

Dante said something to Rossi, and they both laughed.

"Please translate what he just said." Murray asked, clearly irked.

"He said, 'Mr. Rossi, let's agree in principle that thirty days is okay. If there are certain particulars that need your agreement—your further agreement—we can make an exception and take longer.'"

There was awkward laughter around the table.

"Honestly, that's what he said. You understand Italian, Mr. Butler. He said that, right?"

"Exactly," Butler said, grinning.

"May we assume, then, that if we haven't heard anything from you, Mr. Rossi, in thirty days that the transcript has been approved?" Murray insisted.

Rossi shrugged. "Okay. Why not?"

"Is that acceptable to Mr. Montepulciano?" Bray asked.

Dante nodded.

"That is acceptable to my client," Rossi responded.

"Good. With that short clarification, Mr. Murray, is the stipulation as stated okay for the record? Do you agree?"

—◊—

I DIDN'T understand what the fuss was about.

A waste of everyone's time.

I was still thinking of the word "farce."

I thought Caprice would laugh out loud over all of this.

"YES, I agree," Murray affirmed.

"Mr. Galileo, you heard the stipulations at the start of the deposition. Are they acceptable to you on behalf of your client?" Bray said.

"Yes, they are, Mr. Bray," Galileo said.

"We will now ask the court reporter to take Mr. Montepulciano's solemn affirmation that the testimony he will give here will be true and correct."

"One moment, please," said Rossi. "I must instruct my client that this is not an oath, but an affirmation."

"Take your time," said Bray.

"Sirs, this is not about taking time. For me it's a serious principle." Bray said, "Please take your time, Mr. Montepulciano."

"Thank you, Sir."

"Please help us understand your important principle."

"I have made only one oath in my pathetic life. The oath was to serve my king—before Mussolini, King Emmanuel III of Italy, Ethiopia, and Albania. I made an oath to serve him and Italy in WWII. I almost lost my life. For the rest of my life I cannot make another oath."

"Why not?" said Bray, realizing he was deeply exploring a deeply psychological subject.

"Because, sirs, it is my belief."

No one said a word.

—◆—

"THE lawyers must understand that I cannot take an oath, Mr. Rossi," I said.

"I understand."

"But do they understand?" I said, pointing to the Americans.

"Yes, they do."

"How do you know that?"

"I asked John Butler to explain it to them—in English. That's why we are using the word 'affirmation.'"

"Good, because you can only make one oath in a lifetime, and I've already made mine."

THE GOLDEN PACT

ROSSI talked at some length with Dante. It took a while to explain the difference between an oath and an affirmation. Finally, Dante agreed to make an affirmation.

Bray sighed in relief, and instructed Nelson to administer the affirmation. "Let the record reflect that a translation of this affirmation has been given to the witness," Bray said. "The witness affirms that the testimony he gives here will be true and correct to the best of his knowledge. He is nodding, but he must give his assent verbally."

Dante spoke a few words in Italian, and Rossi translated, "Mr. Montepulciano confirms that he has understood the sense of the solemn affirmation, and he affirms that he will tell the truth to the best of his knowledge."

"Thank you, Mr. Rossi. Thank you, Mr. Nelson," Bray said.

"Also, at this point…" Murray said, wanting to remind them to swear in Rossi as translator.

"Yes, I know what you're going to ask, Mr. Murray," Bray said. "I was just getting to it. At this point, Mr. Nelson, would you please swear Mr. Rossi to act as interpreter?"

The court reporter did as requested, and Adam Rossi was sworn to act as interpreter.

—⟪⟫—

AT last the Americans had worked out how the deposition would proceed. Since I could not take an oath—I had made my once-in-a-lifetime oath to my king when I became a military officer—my deposition would use affirmations.

My heart beat faster as I began to wonder how tomorrow's proceedings would go. I felt anxious.

"I do not feel well," I said aloud in English.

The Americans looked slightly startled.

I realized instantly that "I do not feel well" was a weapon.

GUY Bray now had other business to cover. "Let's go off the record for a minute, he said. "I have some exhibits I want to show to Mr. Montepulciano, documents he has seen before. So why don't we go off the record while we give the documents to him, let him read them, and then we will attach them to the record."

"Fine," Adam Rossi agreed.

An animated discussion started among the charity lawyers. They were tired. Bill Bass was particularly tired and vocal. Dick Lambert, it appeared, had dozed off.

After a few moments, Donald Murray spoke up. "Okay, let's go back on the record," he said. "For the record, I want it noted that Mr. Montepulciano has *not* seen these documents. I received them too late, and there was no way I could get them to Mr. Montepulciano before I left Los Angeles. I believe it was explained to Mr. Rossi and Mr. Galileo that Mr. Montepulciano would have his deposition taken pursuant to a California court order. He was asked to bring to the deposition all relevant documents, and all other items relevant to the case, regardless of volume, that were listed in the original Notice of Deposition given last June. I believe I sent a copy of that notice? Right?"

"Yes, that's the order we have here," Bray said. "Also, the documents will be available for him to have them retranslated or to look at, and to have copies made for his own files should he wish to have them."

—⁂—

I HAD no idea what they were talking about. Rossi had already shown me all of the documents that had been sent to him, and we had discussed them. I had already agreed to everything.

ADAM Rossi was asked to read a document titled "Preamble" and to translate it into Italian before they went back on the record.

"You have a copy of that document to read, Mr. Rossi, in front of you," Bray said.

"Yes, I do," Rossi replied. He read the document aloud to Dante, translating into Italian as he went.

"Thank you," said Bray. "Please write at the bottom, 'Translated and read.'" He pointed to the bottom of the page.

"Here, or here?" Rossi asked.

"On the right side—right here," Bray said, pointing specifically.

"And Mr. Montepulciano?" Rossi said.

"Yes, he should initial. And I would like this document to be attached to the deposition as an exhibit. In addition, I understand that all parties have executed our settlement offer—our compromise agreement—tonight, and that's the reason why we are here." He took the documents and gave them to Rossi. "I would like you to show Mr. Montepulciano a copy of the documents that have been executed. This will confirm that those are the settlement documents that we want to negotiate."

WHAT mumbo jumbo.

I was not asking for money. I was just trying to live up to my relationship with Caprice and our mutual solemn pact, the *Atto Solenne*.

I thought everyone knew that money did not interest me. Caprice knew that, and John Butler did, too. A main reason Caprice trusted me and loved me was my indifference to her wealth. She loved my personality and humor.

JACK Orso broke his silence and said, "Before we do that, counselor, as a housekeeping detail, perhaps the record should reflect that the Preamble will be marked as Deposition Exhibit Number One. The Ex Parte Application should be marked as Deposition Exhibit Number Two. The Order Confirming Stipulation should be marked as Deposition Exhibit Three. And the Commission should be marked as Deposition Exhibit Four."

"Yes. Would you please so mark those, Mr. Reporter," Bray instructed. Nelson marked the documents respectively as the charities' Deposition Exhibits 1, 2, 3, and. 4 They were attached and made a part of the deposition record.

"Wait a minute," objected Donald Murray.

"Don't worry, Mr. Butler will show the documents to Mr. Montepulciano," Bray assured him, having anticipated the objection. "Is this agreeable to Mr. Montepulciano?"

"I'll ask him," Rossi said.

—m—

MR. Rossi asked me if I was happy with the steps being taken by these lawyers, and I answered in Italian, "Why is all this paperwork needed?"

"My client agrees," Rossi said.

"No," interrupted Butler. "He asked, 'why is all this paperwork needed?'" said John Butler.

Rossi did not interrupt.

"This is all about you charities," I said. "You are in Italy," I said reminding them.

"No, you are in California," Bass said gruffly.

"There is no California flag on the table," I said shouting.

"You lose," Bass said, taunting me.

In the moment I hated Bass.

I showed the documents to Guido and Lessa.

THE GOLDEN PACT

"WAIT a minute. Please have that translated," Donald Murray demanded.

"It's okay. Dante agrees." Rossi assured. "And Guido says that some of those documents constitute amendments and corrections of others, but the documents speak for themselves. Do you understand, Mr. Bray?"

"Yes."

"The reading of the documents will explain what the documents say," Rossi insisted. The lawyers discussed Rossi's statement, wondering whether Dante had changed the order of documents.

"Mr. Montepulciano does *not* affirm your offer of settlement," said Rossi. "It needs discussion later."

"What?" said Bass, waking up. "Jesus!"

The other charity lawyers all said, "What?"

Bray looked alarmed. "I thought the Compromise Agreement was approved—we understand that he has agreed to accept five hundred thousand U.S. dollars."

Rossi said, "He has not."

"Christ almighty," said Jack Orso. "When will we know what his number is?" asked Bray.

Bray interrupted everybody. "It's important that everyone understand that Mr. Montepulciano has not accepted any number."

"Where did $500,000 come from?" said Bass.

"Not from Dante," said Butler.

"Jeesus Christ," said Bass shaking his head.

—◇—

I WAS tired and wanted to leave. The charity lawyers didn't understand. I pulled Butler's sleeve and told him I was tired.

"I understand, Dante. The Americans have just seen your changes to their offer to settle."

"Yes, I understand."

"So just wait for a few moments."

"I SEE. Then we'll put the Compromise Agreement off for now," Bray said. "For present purposes, I have the English version Compromise Agreement and the Italian translation of the Compromise Agreement, and I would like to offer those to be attached to the deposition as Exhibits Five and Six, respectively," Guy Bray said.

Whereupon the Compromise Agreement was marked Exhibit 5, and the Italian translation of the Compromise Agreement was marked Exhibit 6, and both were attached and made part of the deposition's documentation.

Next, Bray said he had heard something about a document called *Atto Solenne*—a special agreement between Caprice and Dante.

"Mr. Montepulciano," he asked, "do you have a copy of the *Atto Solenne* document?"

"I think I do. I'll have to look for it. I don't have it with me."

"Please bring it tomorrow, then."

"It's a private document, one between a husband and his wife."

John Butler said, "That's a document I drew up for you and Mrs. Taylor, Mr. Montepulciano."

"Yes, sir. I know that," Dante said.

"Do you have a copy of it?" said Butler

"I haven't found it," he lied.

"I'll make a copy of it, Butler said. "You'll need it."

Dante felt badly he had lied. He would discuss it later with Rossi.

WHAT? I did not want the Americans to include that document! It was personal. It concerned only Caprice and me. I carefully and emphatically warned them through Adam Rossi that I didn't know if I had that document.

Although the American lawyers were disheartened by my vague attitude, they were too tired to go into it and simply hoped for the best.

IT was now past midnight.

"Let's put on the record that the deposition is recessed until four P.M. tomorrow. We're all tired and want to conclude for the night," Bray said to the court reporter.

And so they agreed to recess. They also agreed that Dante did not have to bring everything that bore upon the issues. However, they specifically requested that he bring photographs, particularly those in the United States that showed him and Caprice together.

In addition, they asked for a sample of letters written by Caprice, if he had any; any written documents signed by Caprice that dealt directly with the Golden Pact, also known as the *Atto Solenne*; and any documents that would reflect on the creation of a common-law marriage in Colorado.

—⚶—

FINALLY, the first day's done!

I grabbed my brother and Lessa, and we hurriedly left the room. Guido drove me to my flat.

11

DAY 2: Credentials

NO ONE, INCLUDING Dante Montepulciano's legal advisors, could have expected the second deposition day to begin so quixotically. All the handshakes, embraces, cheek-kissing, and solicitous greetings masked it. To begin with, what Guy Bray wanted for purposes of the record was the date, time, and place of Dante's birth; then he would proceed to argue on behalf of the charities. That seemed innocent enough. Bray distributed to his American colleagues copies of the agenda for the day, and then he called for Dante's birth records to be entered into the record.

"No," Rossi objected. "My client wishes to start differently."

This upset the charity lawyers. They demanded private time to discuss this surprise request. Most of them were upset, but Bray insisted on a careful, disciplined response. Underlying his caution was the potential threat of Colorado's common-law judicial rulings. The charity lawyers were in a tough spot.

—⚋—

I WANTED to establish my credentials on my terms. They must agree to this. I would not just play their game. I wanted my documents to lead this California deposition being held in my country. Caprice would appreciate a strong defense by me.

I would agree to give them my birth certificate. But I wanted to insert my own documentation first. My brother Guido agreed, and so did Lessa.

"WE need to be driving this agenda," insisted Jack Orso when the American team were all gathered together in Roberto Galileo's office. "This is getting out of control, Guy."

"I think we all feel the same," said Bill Bass. "I say screw Montepulciano, and screw his request."

"Mr. Bass," said Bray, "let's look at our legal position."

"Screw that too. Montepulciano is trying to take control."

Patiently, Bray explained that in fact Dante was a legal heir under Colorado law. The common-law marriage was undeniable.

The charity lawyers decided to follow Bray's advice.

It was time for the two sides to reconvene. The Americans went silently back into the meeting room, entered single file, and took their seats.

"In the interest of saving time," said Bray to Rossi, "can we first attach a true copy of Mr. Montepulciano's birth record to our deposition record?"

"No offense, Mr. Bray, but that is quite impossible at this moment," Rossi said. "First, Mr. Montepulciano insists that we agree to enter three other documents. And we must agree before we enter his birth record. These documents will establish my client's impeccable reputation and integrity. Please agree to allow these documents, and then we can proceed with the birth certificate."

Bray looked directly at Dante. He was not a man who took surprises lightly. He was upset that Dante was trying to change the order of the presentation of credentials.

—\m/—

GUIDO glared at me, making sure I would shut up. I did.

Except for Rossi, nobody in the room knew that early in our romance Caprice had hired a detective to certify my background. And of course I had passed scrutiny.

If my background had showed a problem, we would never have gone together to Rifle, Colorado.

"NEITHER his reputation nor his integrity are under question," Bray added. That was a lie.

"Of course not," Rossi said, not trusting the Americans' approach.

"So, Mr. Rossi, what are these three other documents?"

"If you will let us attach them to the proceedings, you will find out."

"But we have no prior knowledge of these documents, Mr. Rossi," Bray said, objecting to the lack of protocol in Rossi's request. "We should have received these documents in advance of this deposition."

"Yes, well, we're a bit late. Dante's brother, Guido, wants us to enter into the record three documents, in the following order: first, a letter from a social worker; second, four pages from a novel; and third, Dante Montepulciano's *curriculum vitae*."

"A letter from a social worker?" said Bass.

"That's correct."

"A novel?" Bass said, looking glum.

"Yes—only four pages, though."

"And then Mr. Montepulciano's *curriculum vitae*?" said Bass, looking even more glum, finishing with a "shit" that hung awkwardly in the room.

—⚬—

EVEN Adam Rossi, my own lawyer, had disagreed with Guido. He said that the Americans would not agree. The American lawyers would be upset with us. And they were upset, but they agreed.

Guido was right after all.

The American charity lawyers looked like professional, well-trained estate people—even Bass. They were obviously on a mission—each to maximize their employer's gifts. I must have some strength in my position as the surprise husband or they wouldn't be this considerate. Right? I said to myself.

I looked at Guido and Lessa. Their eyes indicated "shut up."

I didn't say a word.

GUY Bray scratched his head. "But we haven't had a chance to review these documents. And going over them one by one could take a lot of time."

"That's correct," Rossi answered.

"Will Mr. Montepulciano accept just attaching them to the record?" Bray asked. He glanced at Guido, Lessa, Dante, and Adam Rossi.

Guido shook his head from side to side. "Mr. Bray, it's important to my brother that his reputation be viewed as impeccable by your California court in Italy—as it is in California and in Colorado."

"Jesus H. Christ," Bill Blass blurted, but Bray shut him up and ordered the proceeding to go off the record. Again the American lawyers retreated to Galileo's office for a short discussion. Behind closed doors, they again quarreled about how to proceed. Bray again repeated that Mrs. Taylor's will simply instructed them to settle with Mr. Montepulciano. The amount of the settlement was up to them. They would hash that out on the fourth deposition day.

"How much is the estate's holding of Jordan Oil worth today?" said Orso.

"About fifty million U.S. dollars."

"Jesus."

"We all agree," said Bray.

"It would be nice if he didn't get any of that," Bass said.

Bray ignored the remark and so did the other charity lawyers.

HAH, so I was correct.

I asked Butler for a private word. We stepped outside of the meeting room.

"Did someone say fifty-million-dollars?"

"Yes, Dante," said Butler. "Another oil company is acquiring Mrs. Taylor's oil company. This should help everyone in the room."

I thanked Butler for the information and we returned to the deposition room.

Mr. Bass was an enemy. This whole legal circus was an attempt to discredit me and Caprice and our relationship.

I felt anxiety and anger. Mostly, I felt anger.

THE GOLDEN PACT

"WHAT was discussed, Mr. Butler?" Bray asked. "It's a responsibility to report such private conversations."

"Mr. Montepulciano asked to know the current size of the Taylor estate."

"And he now knows?"

"Jesus H. Christ." Bass threw a pen across the room.

Bray immediately asked for a private meeting.

In Galileo's office, Bray reminded the other Americans that if they weren't careful the case might be appealed and go to Colorado, where Dante's lawyers might successfully argue for at least fifty percent of the estate. He insisted they support his judgment and let him lead the deposition, and he warned Bass that another "Jesus H. Christ" would send him, Bass, packing.

That was that. The Americans returned to the conference room, and Bray called the deposition back to order.

"Mr. Rossi, how long will it take to read in these three documents?" Bray asked, trying to figure out how much they could get accomplished in this second day.

"As long as it takes, Mr. Bray," Rossi answered. He didn't want to appear rude, but he intended to do a proper job.

"Um, could you try to do it in twenty minutes?" Bray appealed.

"We're not trying to be difficult."

"Okay, let's read the birth certificate into the record as Exhibit Seven."

ACTUALLY, it was okay with me if they read my birth certificate first—what I wanted in return was the reading of the letter from a social worker, four pages from the novel, and my résumé.

I warned Rossi that I was starting to get a headache. He looked concerned, but I told him not to worry. While the Americans were out of the room, he told me, "Dante, you must not get upset. I know what I'm doing. You know what the American charity lawyers want. You will get what you want. Just remain calm—I'm here to help you. Okay?

"Yes, Mr. Rossi."

DANTE spoke up. "It's important in the life of an Italian to know the exact date—year, month, day, and minute—that a person is born. I have the same birthday as your General Ulysses S. Grant. I read that in a book."

"General Grant?" Bray repeated in astonishment. "Do you want that in the record too?

"Sì," Dante answered, "exactamente."

—⁊⁊⁊—

I GRINNED with excitement.

The Americans yearned for a compromise financial agreement— it showed on their faces and in their agenda. As far as I was concerned, let them work for it.

Rossi kicked my ankle, hissing, "Be careful. Snakes can bite back and kill you. That is the character of the law."

I reassured him that I was being cautious.

Once, when Caprice and I visited Venice, I told her that my birthday was on the same day as General Grant's. I had packed my military uniform, so she insisted that I wear it. I didn't know it at the time, but she had purchased some general's stars—three for each of my epaulettes! We showed off, and she threw a big party and paid for everyone's dinner and wine at a restaurant that was famous for its wild boar.

Although Caprice was careful with her money, every so often she would hold a big, spontaneous party. She knew how to enjoy herself. That night we had a beautiful party.

Still, I worried because of her illness with alcohol. I would say, "Caprice, wine is not good for you."

"Don't be stuffy, Dante," she would say. "I'm almost cured."

Afterwards, we had a wonderful steamy night.

THE GOLDEN PACT

DANTE'S birth certificate contained errors. There were *z*'s where *l*'s and *c*'s should have been used–misspelling his last name as Montepuzziano. A lawyer representing the Italian civil service had appended a note acknowledging the error. Donald Murray spoke up and reported that Dante already knew about it, and that there was no problem with this administrative error.

All eyes turned to Dante. No one believed for a moment that he would let this slip by, and their expectations were met. The American charities' lawyers held their breath, watching Dante's reaction, hoping this time he would actually respond.

Dante whispered something to Adam Rossi. Rossi looked up and smiled. "Mr. Montepulciano says he does have a problem with the misspelling. Furthermore, there is another problem with the name as shown on the birth certificate."

"My proper name is Dante Valentino Caesar Montepulciano," said Dante. "I would like my name pronounced and spelt correctly."

"Of course, Mr. Montepulciano," Bray said, instructing all present to please meet Dante's request.

Everyone agreed—even Bass.

"Thank you," Dante said.

—⟋⟍⟋—

THIS was a small point in Italy, but I would use it to my advantage with the Americans.

Back in the early days of my romance with Caprice, I signed documents using "Valentino Caesar"—"Dante Valentino Caesar Montepulciano." When we were feeling romantic, Caprice loved to call me Valentino. It reminded her of the Hollywood movie star. It was part of our personal theater together, the ability to lose ourselves in each other.

What halcyon days. "Halcyon" is a Greek word describing the mythical kingfisher bird that nested in a floating nest out at sea. But for us it stood for times enjoyed by two idyllically happy, peaceful people.

"DANTE says he is concerned," said Rossi. "His full name is Dante Valentino Caesar Montepulciano. In Italy it is common to use just one's first and last name. The document lists only his first and last name. In error it omits Valentino and Caesar, his grandfathers' names."

"That's okay with us," Bray said.

"No, you don't understand. He has *signed* documents concerning his relationship with Caprice Jordan Taylor using all of his names. He wants you to be exact."

"I see."

"Valentino and Caesar are the names of his grandfathers. He wants us all to understand that."

"We understand. Valentino Caesar," Bray said. "Please assure your client we understand and appreciate his full name. They are the names of his grandfathers. Now would you be kind enough, Mr. Rossi, to let us admit the birth certificate into the record?"

—⁂—

I HAD to go to the bathroom. I excused myself and encouraged them to proceed without me.

Of course they couldn't. California law apparently requires that the person being deposed be present at all times during the proceedings. That makes sense.

As I said earlier, the name Valentino is important to me. When she was a young girl, my mother had a crush on Rudolph Valentino, the silent film actor. After she saw him in *The Sheik,* she vowed that her first son would bear his name. Many girls liked the name, including Caprice, who in our loving moments called me her Valentino, and at times, Caesar.

Caesar needs no explanation.

I insisted the American charity lawyers use my full name. It was part of my relationship with Caprice.

THERE was a short discussion among the Americans, during which Dante returned to the deposition room and sat down next to Adam Rossi.

"We're in agreement as to his full name," said Bray. "Let's continue. We see that a letter of some kind is attached to Dante's birth certificate. It appears to be addressed to you, Mr. Rossi. Would you translate it for us, please?"

Rossi adjusted his reading glasses and read. "It's addressed to Mr. Avvocato Adam Rossi, Via Borgonovo—B-o-r-g-o-n-o-v-o—number nine, Milan, and the object is Montepulciano, Dante."

"Object?"

"That means subject."

"I understand."

Some moments passed while Rossi scanned the letter so that he could translate it into English. Then he continued.

"I attach hereto the Extract of the Register of the Certificate of Birth for the name cited in the premises. The annotation *nessuna* means that Montepulciano is unmarried, as has been confirmed to me by the officer upon the first examination of the register. With kindest regards, Mr. Aldo Zenari."

Dante interrupted Rossi by tugging his sleeve. A short, animated conversation took place between them. Dante spoke in rapid Italian. At one point he abruptly stood and walked completely around the meeting room table, talking loudly and gesturing with both hands. When he reached his chair, he just as abruptly sat down and fell silent.

THIS subject was more important to me than to them. They must recognize my full name and spell it correctly. And they must realize the meaning of *nessuna* and how incomplete records are in Italy.

Both Rossi and Butler had discussed this with me and had told me that they would discuss the problems. They also told me not to worry.

The trouble is that I *was* worried—I had to appear legitimate.

"EXCUSE us, please, sirs," Rossi said, "but Mr. Montepulciano is still concerned about the misspelling of his family name."

Guy Bray moved immediately to dispel any concerns. He asked Adam to please inform Dante that they had already noted the spelling error. He promised that the final record would use the correct and full spelling of all of Dante's names, including Valentino and Caesar.

After some discussion between Rossi and Dante, the matter seemed settled and they gave permission. The deposition could continue. John Butler and Guy Bray smiled because it was not up to Dante to give or deny permission. Somehow he had taken control of the deposition.

Donald Murray watched the estate lawyers while they tried to read their copies of the letter attached to Dante's birth certificate. He kept an eye on Orso, who was discussing with Bass the Italian words that defined whether one was single or married, a fact that was certain to weigh heavily on Dante's settlement. Murray decided he ought to enter some testimony into the record. He was determined to dampen fires before they got out of control, so he went after the Italian phrase *"di stato libero."*

—ɷ—

OOPS. It occurred to me that the phrase *"di stato libero"* might cause misunderstanding. It was obviously confusing the charity lawyers. I also knew it was leading them to a conclusion they wanted to prove: that Caprice and I were not husband and wife.

That's the trouble with bureaucracy. First they make mistakes with my name, and now with my marital status. They should have written "unknown."

This is a mess.

"Excuse me," I said to Rossi, pulling on his sleeve.

"Yes, Dante," he said.

"Would you explain *di stato libero* to the Americans for me?" I said in Italian.

Rossi asked for everyone's attention.

"MR. Rossi, what does *"di stato libero"* mean?" Murray said, letting his question hang out there, inviting anyone to answer.

"*Libero* means free—unmarried."

"*Un*married?"

"Yes," said Rossi.

"Does it mean *never* married?"

"No, it simply means unmarried."

"Could it mean they just don't know?"

"Yes," said Rossi.

Bass jumped to a conclusion. "It says in plain language 'unmarried,' so Mr. Montepulciano is unmarried."

John Butler immediately raised a hand. "Mr. Bray, I would like to speak off the record."

"We're off record, Mr. Butler," said Bray.

"Gentlemen, we are not addressing *libero*. We already know that Mrs. Taylor and Mr. Montepulciano were considered husband and wife under a Colorado common-law statute."

"In my opinion, Mr. Butler," said Bass, "we haven't fully considered the implications of the word *libero*."

"I agree," said Orso.

Butler said, "Mr. Bray?"

"I think we're on a different mission," Bray said. "We're here to try settle an amount on Mr. Montepulciano."

"We don't agree," said Bass.

"No way," said Orso.

—⚬—

MY heart rate doubled.

This could get out of hand.

BUTLER understood Murray's intent and joined the fray, buttressed by his own knowledge of Italian. "There is a difference between *libero* and *nessuna.*"

"What is it?" Rossi inquired, wondering how much Italian the American lawyer knew, and knowing that this conversation could only help his client.

"*Nessuna* means 'no one,' in the feminine gender. *Libero* means 'free,'" Butler said, looking at Jack Orso, eager to prevent him from goading Dante into some unknown reaction that might hurt his own case.

"The thing is," Rossi said, "according to the certificate, Mr. Dante Montepulciano was never married. A prior marriage would have been noted."

"All right," Murray said.

"A divorced person is *di stato libero* as well," continued Rossi. "But then, such a certificate of birth in Italy should show the prior marriage, *and* the divorce."

Murray wanted this definition understood by all. "I see. You mean *nessuna* and *libero* as annotations?"

"Correct. As annotations." Rossi smiled. Dante smiled too. The American charities' lawyers frowned and remained silent.

"Okay," said Bass, disgusted. "It's about as clear as mud."

—〰—

I DIDN'T think it was clear either. Two of the American lawyers were calculating whether they could avoid settling with me. That would leave me little power to negotiate honors for Caprice.

I saw my job as making sure that Caprice's charitable gifts were recognized so that the rest of the world would properly acknowledge who gave the gifts.

I told Rossi this, and he assured me we would win this point.

"SO if a woman's certificate was obtained," Bray asked, "might it contain the word *nubile,* n-u-b-i-l-e?"

"Yes," Rossi said. "But we are not dealing with *nubile.*"

"What would that word—*nubile*—signify?" Bray persisted, partly to annoy Butler and Orso.

"It would signify never married," said Rossi. "But never mind that. Mr. Montepulciano is concerned about being called illegitimate—an illegitimate husband."

"Now I get it," Bray said. He turned to Dante and asked, "Are you the individual that is named Dante Montepulciano, that was born in Verona on April twenty-seven, nineteen twenty?"

Dante nodded his head.

"Please say it aloud. For the record."

"I am that person."

"And when you were in Colorado, did Mrs. Taylor consider herself your wife?"

"Yes," said Dante. "Yes, she did!"

"Mr. Montepulciano confirms!" Rossi said triumphantly.

"Thank you for the questions," Dante said, beaming in turn at Rossi, Butler, and Murray. He clutched his hands above his head as if he had just scored a goal in an international soccer match. He whispered extravagant compliments to Rossi.

"We have documents that we think will persuade you," Rossi said. "We will present them later. First we simply want to submit Mr. Montepulciano's birth certificate."

I GRINNED with pleasure.

I jumped on my chair, bowed to the lawyers, and said, "Thank you for understanding me. Thank you!"

Then I ran slowly around the room in a victory lap.

Why did I do that? I don't know.

BRAY ignored Dante's antics and continued his line of questioning, intent on completing his point for the record. "Other than your common-law marriage to Mrs. Taylor, have you ever been married to anyone else?"

"No."

"Your answer is 'No'?"

"'No' is my answer."

"Then do you confirm that the document, except for the incorrect spelling of Mr. Montepulciano's name, accurately records the facts as you understand them—*di stato libero,*" Bray asked, smiling at Dante.

"Yes, yes. Mr. Montepulciano confirms," Rossi said, clapping his hands over their significant triumph. Dante thumped Rossi's back, whispering cheers of support, *"Bravissimo! bravissimo! bravissimo!"*

Bray glanced at his watch and noted how quickly time was passing. Half of the evening was gone. "Would you remind Mr. Montepulciano that we're anxious to get to his four-page story?" he said to Donald Murray, picking Dante's American counsel to solve the time problem. Bray explained that the more quickly they could enter the required documents into the record, the more quickly they could go back to their hotels.

Bray told Rossi he just wanted to enter the facts for the record. Rossi turned to his client and told him what Bray had asked for.

I SETTLED down.

But the four pages of the novel were obviously important to my brother Guido, who was the one to identify the novel. I was curious what it was all about.

Nevertheless I decided to skip the four pages.

It's enough to have the four pages placed in this deposition record, and I told Guido so.

I wanted to get to a social worker's letter.

THE GOLDEN PACT

MURRAY turned to his client and said in a firm tone of voice, "Mr. Montepulciano, the way a deposition works is that Mr. Bray is to ask you questions, and you are supposed to answer those questions. Additional conversations can be saved until a later time."

Dante waved a hand, merrily acknowledging Murray's little speech.

"Mr. Bray, do you want to—" Rossi started to say, lifting the two other documents they wanted to enter into the deposition record. One of them was the novel excerpt.

Bill Bass interrupted, wondering what in the world a goddamned novel had to do with all this. "Now, that's what I would like to get to. We have two other documents: a letter from a social worker we don't know, and a novel we haven't read. Isn't it out of place to enter an entire novel as an exhibit?"

Rossi replied, "We agree—but we are only submitting four pages. What I can do is briefly give an idea of what each page means. We could then attach a complete translation of the four pages as the exhibit."

"I say we skip them," said Bass.

"I'll briefly describe each page as I read it," Rossi said.

"With the permission of Guido," John Butler said. He wanted to make sure that the entire attending Montepulciano clan was happy. Unhappiness would only stress Dante and lead to more unpredictable behavior.

Bray felt the same way.

"I say we skip it," Bass repeated, but the others ignored him.

—ɯ—

THERE he was again—Mr. Bass, acting rudely. I didn't like him. Not to worry. Mr. Bray was in control.

"OKAY," Bray continued. "The next document is a copy of a letter from a social worker, addressed to—"

"Can we go off the record for a moment and talk in private?" asked Jack Orso. Orso had decided that as the representative the Art Museum, some action from him was necessary.

Once again, the Americans retreated to Galileo's office. Orso complained that the documents Dante wanted to introduce were irrelevant. Valuable time was being lost, and the three proposed documents, in his opinion, added nothing. Bray sympathized but reminded Orso that they probably had to listen. To offend the Italians could have serious consequences when it came to how much each charity would ultimately receive from the estate.

Orso reluctantly dropped his point, and they returned to the conference room, where Guy Bray called the deposition back to order.

"For the record, the original of the novel is before us," Bray said. "It consists of one hundred seventy-five numbered pages, plus the introductions, and the portion that is copied is only a small portion of the novel. How many pages are we talking about?"

—𝔐—

I WATCHED them leave the deposition room.

I contented myself by walking around the table. "Mr. Butler, up to her death, were you Caprice's estate lawyer?"

"Yes."

"Good."

"The others are talking privately. Does that bother you?"

"No."

Okay. If it's all right with Butler, fine with me.

"PAGES? Only four," Rossi said. "But before that, Dante wants us to introduce the letter written by a social worker—"

"Yes," Dante interjected.

"Because the letter is dated twenty-three November, nineteen forty-nine, and the novel is nineteen fifty-nine. It's a sociological novel."

"Okay," said Bray. "Let's start with the letter, if you would now translate."

The social worker's letter was on letterhead that read MILITARY HOUSE FOR THE VETERANS OF THE NATIONAL WARS. It was postmarked in Turate, which is near Lake Como.

Guido began to read in Italian; Rossi simultaneously translated.

"'Dear Sir,

"'I dare to address myself to your noted human sensibility and comprehension to vouch for the honor of Mr. Dante Montepulciano.'"

"Oh, for fuck sake."

"Mr. Bass, apologize to the Montepulcianos," Bray said shocked by Bass's outbreak.

"No."

"I will end tonight's deposition, if you don't apologize."

The other charity lawyers urgently demanded that Bass apologize.

"Well, I guess I did overreact," said Bass looking uncomfortable. He rose from his chair, turned, and looked at Lessa, Guido, and Dante, saying, "Gentlemen I apologize for my comment and bad manners."

CAPRICE must be looking down on me.

Guido refused to look at me. This was both a true testimony and to my advantage.

John Butler just stared straight ahead.

I knew the charity lawyers were not happy.

"'I AM writing this because I have a debt of honor to this young person, who for three years has volunteered to help me, and who is doing his best for the happiness of the poor and elderly soldiers who have recovered from service injuries and are guests in this house. Faith—'"

Guido stopped and asked, "What do you call people who, you know, just think about their faith?"

"Philosophers?" Bray suggested.

"No. They only think about the faith, and forget about the world," Rossi said.

"Meditators?" Bray said.

"Yes," Rossi said.

"Like nuns. Nuns in a cloister. That's the closest I can get," Bray said.

"Okay," Rossi accepted, motioning for Guido to continue.

"'The faith of a cloister and enthusiasm of an apostle make Dante Montepulciano an athlete of that principal social virtue which is the love for people, people who suffer, the desperate, a love with vibrations that are high and very deep. He is very serious for the following: He feels in his heart more for others than for himself.'"

—m—

I REMEMBER the social worker. She worked at a Catholic hospital dedicated to veterans. I was still recovering from the head wound I had received in North Africa during World War II. She cared for soldiers with brain injuries. She helped me through a bad time in my life. My recovery was difficult. I had to learn to speak again, to walk, and had to recover many of my memories. Guido was helpful too, but this middle-aged nun was the key to my recovery.

"'IN a recent case that occurred in this institution, he once again demonstrated his generosity and his willingness to sacrifice himself, with very little money and with an immense faith. He went to Rome, where he bravely battled for a cause that I would call saintly.

"'The continuous gift that he makes with purity of his own heart and of his own activity is a very rare gift in this world. In light of which any noble person would forgive this man for small mistakes he may have made.

"'That is why I admire him and love him as a son, a son who must be understood and helped.

"'I am sorry to dare so much, and I remain,

"'Sincerely yours,

"'Commendatore Tramonti.'"

Guido spelled out the writer's last name, "T-r-a-m-o-n-t-i."

"This will be Exhibit Eight," Rossi said. "You'd better photocopy it."

"Mr. Nelson," Bray said, "at the next recess, would you please take the document that was just read by Mr. Rossi. Mark it as Deposition Exhibit Eight, and attach it to the proceedings of this deposition."

MY memories of it all were still fresh—as if I were reliving the moment.

A shell exploded overhead.

I was wearing my helmet. The soldiers in front of me and behind me were killed instantly. I fell unconscious. My helmet disintegrated, and a part of my skull was blown off .

I was left with vivid scars running from the back of my head to halfway down the left side of my forehead.

NEXT, Rossi distributed copies of a novel to each of the lawyers. It was titled *Aspirante*, and the author was Mariuccia Bergomi. Some discussion ensued about the meaning of the title.

"Aspirations?" Bray guessed.

"No," said Rossi. "Aspirant. A person who aspires to something—you know, one who is starting law school is an *aspirante*. The novel is about an aspiring social worker."

Rossi began to read from the text.

"'The past winter, I remained for a whole night close to the man who removed the snow, and I learned much more during that night than I learned during many years at the university. The man seemed to come directly from a painting of the eighteenth century. He had a heavy beard and wore a scarf over his nose and mouth, so that one could see only his forehead.

"'Marco had just introduced me to him, and we three started walking along this street full of lights. The cold wind had cleaned the sky, which was full of stars above the houses that lined the street. There were many people around, happy and walking in a hurry, people who had left their offices, girls looking at the windows of the shops, people happily talking how little bit about everything. In the Piazza Cavour we stopped before the red lights at the streetcar tracks.

Rossi continued reading.

"'The conversation was getting thicker, and we were getting to know each other better, and I could study my new friend and relate his words to his gestures and the expressions on his face. I learned that he was a former officer who had fought in Africa. He had to quit the army and had attended various universities, passing some sixty courses without ever graduating. And now, wanting to become a social worker, he was observing the shame of a society without any order and was trying to rescue somebody who was sinking.

—⚊⚊—

THIS was going well, so far.

"'WE stopped under a street light, very happy to talk to each other and to understand each other. Shadows and lights played on our faces, giving us many different images. It occurred to me that the game of reality is always the same and always different. My new friend would never get tired of talking. His voice was slightly hoarse, like that of someone who passes most of his time in discussions.

"'He said, "There is a precise cause for any guilt, a precise and remote reason. And there is always a story that precedes the guilt and this I've researched with love. For young people, what we call guilt is usually no more than an act of rebellion against society, and sometimes against a bad destiny."

"'Marco said, "If we stop making excuses and look for justifications for people, we will an fact favor what's happening."

"'I was attempting to reconcile them, as I was in the middle. And for the most intelligent ones, those who have understood life well who have seen prostitution in the house and outside, for them there is rebellion against society. The others are dead weight that we must carry."'

—ɯ—

I LOOKED at the charity lawyers. They appeared to be listening.
    I looked at John Butler and he smiled back.

"'…HE had dreamed of glory in Africa, and now he was trying to do something noble and generous to feel alive and heroic.

"'He had dedicated himself to restoring society, which was falling to pieces because of a war in which he had fought earnestly.

"'Marco asked, "And what is society giving you for all you do?"

"'The aspirant replied, "My dream is to work as a social worker in schools. For now, I look out for the boys, give some lessons, and I have a bit of money on which to support myself. I would like to teach soccer and philosophy—probably in a parochial school."

"'Now I understood. A St. Francis with a small bank account. "It's a pity," I said, "that society does not want to be restored, at least by you." He laughed, amused by this, and then he left, smiling. He went away, walking…'"

—◊—

I GOT up and walked around the room, pantomiming the walk.

The Italians and John Butler laughed. They understood Italian farce, which involves absurdity. The humor of Charlie Chaplin is like that. I wished I had on baggy pants and a beaten-up black hat and was carrying a cane.

There I was, a broken soldier with a Medal of Valor, being confronted by a bunch of charity lawyers.

I was happy I got them to laugh, even though their laughter resulted from being startled—not from my Charlie Chaplin walk.

"'...WALKING clumsily along the now deserted street, until his shadow disappeared into the night.'"

Rossi was finished reading and looked up. Except for John Butler and Donald Murray, all of the Americans looked bewildered, wondering what the last seemingly interminable minutes had been all about. But no one questioned Rossi. They were content to let sleeping dogs lie.

Bray broke the silence.

"Mr. Nelson, at the recess, if you would, please make a copy of the first page, which appears to be the cover of the book from which this comes; the second page, which is an inscription bearing the date February twenty-second, nineteen fifty-nine; and the third and fourth pages, which are pages one-twenty-three and one-twenty-four, respectively, which have just been translated, and mark the true and correct copies as Exhibit Nine."

—m—

SO much for that.

A DISCUSSION ensued off the record. There was much pointing to watches, yawning, and general boredom. It was agreed that Bray would call a recess. Then battle plans could be reassessed and more productive directions pursued, at least according to the American estate lawyers.

"Thank you, Mr. Rossi. Can we move on now?" Bray said, noting that Rossi was listening intently to Dante.

With a vigorous nod of his head and reassurances to Dante, Rossi declared that they did have just one more thing.

"Yes, thank you," said Rossi. "As previously stated, we would lastly like to introduce into the record Mr. Montepulciano's *curriculum vitae*. This will give a fair and accurate account of his accomplishments and credentials."

An audible groan went around the meeting table. Rossi understood that he had already exhausted the lawyers' patience. But everyone quieted down, hoping that this last exhibit would go quickly.

"Thank you," said Bray formally but with a note of weariness. "Would you please read that into the record, Mr. Rossi? We will mark it as Exhibit Ten."

Guido grinned at his brother. Dante averted his eyes.

—◆—

Guido had written the *curriculum vitae* the night before. I was grateful, and I was also curious to find out what it contained.

"THIS is just to give an idea of his education and the specialization of his studies," Rossi added. "This is important to Dante's brother. He composed it last night with the help of Mr. Butler and Mr. Murray."

Orso interrupted. "Perhaps you should read into the record who exactly prepared this document, whose handwriting it is, and so forth." He apparently wanted to discredit the document's authorship as being the work of a third party, not of Dante himself.

"This *curriculum vitae* was prepared by Mr. Guido Montepulciano, the brother of Mr. Dante Montepulciano," Rossi said, addressing the court reporter directly.

"I see," Orso said. "And does this come from his personal knowledge of his brother's activities and education?"

"Yes, it does. It is entitled Memorandum: Demonstration of Specialization."

—⁂—

I TOOK many specialized courses at the university level in psychology and social sciences. But because I have no formal degree, I cannot teach those subjects, and my pay remains lower than what it should be.

But I make do. I live happily, even if I suffer from terrible headaches from time to time. I am happy in my poverty, strange as that may sound.

ADAM Rossi began to read.

"Classic High School. Officer in the Army in Northern Africa, El Alamein. University of Philosophy and Letters, Milan, nineteen forty-four: examinations in psychology. U.S. Army, Milan, Rome, and Palermo: courses in military psychology. School for Social Workers, Milan: Professor Musty, psychoanalysis. Catholic University of Milan: Padre Genelli, laboratory of psychology—Padre Genelli was a master of the University for twelve years. Institution of Psychology, Russeoux, Geneva: experimental international course with Master Mastropolo.

"He was also a student of Marly Leroi, Paris. SPA Liegi, which is in Belgium. Le Paradis des enfants. TESS. Discussed and presented before Professors Musatti, Medugno, Sala, and Mastropolo (London). Course of physiotherapy at the University of Milan. Course for the helpers of people who have a normal character in psychology, 1950, and second course in nineteen fifty-four.

"He participated in a congress in Naples in nineteen fifty, discussing the defense of young children for the psychology section. The chairman was Professor Musatti. Participated in the World Congress in Vienna for the Defense of Children."

Rossi finished quickly, and laid the paperwork aside. He made a gesture to everyone around the conference table, indicating that their ordeal was over. The deposition could now move on to other subjects.

I WAS in tears.

My brother was sweet and considerate.

12

DAY 2: First Meeting?

THEN THE DEPOSITION that began so quixotically took another turn. With the birth certificate, the letter from the social worker, the novel, and Dante's *curriculum vitae* now on record, Guy Bray happily moved on to the charities' lawyers' next agenda item: the first meeting between Dante Montepulciano and Caprice Jordan Taylor. The lawyers' goal was to create at least two impressions in the deposition record. First, they wanted to discredit Dante in a general sense. Second, they intended to weaken his claim of being Caprice's husband. If they could accomplish these goals, the charities might be able to claim the majority of her estate.

—ɯ—

I WAS quite certain the American charities' lawyers would now begin their humiliation of Caprice and me—and of our relationship.

I knew they would try to belittle our marriage. I just didn't know how.

I wasn't hysterical about the coming storm. I was in a good mood. I just felt that Caprice deserved better—after all, hadn't she given each of these Santa Barbara charities wonderful and generous gifts? Demeaning me was demeaning her. Wouldn't private meetings with me, Guido, and Rossi been better? More respectful? Less publicity? Strange how money works.

BRAY looked across the table at Dante, who appeared relaxed and unpretentious. Bray smiled and asked a question in which everyone was interested. "Mr. Montepulciano, tell us, how did you meet Mrs. Caprice Jordan Taylor?"

Dante panicked. He glanced at John Butler on Bray's right. Then he looked at Adam Rossi, then at Guido, on either side of him. He licked his lips. His mouth was as dry as the Sahara Desert, as dry as Death Valley. He was convinced the American lawyers intended to disparage him, which was the exact truth of the matter.

"May I have a glass of water?" he asked weakly.

"Of course," Rossi said, passing a glass of water to him. He grasped Dante's arm, soothing him, speaking softly in Italian. "Don't worry," he said.

—〰—

"WELL, I *am* worried," I said.

"They have to ask you this question," Rossi said. "It's not a bad question, it's a necessary question. We've rehearsed your answer at least a hundred times."

"I have forgotten my lines." My broken brain honestly could not recall my rehearsed answer.

I must protect Caprice. It is in our Golden Pact.

I must protect us!

Rossi tried his best to calm me down. "Just tell the truth. That's all you have to do. Just give the facts."

As I thought about what Rossi said, I smiled.

The facts are comical. Caprice and I often laughed at our first noticing each other. My whole soccer squad noticed it. Even Clarissa was there.

I looked at Rossi, saying, " Of course, this is perfect. It's a good story."

But first these Americans must learn the distinction between 'meeting' and 'noticing'. Especially concerning a wealthy oil heiress and an officer of King Emmanuel III.

ROSSI felt compassion for this honest man who most of all feared humiliation at the hands of the American lawyers.

"They intend to shame my relationship with Caprice," Dante whispered. "They want to defile us, and turn our love into something dirty, something trivial. I want to honor Mrs. Taylor."

"Of course they do," Rossi answered. "But we will not let them do that to you. You must trust me. You must trust your friends, including Mr. Murray and Mr. Butler. You must answer the questions, Dante. Believe me, we will make sure Caprice Jordan Taylor is honored. Just tell them the same story you told us earlier. It's a beautiful story, full of integrity and honor."

Silence enveloped the room. All eyes were on Dante.

Dante took a long drink of water, closed his eyes for a moment, opened them, took a deep breath, looked Guy Bray fully in the eyes, and answered. He spoke thoughtfully, clearly, and slowly, in control of himself once more.

"It depends," he began, in English, choosing his words carefully and speaking with fierce dignity and pride. He let his words sink in for a few moments.

"It depends," he repeated, speaking Italian now, staring into his weathered hands and long, slender fingers. Rossi provided instant translation. "Are you asking about when she first *noticed* me, or when we were first *introduced*?"

"I will tell of our first noticing each other," said Dante.

"Jees… ." said Bass, but stopped because of Bray.

"Don't go there," Bray said curtly, his looking straight at Bass.

—⚹—

GUIDO LOOKED at, laughing, raising his right hand in a welcoming way, encouraging me on.

I gestured back, assuring him that's what I was about to do.

"MR. Montepulciano, *per favore*, I asked how you *met*. How did you first meet Mrs. Caprice Jordan Taylor?" Guy Bray repeated in the friendliest tone of voice he could muster.

"It is not that easy in Italy, Mr. Bray," Dante said, with Rossi translating. "Especially if you are an officer of the king's army."

"You must understand," Rossi explained, "Mr. Montepulciano was an officer, a gentleman. An officer doesn't just go up to a woman and introduce himself. Not to a woman of station. Another person must introduce you. Caprice Jordan Taylor was a woman of position, a woman of means. Everyone knew that. She was a woman who must be respected and approached in just the right manner."

"On the other hand," Dante continued, with Rossi translating, "if you are asking me when she first *noticed* me, that is a simpler matter. It was sometime in nineteen fifty-nine or early nineteen sixty."

"Was it nineteen fifty-nine or nineteen sixty, Mr. Montepulciano?" Bill Bass pleaded, frustrated with yet another piece of ambiguity. It seemed to him that Bray had asked a simple enough question.

"Either nineteen fifty-nine or nineteen sixty," Dante answered.

"Choose one of those years," said Bass demanding an answer to his question.

"I don't remember," Dante said.

Bray asked Dante to continue his story while insisting that Bass stop.

THAT made me angry. Bass was a man who lacked nuance and manners. I wondered if he was married. I doubted it very much.

And he was always sweating. He had loosened his tie and hung his jacket on the back of his chair. His hair was oily. What woman could stand him?

Rossi whispered to me, advising me to control myself.

I decided to say nothing in reply to Bass. John Butler looked relieved.

I looked at Guido and Lessa. They were grinning at me, which infuriated Bass even more.

I turned away from them, worried I would carry things too far.

"I DON'T remember the year exactly," Dante said, his anger barely suppressed. "It was many years ago, and the exact date is not important anyway. Your original question was *how*, not *when* I first met Caprice Jordan."

Bass retorted, "That may be so, but I have just asked you—"

Bray interrupted him. "I think it's best if we first let Mr. Montepulciano answer the question. Afterwards you can ask anything you want."

Rossi asked to go off the record. Bray agreed, and they took a short break. Bray went over to Bass and whispered to him not to interrupt. Bass reddened at the public reprimand, but kept his peace.

Meanwhile, Rossi calmed Dante. He explained that the Americans only wanted to know how Dante and Caprice had met. He reminded him that they had a perfect right to know. Dante insisted he didn't want to answer Bray's first question, but he could not overcome his counselors' insistence that he respond truthfully and right away.

Rossi told Bray they were ready to resume.

—⁓—

FOR a charity lawyer, I thought, Bass was not trustworthy. He seemed devious.

I decided to do my best to forget him. I'd deal with him later. I'd teach him an Italian thing or two about etiquette.

I fondly remembered our first noticing each other. We used to laugh about it. It was obvious that Americans don't put much importance on noticing. Perhaps I was mistaken, but these charity lawyers seemed to miss the importance of distinguishing between noticing and meeting.

"WOULD you please read back Mr. Bray's last question?" Rossi asked the court reporter.

"'How did you first meet Mrs. Caprice Jordan Taylor?'" Nelson read.

"We didn't have a 'first meeting,' as you imply," Dante replied reluctantly.

"So how did you first meet?" Bray said.

"She *noticed* me," Dante said, smiling inwardly.

"Noticed?" Bass said.

"Yes, she noticed me," Dante said.

Now Orso uncharacteristically threw up his hands. "This isn't going to get us anywhere," he snarled. "At this pace we'll be in Milan for the rest of the goddamned millennium. I can't in good conscience accept such evasive answers." He glared at Bray. "My client, the Museum of Art, is not getting good value. Mother of Christ, counselor."

"Mr. Orso, you're out of order," Guy Bray snapped. "Strike Mr. Orzo's outburst," he told the court recorder. "We're off the record."

ORSO surprised me. He was a gentleman and had served in the military, which I respected. I still liked him, but his outburst caught me flat-footed. The charities' lawyers were under more pressure than I was. Charities. *Mama mia.*

And yet this realization helped me relax. I did have the upper hand on this topic. I just needed to keep this in mind.

My responsibility was to tell it accurately and well, so that Caprice (and Clarissa) benefit from my choice of words. And when I recall our 'noticing', it's an easy story to tell. I loved our first 'noticing' of each other. Caprice always said it was the first time in her life when meeting a man thrilled her.

BRAY took Orso and Bass outside to talk. When they were out of earshot, he turned and scowled at both of them. "If you two don't behave, I'm going to stop this deposition and order you home. And if I do that, we stand a good chance of the Santa Barbara court referring this matter to Colorado, where Mr. Montepulciano stands an excellent chance of getting at least half of the estate. We're talking about the loss of at least thirty million dollars," he said, thumping a finger on Bass's chest. Then he told Orso also to get control of himself, turned angrily, and went back into the room. The American lawyers, chagrined, followed behind.

"This deposition is back in session," Bray announced wearily. He took his seat and tried again. "Mr. Montepulciano, when did you meet Mrs. Caprice Jordan Taylor?"

"If you mean when did she first notice me, it was sometime in nineteen fifty-nine," Rossi translated.

"Mr. Montepulciano, was it in nineteen fifty-nine?"

Dante paused. "It's not that easy," he said.

Orso and Bass fidgeted in distress, but they did not protest.

"Mr. Butler, would you ask Mr. Montepulciano about this important matter?" Bray said, passing the ball to the only lawyer among the Americans who could work in Italian.

—m—

MR. Bray was good. Very patient. I trusted Mr. Butler, and I was happy that Bray had turned to him for help.

Much earlier—maybe fifteen years before she died—Caprice and I went Santa Barbara and were invited to Butler's house. We met his wife and children. We shared dinner and talked late into the evening. From that time on, we were friends. Even then Butler spoke Italian.

Caprice seriously started to learn Italian after that. I looked at Butler, welcoming his questions.

"OF course," said Butler.

Guy Bray grinned. Dante Montepulciano would not be rail-roaded into anybody's version of the truth. He smiled at Butler, and Butler smiled back.

"Mr. Montepulciano, when did Mrs. Caprice Jordan Taylor come to Lake Como? I mean when she noticed you?" Butler asked in fluent Italian.

"Nineteen fifty-nine, in May. But we didn't meet right away, Mr. Butler," Dante answered in good English.

"I understand. Thank you, that's quite clear: May, nineteen fifty-nine." Butler said. "And when, to the best of your recollection—I know quite of bit of history has passed—did she first *notice* you?"

"I understand, and that's what I said: 'noticed,' only 'noticed.'"

Butler nodded and said, "Yes. Please tell us when Mrs. Taylor noticed you."

The room became quiet.

"Almost immediately," Dante said in Italian. Again, Rossi translated. "Later, she mistakenly thought it had been in September, not May. But it was in May," Dante said. "It was on the soccer field where I was coaching, helping to select the Italian Olympic national team that went on to place fourth in the nineteen sixty summer Olympics," Dante said, beaming with Italian pride.

—⚡—

AT last I was getting somewhere.

We were in the old city of Como, which is located on the south shore of Lake Como. Como had luxurious soccer facilities and lake shore parks.

The soccer camp would invite certain ranked soccer players and they would compete for selection to Italy's national team. The competitions were intense and everyone took the camps seriously.

I was honored to be one of the coaches.

Before the war I was known to be a good player.

"I WAS very athletic in those days, and Mrs. Taylor liked to walk around the athletic fields, looking at the athletes. She liked to do that, you see," Dante said. "With her nurse who was also a friend, a companion—Miss Clarissa Crane."

"So you met in nineteen fifty-nine?" Bray concluded.

"I didn't say that," Dante protested loudly.

Bray sighed. "What? I'm getting confused."

Butler rescued the moment. "Mr. Bray, Mr. Montepulciano is talking about *noticing,* not meeting. This is an extremely important point to Mr. Montepulciano, as he has told us already."

"Okay, I understand," Bray said. He turned and addressed Dante. "Excuse me, sir, I now understand what you are emphasizing —*noticing*, not *meeting*."

"Yes, thank you."

"What in the name of God is the difference?" Orso asked.

Dante immediately caucused with Rossi and Butler, complaining that the American lawyers, especially Bass and Orso, were not listening. He asked if a new team of charity lawyers could be sent to Milan. Rossi told Dante there was no way, at this late date, that the American lawyers could be replaced. Dante fumed. He reminded Rossi that it was still his solemn duty to protect Caprice's name. Rossi assured him he understood that.

—m—

THAT was such a sweet noticing—running down the path of the broad jump so fast that I catapulted out of the pit, landing in the grass in front of Caprice and Clarissa.

My soccer team complimented me on my stroke of good fortune.

ROSSI looked up and addressed Bray. "Mr. Montepulciano has said he was first *noticed* in May of nineteen fifty-nine. They did not *meet* at that time."

"I understand, Mr. Rossi," Bray affirmed.

Despite Bray's admonitions, Bass could not hold his tongue. "Noticed. Met. What's the distinction here? All we want to know is when Mr. Montepulciano met the deceased. Is that so difficult?"

"Don't put Mr. Bass's question in the record," Bray instructed the court reporter.

Then he addressed Rossi. "Okay, so he was first *noticed* by Mrs. Taylor in May of nineteen fifty-nine. Let's take it from there."

Dante complained to his lawyers that men like Bass lacked sensitivity concerning such matters involving women, especially how proper Italian officers should behave with ladies. He warned Rossi that he was going to aggravate Bass and Orso every chance he got.

Bray asked for the proceedings to continue.

—⁑—

I REMEMBERED Caprice's amusement.

First, I'm running furiously down the approach, as I said, and I leapt into the air, stretching to gain distance—then I almost crashed into two women looking down at me, sprawled in the grass.

Both women jumped back. They looked like two angels dressed in summer all white blouses and shorts. One said, "Oh my god, what a handsome man." (Later, I learned her name was Caprice.) They were Americans.

My soccer players were clapping and cheering and acting crazy.

Then I too saw the comedy of it all and started clapping, but not before bowing deeply to them both.

"SO, Mr. Montepulciano, after you were first *noticed* by Mrs. Taylor, when did you first actually *meet* her?"

Dante decided it was time to talk about meeting Caprice.

"It's not so simple," Dante said through Rossi's translation. "During the nineteen sixty Olympic soccer training camps, we noticed each other many times. She watched from the sidelines, and she would sometimes stroll by and acknowledge me."

"And, at some point, did she speak to you?"

"Yes," Dante said.

"Did you consider that to be a meeting?" Butler asked.

"No. We had not yet been introduced. An Italian officer and gentleman does not directly meet a woman of good station. He must be formally introduced by a third party."

"You mean you greeted each other verbally, but that doesn't count as meeting each other?" Bass interjected.

"Correct," Dante replied.

"So Caprice—"

"You must refer to her as Mrs. Taylor," Dante said, his voice rising. "I may call her Caprice, but not you."

"I beg your pardon?"

"You must refer to her as Mrs. Taylor, or Mrs. Caprice Jordan Taylor. Not Caprice. I was her husband. Only I may call her Caprice, Mr. Bass."

Dante felt pleasure for a change. *Ah, at last, Bass is publicly embarrassed.*

Bass let forth a long sigh and asked for a break so that he could meet privately with the other lawyers.

I DON'T like to embarrass people. It is an unnecessary rudeness. But Mr. Bass was constantly uncivil.

Guido reprimanded me in Italian. "Dante, control yourself. Take the high road. I beg you."

Unexpectedly, John Bray interrupted us and announced, "This deposition will recess for the evening. Thank you, everyone. We will reconvene here tomorrow at seven-thirty P.M."

13

Day 3: No Show

IT WAS 8:15 P.M. The lawyers were all gathered at the law offices of Galileo & Rossi, ready to resume the deposition. The meeting was to have begun at 7:30. But at a quarter past eight the phone rang. Rossi picked up.

It was Guido. Dante was unwell, he said. He had been stricken with a migraine headache, and taken to his bed. Guido was profusely apologetic, but his brother would not attend the deposition tonight.

—⁂—

JUST before last night's deposition ended, I began to see a few auras—visual disturbances, like flashes of light. Now I had a severe, throbbing headache on the left side of my head.

The headaches come from my war wound. They are utterly debilitating. When one of these headaches comes on, I think of North Africa, and of the man in front of me and the man behind me. They were good soldiers, but they died. Then I feel lucky to be alive, and I just wait until it ends.

Fortunately my school's administrators understand. They do not even dock my pay. I wasn't sure the American lawyers would understand as well. But I didn't care.

"LET the record show that we're gathered pursuant to the recessed deposition, which was to reconvene this evening at seven-thirty P.M.," said Guy Bray.

"So he's a no-show," Jack Orso said, disgusted.

"We've just heard from Guido Montepulciano that his brother, Dante, is unwell—mentally as well as physically," Bray explained. "Mr. Montepulciano is unable to attend."

"Well, that's that," Orso said. "Now what?"

"Day three of four days shot to shit," Bass said.

"Mr. Montepulciano says he will be able to attend tomorrow afternoon at four o'clock, or shortly thereafter," Bray said, ignoring Bass. "He's requested that the deposition be continued at that time. I don't think we really need to put anything else on the record. We are here. The deposition is adjourned until tomorrow at four P.M."

The meeting ended, and the entire gathering dispersed into the night.

—〰—

. . .

14

DAY 4: The Final Deposition Day

THE FOLLOWING DAY, Saturday, October 27, 1979, was the fourth and final day of the deposition of Dante Valentino Caesar Montepulciano. Dante had recovered from the previous day's migraine, and the lawyers were anxious to proceed and put an end to their thus far unproductive efforts to eliminate him from Caprice Jordan Taylor's will. There was little doubt now that the Italian was her legitimate common-law husband. Rather, it was time for damage control. Now the 'charities' lawyers simply wanted to keep Dante's share of the estate as small as possible.

At a luncheon held earlier in the day at the Palazzo Sempione, where the American charities' lawyers were staying, Bray reported that Mrs. Taylor's estate had now grown to almost sixty-eight million dollars, and that Dun & Bradstreet had given a strong "buy" recommendation to Jordan Oil.

—⚍—

I WAS lucky this time. My migraine ended early in the morning— around three A.M. Just in case my headache came back to torment me, I brought medicine that would help me.

I also felt good because this was supposed to be the last evening of this infernal charade.

AS usual Guy Bray opened the deposition. He, too, was looking forward to concluding the deposition. But his optimism was tempered when, in a private moment, John Butler advised him that this final session would not be without more drama, more surprises, more Dante.

"We agreed, because Dante was unwell yesterday, to continue the deposition today," Bray opened, addressing Adam Rossi. "This will be the last day of the deposition, and I would like you, Mr. Rossi, to ask Mr. Montepulciano if he is feeling well today. Also, if at any time during the deposition he feels tired or feels that he is unable to proceed without a rest, ask him, please, to tell us. Let's pace ourselves, so that we can finish today as planned."

"Okay," Rossi said.

"Okay?" Bray repeated, looking Dante straight in the eyes.

Speaking English, Dante generously thanked Bray for considering his health. Perhaps Bray was more trustworthy than he had originally thought. Perhaps Dante could place confidence in him. Yet he remained convinced that the others sought to destroy him and dishonor Caprice.

—✺—

ROSSI had prepped me about the agenda: my stay in Colorado with Caprice, our solemn oath (the Golden Pact), and what I wanted as a settlement from her estate. He also encouraged me to be straightforward in my account, so that we could finish tonight.

For myself, I wanted mostly to honor Caprice.

I told Rossi that I still did not like Mr. Bass. He swore unnecessarily, and he sweated too much. Very unprofessional.

Rossi patted my arm and told me to ignore Bass. The most authoritative American here was Mr. Bray. He also reminded me that Mr. Orso was of an Italian background. He was just doing his job.

BUTLER had a few words in Italian with Dante, then addressed the assembled lawyers. "Mr. Montepulciano apologizes for missing yesterday's session. He wants to underline that because of his war wound, his physical health is sometimes not what it should be or what he would like it to be. He hopes you understand this."

"Dante, Dante," Guido whispered, emotionally.

Butler interrupted, wanting to complete his statement.

"Excuse me. Mr. Montepulciano has also explained that his heart is not strong, due to having remained so long at a high elevation in Rifle, Colorado—with Mrs. Taylor—during their residence there."

"War should be criminalized," Dante said. "Nothing is more inhuman than hand-to-hand combat."

"Take your time, Mr. Montepulciano," said Bray,

"And the killing of civilians is an ugly stain on humankind."

Dante looked at Bass whose eyes were closed, giving him a frog-like appearance.

—◊—

BASS seemed not to pay attention. He looked like he might be sleeping. Orso saw me looking at Bass. Suddenly Bass's eyes opened—maybe Orso kicked him under the table.

Mr. Bray, on the other hand, listened carefully.

Mr. Orso seemed glad he had missed World War II, and I didn't blame him. Hand-to-hand combat is horrible. No mother should ever let her son go to war.

The second battle of El Alamein went badly not only for me, but for the Italian and German forces, and for General Rommel, who had replaced our General Bastion in the first battle of El Alamein. The Italians had been losing that one too until Rommel came and soundly defeated the Allies. But a great price was paid. The casualties were high. War is hateful.

It is because of war that I became an educator and social worker. I wanted to change the world.

GUY Bray interrupted. "For the purposes of the record, could we stay with Mr. Montepulciano and Mrs. Taylor's Colorado experience?"

"Okay, we will," Rossi said.

"Thank you," Bray said. His goal was to get Dante back to the subject of Colorado, in order to confirm the length of his stay there. As soon as he could, he broached the subject.

"Now, Mr. Montepulciano, how long did you stay in Colorado?"

Rossi translated as Dante said, "I remember our arrival. Mr. Edward Winslow, our first lawyer at Mr. Butler's firm, can confirm the date. We arrived in Colorado after leaving Tucson, Arizona. We left Tucson and went straight to Colorado after a phone conversation we had with Winslow."

"Was that in nineteen sixty-four, or sixty-five?" Bray asked.

Dante paused and tried to remember the exact date. He was having trouble remembering because so many years had passed. "Tucson..." he mumbled. "Tucson, Denver, and from that moment we remained in Colorado. Yes, it was nineteen sixty-five."

—⚹—

I ASKED Rossi if he could confirm the exact year.

He could, and waved a record at the American charity lawyers.

Exact dates are difficult for me. I think it's due to the war and my injuries. Parts of my brain work perfectly while others do not.

Post war research brain doctors were interested in my case. Based on my performance on many occasions.

DANTE broke into English, unaware that he had done so. Rossi let him go on, trusting that his client wouldn't get them into trouble.

"I have the exact dates, because when I purchased this little statue, I remember exactly—Colorado Springs—okay? I don't remember exactly all of these names: Colorado Springs, Springfield—no, not Springfield."

What do you mean by 'I don't remember exactly'," Orso said wondering if they could find something discrediting Dante.

"It was thirteen years ago," said Dante to Orso.

"We're just trying to establish your residency in Colorado, sir."

Dante turned to Rossi and said, " I thought that matter was already settled, Mr. Rossi."

"It is," Rossi said turning to John Butler.

"It is, Mr. Rossi," said Butler confirming Dante's statement. Butler turned to Bray and requested they move on.

—⚹—

ROSSI and I had gone over the dates earlier, but it was hard to remember. I tried my hardest. I knew this last day of the deposition was important. I knew I was being tested on the issue of common-law marriage.

The American charities' lawyers wanted to prove I was not married to Caprice, that I am a fortune-hunter or something like that, or worse.

I was her coach and physical therapist. We were in the spring of our love, and we would hike, play tennis, and spend long hours in bed. She thought I was a good lover—she told me many times, and said I have strong, gentle hands. Caprice felt alive. She was vivacious.

Caprice was not drinking—only water.

She told me that for the first time in her life she was truly happy. So was I.

"WE took care of each other. I took care of her and she also took care of me," Dante continued. "I had headaches, like I did yesterday, and Caprice would gently caress my head wound and quietly sing children's lullabies. When I awoke, the pain would be gone.

"We spoke Italian, and I was her teacher," Dante said. "Those three years were the spring of our love. That is the truth.

"All of the legal documents that she signed during those years were signed Caprice Montepulciano.

"As I remember," Dante continued, intent on clarifying the exact date, "we were visiting Colorado Springs. I purchased a little statue. I remember very well, because they made me pay three percent on the invoice. I have the date on the receipt. In America, whenever you buy anything, you get a receipt with three percent added on."

Dante rambled on, Rossi translating simultaneously, United Nations style. "I also have receipts from the hotels where we stayed in Colorado. I also recall that in Palm Springs, in California, where we visited, I saw—visited, is the correct word, I believe—the villa of Frank Sinatra."

Bass interrupted. "Frank Sinatra? His villa? What does that have to do with—"

"Yes, Frank Sinatra," Dante said. "I prefer to discuss some of the places we visited, before going on to our time in Colorado—and then I will tell you exact dates of all of those places."

—⚌—

I LIKED Colorado. The Rocky Mountains are dramatic in all seasons. It was hot and dry from June until the end of August. It was a little like looking at the Italian Alps across Lake Como from the town of Como—that magnificent, historic Italian city on the south shore of the lake—except that of course there was no Como.

I liked our small house. It was just right for us. We had hiking trails nearby, and there was a tennis court a block away, and we played almost every day. We kept barbells and weights in the front yard, so that we could keep physically fit.

"MR. Bray," interjected Bass, "do we need all this irrelevant testimony?"

Bray quietly asked the charities' lawyers to please listen and not interrupt Mr. Montepulciano or Mr. Rossi.

"And where did you live in Colorado?" Bray asked Dante.

"We lived in Rifle, Colorado, for approximately three years, from nineteen sixty-five until the early spring of nineteen sixty-nine. Caprice even purchased a house for us—not under her own name, but using my last name, Montepulciano. She insisted on using my last name, signing herself Caprice Montepulciano."

"You both bought the house—using your name?" said an unhappy Orso.

"No, sir," Dante said. "She bought the house, but she used my name, Montepulciano."

—◊◊◊—

I REMEMBER so much.

Caprice was like a girl experiencing life for the first time. There was no press. She was not hounded for interviews. She was free from gossip, and our neighbors did not care who she was.

I loved her even more because of her enthusiasm. Her health improved. She worked hard at becoming physically fit.

I knew about her alcoholism because, bit by bit, she revealed parts of her past life to me. She grew up in a contentious family. She felt much shame because of her family and herself. That shame made her drink. Those were out-of-control times. The drinking, together with her stays in hospitals while drying out, became the object of too many newspaper articles. Gossip. Gossip was her dread of all dreads.

Her sharing this helped our intimacy flow unrestricted.

"MR. Montepulciano," said Bray, "was Mrs. Taylor drinking alcohol at that time?"

"No," Dante said.

"Are you certain?" said Bass.

"Before that, I never realized how powerful the psychological attraction of drink can be for people suffering alcoholism," Dante said. "Needless to say, we glorified water, coffee, and tea. We didn't keep alcohol in the house. Visitors brought their own or, more often, went without, out of courtesy to Caprice."

"What was living like in Rifle, Colorado, at that time, Mr. Montepulciano?" said Dick Lambert.

"I was new to Colorado, Sir," said Dante, "but I was fascinated by the American west—all the ranch people wearing cowboy clothes. In Italy in those days movies about American cowboys were being made—we called them 'Spaghetti Westerns.'"

"Spaghetti … ." Bass said laughing, making Dante laugh.

Montepulciano proved informed on this topic. "Yes, my favorite was *A Fistful of Dollars*, starring Clint Eastwood. It was his first Spaghetti Western film. People said he was paid $15,000 U.S. Dollars."

Bass laughed. The whole room laughed.

—⚭—

I HAVE only good memories of Rifle, Colorado. The cowboys and townspeople at grange hall dances drank heavily, but that never influenced us. We just learned their cowboy dances and partied along with them, drinking sparkling water laced with lime or lemon juice. We stomped our way through many joyful weekend evenings. I learned that Americans work harder than Italians.

The town had little to offer in the way of business opportunities. There were farmers working small plots of land, cowboys handling horses and cattle—mostly on federal land. We had a few merchants, and a doctor and a dentist. A hospital was only a few miles away, across the Colorado River in Grand River.

Caprice loved the time we spent in Rifle. She was able to remain anonymous, without the tabloids haranguing her. She experienced freedom, life without criticism.

"MR. Montepulciano?"

Dante looked up at Guy Bray and immediately refocused.

Bass didn't understand the relevance of what Dante had just said. He looked quizzically at Guy Bray, hands raised, eyes rolling up at the ceiling.

Bray asked Rossi whether Caprice was with Dante the whole time he was making "stops" in Colorado, Nevada and California, especially in Colorado.

"Of course," Rossi answered. "It was Mrs. Taylor who took him around. Without her, he couldn't get along—he couldn't afford the travel. You know that he had given up his job as a teacher and as a soccer coach. He had no money of his own whatsoever."

"I have no shame about that," said Dante. "I had no money. Caprice did, and she freely offered to take me on frequent vacations. She wanted us to be together."

—∽∞∽—

CAPRICE craved privacy. She didn't like being a famous oil heiress. Journalists always took the low road and made her mad.

I was happy to be part of her life—her "Montepulciano life." In this way she could be herself, and I was not just a coach and therapist. She was free. I too was free. Whoever heard of me, Dante Valentino Ceasar Montepulciano? We had freedom.

By that time, Caprice spoke good Italian, good enough to pass for an Italian. Except for one thing: she had red hair, flaming red hair, and some of our friends didn't think she could be Italian. We ignored those people.

"BESIDES," Dante continued, "we were husband and wife by then—well, not at first—but she told people her name was Caprice Montepulciano. She never used the name Taylor. We spoke so much Italian that I think everyone thought she was Italian."

"So that I'm clear," Bray said, "this was *after* the Golden Pact made in February nineteen sixty-eight?"

"No. The Golden Pact was made in Lucerne, Switzerland, on the third of February, nineteen sixty-eight," Rossi said. "Colorado happened before—starting in nineteen sixty-five. Mr. Montepulciano insists you are clear on this point."

"I understand," Bray went on, looking at Dante. "Now, I asked you this before, but I will ask it again. You and Mrs. Taylor held yourselves out and acted as husband and wife from nineteen sixty-five, when you arrived in Colorado, and in nineteen sixty-eight, when you made the Golden Pact, and even until today?"

"Correct, starting in Rifle, Colorado," Dante said quickly.

Jack Orso asked to see documentation proving the length of their Colorado stay.

Dante tugged at Rossi's sleeve, whereupon the two went into a huddle and whispered for a long time.

—∞—

I KNOW that Caprice gloried in the fact that she was unknown. As Mrs. Montepulciano, she luxuriated in privacy.

No journalists. No hateful gossip.

Free to live her life. She was happy.

We loved each other.

She could laugh.

Life was good.

But privacy is a poorly guarded circumstance. Our society has come to regard that private people belong to the public domain. And because of her wealth and past alcoholism, Caprice was considered to be eligible prey for the gossip newspapers. But here in the Rockies and with me—a virtual unknown—she could maintain privacy.

"IT wasn't until sometime later that Caprice told me we were common-law husband and wife," said Dante. "I was surprised. In Colorado, if a couple lives together for two years, they are considered married. What's mine is yours, and what's yours is mine."

Rossi looked up at Bray, saying, "I think Mr. Montepulciano may be confused here. Perhaps I didn't translate correctly. You said, 'You *held yourselves out*,' and I translated it as, 'You *behaved yourselves*.' I'm not quite sure of this American idiom."

"I will ask the question differently, Mr. Rossi," said Bray. He paused, thinking of a better way to phrase his question, knowing this was a sensitive subject for Dante.

"Mr. Montepulciano, in your heart, and in Mrs. Taylor's heart, when you entered into the Golden Pact, did you love each other as husband and wife?"

"Momento," Dante said, holding up a finger. Once again Rossi and Dante huddled, only this time they were joined by Galileo. They went on for some time.

—◊◊◊—

I HAD trouble with Bray's question.

Caprice and I were in love and, according to her, we were already husband and wife—the common-law thing.

Our *Atto Solenne*, our solemn pact, the Golden Pact, was for a different purpose.

Caprice was drinking again—too much—and it was affecting her health. She was sick and afraid she was dying. She was often hysterical, a thing I told no one.

Her sickness for alcohol frightened me. I felt our love for each other was ebbing, like an ocean tide. It was a sad time and discouraging. Caprice felt me withdrawing. I didn't want her to destroy our relationship. I didn't want her to drag us onto the rocks of despair and destruction.

I must protect Caprice from these American charities' lawyers.

ROSSI looked up from the huddle and addressed Guy Bray. "You must look Mr. Montepulciano in the eye when you ask a question," he said. "He learned to speak a little English when he lived in America. Now he understands quite a lot, but he's not fluent. Just speak slowly. He says he wants you to look him in the eye so that he can understand what you say, and you can understand him."

"We'll do that," Bray said, smiling inwardly to himself. This Italian warrior understood full well what they were all about. He knew the estate would have to settle. And probably for big bucks. Bray only hoped that Dante would be reasonable.

"Are we not already looking Mr. Montepulciano in the eye," said Orso concerned about his relationship with Dante.

Rossi answered. "No, no, Mr. Orso. Everything appears to be fine. My client just wanted to stress the point."

"Got it," said Orso.

"But he makes a good point about speaking English," said Rossi. If everyone speaks slowly, he can for the most part understand what you say."

"Jeezus … ."

Bray interrupted, ignoring Bass, and asked for the deposition to proceed.

"Would you go ahead, please?" Rossi said to Dante.

—〜—

I DIDN'T believe the charity lawyers cared.

I needed to protect Caprice, but I also needed to be able to explain my motives and memories.

"OKAY," Rossi said. "What he says is—Dante says, "We must always understand what a person means by love.""

"To repeat," Bray continued, "I understand that you, Mr. Montepulciano, loved Mrs. Taylor, and Mrs. Taylor loved you, as husband and wife."

"That's correct," said Dante through Rossi. "We must always understand what a person means by 'love.'"

"And furthermore—"

"Okay." Again Dante interrupted, affirming their agreement.

"Please translate what 'okay' means," Bass demanded.

"This is his whole concern, you see," said Rossi. "The feeling of love they had for each other was so noble that it can't be talked about, and it is also secret. That's how I understand Mr. Montepulciano's wish to tell what he feels you need to know.

"Mr. Montepulciano asks that I tell what I know about him, because there are things he's told me already and that we have discussed thoroughly, and it is on that basis that he would like to start. He would also like Mr. Butler to tell what he knows, so that Mr. Montepulciano doesn't have to talk about things he feels should remain secret. His loyalty is to Mrs. Taylor, because of their intimate relationship."

Orso nodded in agreement. Murray and Bray agreed as well.

"Are you talking about the Jordan family?" said Bass.

"I think so," said Rossi.

Butler chimed in. "The family was confrontational, which Mrs. Taylor confessed to him, and Mr. Montepulciano does not want any of that on a public record, if it can be helped."

Again, the Americans said they could understand that,

—◊◊◊—

I NEEDED to use the restroom. I asked Mr. Rossi if we could take a break. He agreed. Everyone waited while I got up and left the room.

BRAY thought for some moments about what Rossi had said. "When Mr. Montepulciano returns, would you explain to him that we certainly can do what he asks. In fact, we have talked to Mr. Butler at length about it."

"Okay, Mr. Bray," Rossi said. "I know Mr. Montepulciano will say okay. He feels that he is bound to secrecy, and he does not want to have the responsibility for saying certain things before third parties. He also has some questions, things he wants to know. He wants to know the shames of the Jordan family. Then he can talk, but he doesn't want it to come from him in the first instance. He doesn't want his words on that subject written into the deposition records. So he would like Mr. Butler to speak, in particular with regard to one telephone conversation we had. Do you remember it, John?"

Butler nodded.

"Thereafter, Mr. Montepulciano will speak."

Butler realized that Dante wanted him to help. Dante was looking for guidance. "Mr. Montepulciano has many secrets," Butler said, addressing the charity lawyers, "which we respect. But there is one thing on which I do not believe he keeps a secret."

Dante returned and sat down.

—m—

I RETURNED feeling more comfortable and focused.

As men age their bladders seem to weaken. I was relieved and felt I could cope more easily with this California deposition.

"Thank you, Mr. Bray," I said, "we can proceed now."

Bray thanked me and looked at his fellow lawyers.

"Where were we?" he asked confused about where to pick up the thread of their proceedings.

"I think we were discussing relationship privacies," said Lambert. "Mr. Butler had been asking to speak for Montepulciano.

WHEN Dante had returned, Butler turned to Rossi and said, "Mr. Rossi, excuse me, may I help Dante? Would you ask Dante to speak through me? I'll translate for the record."

"Pardon?"

"Would you have Dante repeat what he said earlier? I would like to advise him of something, something important."

Butler knew his phrasing would get Rossi's attention. He wanted to build Dante's trust in him.

"There are many things that Dante and Mrs. Taylor held as secrets between them," said Butler. "We have to respect their privacy. But some things are not secret, and I want to ask Mr. Montepulciano a question about something that is not a secret."

Suddenly, something in Bill Bass changed. It was as abrupt and unexpected as Saul's conversion on the road to Damascus. He now seemed to understand Dante.

"I fully agree," said Bass, "Mr. Montepulciano, we should not ask about your secrets."

"Pardon?"

"Yes, you and Mrs. Taylor should keep your secrets."

Dante looked at Bass. His jaw dropped. "Thank you, Mr. Bass," he said, looking startled and confused. He even blushed.

Bass repeated himself. "We are not trying to invade your private relationship secrets with Mrs. Taylor, sir. At least I'm not."

Each charity lawyer immediately swore the same thing.

Rossi turned to Dante, looking pleased, saying, "So don't worry, Dante."

—⁂—

BASS had surprised me.

I found it difficult to accept his apology. I would wait and see if he meant it.

A tiger does not change his stripes.

NOW Dante spoke rapidly, pouring his heart out.

"Okay," Rossi translated. "These things are all linked together. He wants to know what your question is—what is it that you think he does not keep secret. Go ahead and ask him."

Butler looked Dante in the eye and formed his question. He already knew the answer, but he wanted it in the deposition record.

"Mr. Montepulciano, after you and Mrs. Taylor became common-law spouses, did you ever get divorced under the laws of any country?"

Rossi listened to Dante, then translated. "He says this is something he has already told me about, and he says that before talking about his common-law marriage, we should ask for someone to define for us exactly what common law is."

"Yes, but first Mr. Montepulciano must answer my question," Butler said. "I'm not asking about the common law. I'm asking about divorce."

"There was no divorce," said Dante, looking exasperated.

"If there was a record, Mr. Montepulciano," said Bass, "where would they be kept: In Italy? In California? Maybe in Colorado?

Dante showed increasing stress.

"Hold on," Butler said. "The facts say that they were automatically common law husband and wife—legally—according to Colorado law. That's it. Mrs. Taylor was even going around Rifle and wherever signing documents as Caprice Montepulciano."

"My question was about divorce," Mr. Butler, said Bass reminding Butler.

—⁓—

WE were never divorced.

In private meetings, days ago, I said as much to both Rossi and Galileo. I never divorced Mrs. Taylor.

But because Caprice and I have not communicated in more than nine years, she may have divorced me without notifying me. If, that is, a common-law husband can be divorced.

THE GOLDEN PACT

DANTE again huddled with Rossi and began a long explanation in Italian about trusting Butler but not trusting the charity lawyers. Butler's question was a good one, but it was dangerous. After all, he reminded Rossi, the American lawyers wanted to destroy his reputation as Caprice's husband—and he suspected they wanted to destroy Caprice too.

Galileo was concerned by Dante's heated speech and vigorous gesticulations. He was afraid they would alarm the American contingent.

"Can we take a break?" Galileo asked.

Bray agreed, but Bill Bass objected.

"No! Before a taking a break, Mr. Bray, I would like a translation of what was just said," Bass demanded. "I think we should know what's being said—just like in a regular deposition."

Bray frowned and shrugged his shoulders. "Mr. Butler," he said, "would you be kind enough to tell us what Mr. Montepulciano just said?"

Butler said he would, and assured the charity lawyers that there was nothing to fear.

—— ∞ ——

ROSSI knows I never divorced Caprice. Mr. Butler knows it too.

She may have divorced me, for all I know, but no papers were ever sent to me.

I am her husband in common law. She never forgot. After all, her will instructed the charities to settle with me.

We were married through thick and thin. Caprice would never divorce me. We were married (common law) and enjoyed good times. When she began drinking again, I tended to her miseries faithfully and with love. She even signed our Golden Pact "Caprice Montepulciano."

BUT before Butler could translate what Dante had said, Rossi interrupted him. He didn't want any more conflict than there was already.

"Mr. Bass," Rossi said, "Mr. Montepulciano says he wants to have the law of Colorado explained for the record, because he is afraid that we are going to cheat him. He wants to have the testimony of two experts: one in religious law, and one who understands the text of the law of Colorado regarding divorce."

"Goddammit." Bass banged the table. "Why can't we just get a straight answer? Were they ever divorced, or not? Yes or no? I don't know how Italy has survived all these centuries! Okay, let's take that break now, Mr. Bray."

Bray then called a break, but the moment he did so, Dante shouted.

"Ingiuria!"

Rossi jumped in to translate. "*Ingiuria* means 'insult.' Mr. Montepulciano means to say, 'You have insulted me!'"

Dante tugged on Rossi's sleeve and told him something. Then Rossi explained.

"Mr. Montepulciano says that he and Mrs. Taylor arrived in Colorado—Rifle, Colorado, to be exact—to purchase a home. He wants, you see, to save his emotions and his time," Rossi said. "He wants me to tell things he has already told us—a waste of our time. And he wants Mr. Butler to tell us what documents he himself has seen already, from his investigator's trip to Colorado, and from Mr. Butler's own side trip to Colorado on his way to Milan this month."

—∞—

I AM tired.

"GRAND Junction," Dante interjected, which made no sense to anyone at the table, including Rossi.

Rossi continued, "By telling what we know, without making Mr. Montepulciano tell it all again himself, we can spare him emotionally. He is still not well, and he wishes to conclude the deposition."

"Grand Junction! Carbondale! Rifle!" Dante shouted.

"Rifle is where Mrs. Taylor purchased a home. But they also looked for a home in Denver. And in Colorado Springs. They looked at many homes, in all kinds of places."

"Good, Mr. Montepulciano," Bray said. "But we haven't asked a question about this line of information."

"What? Pardon?"

"We looked at homes in many places," Dante said.

"I'm sure you did," Bray said. "However, that was not a question."

—⁊⁊⁊—

THIS reminded me of how Caprice liked to travel. It must be an American trait. A part of their culture, a part of feeling free.

When Caprice and I lived in Rifle, we were happy and really had no need to travel. But with her Western spirit, Caprice always wanted to travel. And she had a fabulous car, a 1966 Cadillac. A big one, a Fleetwood Sixty Special Brougham, which she drove herself. It had everything: leather seats, and air conditioning in the front and back.

Sometimes I rode in the back, where I could put my feet up on the carpeted footrests. The rear reading lights were adjustable, and there were two reading tables, one on each side. I would be thrilled and shout the English word "fabulous!"

It was Caprice's car. Not mine. But I enjoyed it as much as she did, and we were happy.

So going on a trip was never dull, and everywhere we went people stared at that car. Most Americans love their cars and appreciate special ones. I think Americans express their freedom with their cars.

But I think we traveled too much.

JOHN Butler talked quietly with Guy Bray, acknowledging how far from the topic of divorce Dante had brought them. Bray chuckled and said he would let things go on for a bit and see where it took them.

"*Memento!* Buena Vista!" Dante said, again shouting.

Rossi translated as Dante continued. "Mr. Montepulciano visited the prison at Buena Vista, Colorado. He had dinner with the prisoners there."

Everyone in the room was startled by the change of subject.

"Gentlemen," said Dante in English, "you know where the prison is?"

"It's in Cañon City, isn't it?" Dick Lambert said.

"Cañon City? No. Buena Vista," Dante said.

"It's near both of those places," John Butler said.

"Yes, okay. Cañon City is nearby. But the prison is in Buena Vista." Dante said. He continued in Italian, with Rossi translating.

"We visited there many times. Whenever Caprice got an urge to travel, we would go there, and other places in Colorado. We would stay four days in one place, three days in another—always in Colorado. Glenwood or Aspen was always the base for our trips. She would buy a flag wherever we went. I still have the flag from Buena Vista."

"Can we move on?" said Jack Orso and Bill Bass in unison.

"Yes," Bray said. "Gentlemen, let's move on. Mr. Montepulciano, we are moving on to the deed on your house in Rifle."

—◆◆◆—

I WAS only too glad to move on.

I had run out memories of looking for a place to stay in Colorado. So moving on was fine with me.

That entire experience for me was a real eye opener. Until Caprice started looking for a house for us, I had no idea about how much space Americans require. In Italy, people lived in small spaces, or if you were rich, expensive villas. Mama mia!

THE GOLDEN PACT

DANTE'S head jerked, and he refocused. "I am glad to move on," he said. "But first let me ask—Mr. Butler, did you see the house in Rifle?

"Yes," said Butler. "I stopped there on my way to Milan, on a tip I received from my investigator, Mr. Kennedy, last year."

Dante had another private aside with Rossi. Rossi then looked up and explained what his client just said.

"He wants you, Mr. Butler, to tell all you know and all you saw there, and what they told you there. Then he will fill in the holes."

Butler asked for a five-minute recess. Everyone agreed. During the break Bray showed a photocopy of the deed to the Rifle house to Dante, and asked him to confirm that the signature "Caprice Montepulciano" was in fact that of Mrs. Taylor. Dante confirmed it. Bray said that after the break, he would show him the deed again and ask Dante on the record whether he recognized the signatures, and to confirm that they were his and Mrs. Taylor's.

When the deposition resumed, the photocopy of the deed was marked Exhibit 13, and was attached to and made a part of the deposition.

But Dante could not let a sleeping dog lie. In a sarcastic tone following a derisive laugh, he whispered something to Rossi.

"Translate, please," Murray said, not wanting the lawyers to get upset further.

WHY am I doing this?

I think my brain is acting up again. I must calm down.

I'm causing my own problems.

I ask Rossi something in Italian—something of little consequence—a slur on the process that will take its course anyway.

They have every right to know what I whispered.

I apologized to Rossi and asked him to make right my wrong.

ROSSI grinned. "Okay. Mr. Montepulciano confirms that the signatures are his and Mrs. Taylor's. he also points out that the deed has also been certified by a notary public. As far as Mr. Montepulciano is concerned, therefore, it's unnecessary for him to confirm the signatures himself."

"Okay. But he does confirm them, verbally, himself?" Bray asked.

"Of course. But he must also confirm something else," Rossi said, his voice cautioning that life is not always simple.

"But these are in fact his and Mrs. Taylor's signatures?" Bray said.

"Yes," said Dante. "But it is absurd in light of the petition to the judge in which…" He hesitated, trying to think of the right words to use.

"I am concerned about the fact that in the petition Mr. Winslow—Butler's boss—only mentions some of the names by which Mrs. Taylor was known. In Latin you say *no solum sed etiam,* which means "not only, but also." Caprice in that period also was known as Mrs. Montepulciano, Mrs. Dante Montepulciano, L'Italiana, and La Americana."

—⚏—

I COULD tell I was driving Mr. Rossi a little crazy. I needed to stop and take a deep breath. I thought Galileo was also getting tired of me. The only thing for me at that point was to make it clear that I was not divorced. But I decided this was not a problem. You can't prove a negative, but nobody had any documents to the contrary. I figured Mr. Bray just wanted to make sure.

"WHEN she was here in Italy, she was called the American," Dante said. "When she was in America, they called her the Italian. She was also called the Red. In America they called me the Italian too."

"What do you mean the Red?" Dick Lambert asked Dante. "You mean red the color, or Red the communist?"

"The color. She was a redhead, as you know. Therefore, it is *not only but also—no solum sed etiam*. To some she was known as Mrs. Montepulciano. To others she was known as Mrs. Dante, or Mrs. Monte—short for Montepulciano—or Mrs. M. She was addressed in many ways."

Rossi stopped his client. They talked briefly. Dante leaned back in his chair, quiet, letting Rossi take over.

"Mr. Montepulciano is concerned about being considered Mrs. Taylor's 'Latin lover.' He told me earlier that he was concerned that if in his testimony he gave the name of a witness—someone at his school, for instance—and if one of us were to interview that witness and asked who was Mrs. Caprice Jordan Montepulciano, the witness would certainly respond that he didn't know any such person—despite the fact that everybody knew that the Redhead, or the American, or Mrs. M. was waiting for him."

—⚏—

I HOPED this would end soon, because my head didn't feel right. I told Rossi, but he didn't reply. He was busy with the deposition.

I wanted to rest. I wanted this interference in my life to end.

Even in death, Caprice, was causing trouble for me. Then I felt bad—I need to behave better and honor her.

My brother, Guido, Lessa, and I are here to honor Caprice, not cause needless confusion and dislike. I vow to do better.

Again I apologized to Rossi.

BUTLER ignored Dante, refusing to be led down another blind alley.

"I talked to Mr. Ford, the proprietor of the Kenrose Hotel in Glenwood Springs, Colorado, where they stayed several times," Butler said.

"Yes?" said Dante.

"He told me that Caprice signed the register as Mrs. Montepulciano." He hoped Dante would understand he was making a point in his favor.

"Exactly," Dante said.

"Exactly," Rossi echoed.

Rossi then explained to the Americans that Dante was angry with him because he had translated the deposition petition. Dante blamed him for having not only translated it, but also participated in writing it.

Butler stepped in to say, "Mr. Winslow, who was Mrs. Taylor's American lawyer before me, knew all of the names Mr. Montepulciano has just mentioned. But under Italian law, the Colorado deed clearly shows that he was Mrs. Taylor's husband, because of the signature."

—∽∾—

I REMEMBER how insistent Caprice was in Rifle, Colorado. She insisted on signing as Caprice Montepulciano. She was in love with me, was romantic with me; and with me, for once, she was not the oil heiress.

We loved our privacy.

She protected her privacy.

She reveled in her privacy.

I reveled in her.

There is an old Italian saying: "If you love someone, you will love everything about them."

NOW John Butler spoke up with a wrinkle he had been keeping to himself until the right moment to reveal it to the assembled lawyers.

"As we mentioned before, I visited Rifle, Colorado on my way here to Milan," he said. "In Rifle I met with a judge, following a lead given to me by my P.I. Jeff Kennedy. The judge told me exactly what Mr. Montepulciano is telling us now: that Mrs. Taylor used many different names at various times, in various circumstances. But during her stay in Rifle, she used the last name of Montepulciano exclusively, for all legal matters."

"Exactly. Thank you, Mr. Butler," Rossi said.

"The judge also told me that he remembered meeting her husband, Mr. Montepulciano," Butler added. "And he also helped Mrs. Caprice Montepulciano buy the house in Rifle. Further, the judge told me that he prepared the deed for the house, and he showed me a copy of the deed, the same that is before us now—in the names of Dante Montepulciano and Caprice Montepulciano."

"Exactly. I confirm," said Dante through Rossi.

"Slowly we come to the truth. Mr. Montepulciano also points out that the name Caprice in Greek is pronounced 'Capritsio,' meaning unpredictable or capricious. Which is why we're here today!

"You all have copies of the deed in front of you, in the folders I prepared for you," Rossi said, holding up his copy of the Colorado deed.

"That's it," said Dante, interrupting. "This is a copy of the legal paper for our house. After we signed it—I remember the time, it was nineteen sixty-five, just after Christmas—I called my brother Guido in Italy and told him about it."

—∽∞∾—

THE deed was perfect. It was signed by "Caprice Montepulciano" and "Dante Montepulciano." It was definitely her handwriting.
Perfetto!

15

DAY 4: Love in the Rockies

THE DEPOSITION RECESSED for supper. At 8:00 the Americans and Italians filed back into the conference room. On behalf of the charity lawyers, Jack Orso intended to inform Adam Rossi that they had decided to accept the fact that Dante Valentino Cesar Montepulciano was Mrs. Caprice Jordan Taylor's husband—at least under Colorado common law. So, since her will stipulated that they were to settle with her husband, the big questions were: First, would he settle? Second, if he would, for how much? Third, if he wouldn't agree to settle, would they sue him? That would cause the charities a lot of grief and a lot more time. John Butler said he felt sure it would not come to that.

—⁂—

IT was still early in the evening, and I suddenly felt fine. Rossi and Guido were saying good things to me.

I wondered how Caprice felt about the deposition. I wondered how John Butler felt about the it.

Mostly, I remembered my responsibility to Caprice.

Rossi had told me that Caprice had stipulated that no charity could receive her gifts until all of charities reached a settlement. And, being a good businessman, he had said his firm's fees for this might approach U.S. $300,000. Maybe more. That was okay with me. I didn't even ask what I would get. But I did care that Caprice and her gifts be honored.

BUTLER asked Dante to talk about their home in Rifle, Colorado.

First, Dante described the house to Guido. Then Dante told how he and Caprice celebrated the event. "We celebrated by having a drink—champagne—because in that moment that was our house. Up to that point, we were always staying in somebody else's house. Before buying a house of our own, we rented other people's houses: Mr. Rosa's, Mr. Bosco's, and Mr. Ford's homes."

"I see," Bray said.

Bass slumped in his chair. "Do we have go through the rentals part," he said. "I don't care one whit about rentals. We're here to negotiate, Mr. Bray."

Dante looked angry.

"Mr. Bass," said Bray, "we are here to hear Dante's accounts of their marriage. It has a great deal to do with the settlement."

"I agree," said Butler.

"You don't have any skin in the game Butler," said Bass in an ugly tone

"Strike that from the deposition record," Butler said addressing Bray.

"Strike these last remarks from the record," said Bray looking at the deposition recorder.

—◆—

CAPRICE was always careful with her money. Being careful with money was part of her character. Her father taught his children to be careful—prudent, you would say. She frequently cautioned me with this quote from Shakespeare: "Let every eye negotiate for itself and trust no agent."

When she negotiated, I kept quiet. She was the oil heiress, and knew how to handle money. She was familiar with people who thought she wouldn't care about overpaying. In fact, Caprice was a tiger of a negotiator. Maybe that was why it took us three months before we settled on a house.

I was a poor man. Caprice trusted that. I stayed out of money decisions, and she liked it that way. It was part of our relationship, part of our love.

"AH-HA, we are arriving at the truth," Dante said. "We hunted three months before finding the house we liked. I still have all the pictures we took. Caprice was very particular."

"I went to see the house in Rifle—" Butler began, but he was interrupted by Rossi, who had been listening intently to Dante.

"Mr. Montepulciano has a picture of that house—also a painting. He painted it himself," Rossi said. "He says it was not a very big house, not at all grand. What was most important was that Mrs. Taylor could spend a week, or two, or even three without leaving the house. She would remain close to the house. She found the house comfortable. The house also had at least one more positive attribute for Mr. Montepulciano."

"Did you see the back yard?" Dante asked Butler, through Rossi.

"No. There was a fence, and people were living inside."

"That's too bad," said Dante. "There was a back yard with a lawn. Caprice liked to walk with bare feet on the grass."

"Mr. Montepulciano liked that," said Rossi. "It was a positive thing for him. He says they often went a long time without leaving the house."

"Like the Arizona Inn?" Butler asked.

—⚬—

WHEN I think of those early days in Rifle, I feel good. We were both becoming healthy, and I was having fewer headaches. We should never have partied and drunk champagne and whiskey.

Our celebration was the beginning of trouble.

I have always felt bad about that small, joyful celebration. Because that was where I learned that Caprice was a mean drunk—although she was always remorseful the next day.

I decided to avoid having alcohol in the house. Whenever I found some in the house I would throw it into the garbage.

That inspired arguments.

Unhappily, Caprice started hiding the alcohol.

I dreaded that because all I wanted was for the good times to return.

"THAT'S right," said Rossi. "And he did walk barefoot there. That's what he refers to. The nice thing about that house—it wasn't very large or pretty, but the nice thing about it, and the reason Dante and Caprice finally purchased it, was the lawn. That and the heating system.

"Dante mentioned that in Glenwood, Colorado, they went to look at the villa of an optometrist," Rossi went on. "He wants to know if you called him."

"Yes," Butler said.

"Yes," Bray repeated, turning to the court recorder to make sure this was put into the record.

Dante leaned back in his chair and reminisced about looking at the villa in Glenwood. He spoke aloud in Italian, with Rossi translating.

"The villa of the optometrist was very beautiful, and was very nice for me because it had an organ. But Mrs. Taylor had a look at the heating system, and it wasn't good."

"He was also doing music therapy with Caprice," Rossi explained as Dante went on. "He was distracting her with the music. And for both of them the positive thing was that in the back yard there was a basketball hoop. He says he is very good at basketball."

"Let's move on, Mr. Bray," said Bass with a groan.

I WANTED to talk about basketball.

Caprice enjoyed basketball.

As soon as I discovered her interest, I tried my best to interest her even more. She enjoyed the movements in the game and the competition of it. And she was a good shooter.

She loved our one-on-one contests, where I joked around a lot, often playing the clown—lots of sweat and laughter.

I started to tell the lawyers about this, about our shared love of the game.

Rossi told me the deposition would be shorter if I kept quiet.

That shut me up. I laughed to myself.

AT that point, Dante leaped up from his chair and started moving around the table, dribbling a make-believe basketball, talking all the while, caught in his memory of playing basketball in Italy with an American soldier. Every so often he would feint and pretend to pass the ball to one of lawyers. In turn the lawyer would jerk back spastically, caught off guard. Bray, Butler and Rossi tried desperately not to laugh at their discomfort. It was like a Keystone Kops sight-gag.

"You see," Rossi explained, "Mr. Montepulciano was taught to play basketball right after the war by a lieutenant of the United States Army. He was short, like Mr. Montepulciano. He said that Mr. Montepulciano was pretty good, in fact. But in Italy nowadays, after the Americans showed them how to do it, they choose only very tall players.

"After a few years dedicated to the sport," Rossi said, "Mr. Montepulciano couldn't do any more, because he was off of the team. The American lieutenant had very good aim. He shot with one hand, and almost always sank it. He was very good from far away."

All the while, Dante was out of his chair, crouching, taking careful aim at an imaginary basketball hoop, leaping up, pushing his imaginary basketball toward the basket.

"Mr. Montepulciano. Excuse me, Mr. Montepulciano," Butler said.

"Excuse us, but we are in a formal deposition," he repeated.

"What?" Dante said.

"Would you please stop playing imaginary basketball and sit down?"

"Excuse me, excuse me, sir," Dante said.

He went to his seat and sat down.

Bass burst out laughing, enjoying himself. "This witness—Mr. Montepulciano, is the best I've seen in years."

Dante laughed with him, happy Bass was appreciative.

BASKETBALL is a wonderful sport. The lieutenant told me basketball had been invented in 1891, and at first it was played with a ball and peach baskets. The game started in Springfield, Massachusetts.

I played guard. I was quick, and a good shooter.

"GOING back to Rifle, Colorado, gentlemen, Mr. Montepulciano was happy," Rossi said breaking Dante's antics and guiding him back to his chair. "Even if he had to stay home, he had something to do. He purchased a backboard."

"It was made of wood," Dante said. "In America you could find them, but in Italy you couldn't. Not in those days. Basketball is the sport I preferred. I needed something to do."

"Mrs. Taylor, on the other hand, liked golf," Rossi said, translating Dante. "In fact, she refused another villa because it was too far away from the golf club."

This was all very amusing, but it wasn't advancing the deposition. Butler interrupted Dante and tried to get things back on track.

"Mr. Montepulciano, did you and Mrs. Taylor live in the house in Rifle, Colorado for about three years?" he said.

"Yes, about three years."

"Long enough for common law marriage," Butler emphasized.

—⁊⁊⁊—

I WAS still uncomfortable.

Lawyers live in a dark world of personality destruction and closed questions. I think they slip into that darkness without even knowing it.

They are trained in closed questioning.

It's apparent from this deposition of me.

Closed-ended questions are meant answered by a "no" or a "yes" or an "I don't know." To me this does not help. It's about power and a lawyer spinning a story in his favor.

Closed-ended questions can turn day into night, a tomato into a cucumber, gossip into truth, and lies into facts.

And these people get university law degrees for this. Even worse, everything rests on the past, which holds mankind's greed and peccadillos. There is no evolution in law—I better keep this to myself---the ramblings of old age.

"THREE years, but we took many vacations all over Colorado." Dante said.

"I know they went to a hotel in Glenwood Springs and spent a night there," Butler said.

Rossi translated Dante's reply. "He claims that they left immediately, in one minute, and Mrs. Taylor told him, 'Dante take care of things. I'm leaving. You take care of the room and everything. She handed him cash and the room key. And although they had reserved the whole month there, instead they went to another hotel, close to the Colorado River. At that time, the latter hotel was owned and run by an Italian from Piedmont, in northern Italy, where the best red wines were harvested. His name was Rocco. Another river joins the Colorado River there. Mr. Montepulciano forgets the name—Something Fork."

—⚏—

I WAS mixed up on dates and places.

I wasn't making sense and I knew it.

How did I get onto the subject of basketball? Why?

Should I change the subject to Matt Dillon?

But we used to laugh because we never met one Italian cowboy while we were in Colorado. Imagine a cowboy named Luigi or Cosimo or Valentino. Imagine a cowboy named Valentino walking into a saloon with chaps on and spurs on his cowboy boots.

Caprice and I would collapse in laughter.

Then we saw the spaghetti western called *A Fist Full of Dollars*. From that moment I would periodically walk around our house pantomiming Clint Eastwood with a serape over my shoulders, wearing spurs on my tennis shoes, and puff with a stick in my mouth for a cigarillo.

Caprice would begin laughing uncontrollably, knowing what came next.

At some point I would undo my fly, pull out my shirt which was tucked in my pants, arch my back, and parade around the room like an Italian male peacock.

She would fall down screaming with laughter.

Apparently I don't look at all like Clint Eastwood.

"DANTE wanted me to call a lawyer named Mr. Zenari," said Rossi. "I was to ask Zenari for a telegram certifying the wrong spelling of Montepulciano. I tried to call him, but he wasn't in. Dante is still worried about the misspelling of his name."

Rossi explained that Mr. Montepulciano wasn't sure of the name of the hotel. It was maybe the Hotel Colorado or Hotel Denver. "But my client remembers very well the—"

Dante interrupted, wanting to talk. "We were going off to that hotel—the name is... I can't remember name. What is name of a hero of Colorado? There's a bar in Glenwood Springs by that name. That's where Caprice told me this man was killed—by Matt Dillon."

"He says Matt Dillon was a U.S. marshal," Rossi said. "Marshal Dillon shot a bad man. He uses the word 'desperado.'"

Bass broke in saying, "Gentlemen, I can't believe what we are talking about."

"Pardon," said Bray.

"Just listen, Mr. Bray, we're talking about Matt Dillon," Bass said "We're wasting valuable time—this is our last day."

Bray turned to the other charity lawyers and said, "Mr. Bass is correct. Can we move on?"

"Mr. Rossi, let's move on."

"Fine, Mr. Bray," said Rossi, huddling with Dante, recommending he end his story so that the deposition could continue. The two went back and forth for a short time. The Rossi turned his attention to others in the room.

"My client asks only to complete this subject."

Bass laughed and suggested that Dante be allowed to complete his story.

—〰—

THE American charities' lawyers think I'm crazy. What am I doing, talking about Matt Dillon?

This bothers me, but I think this a true story. Perhaps not.

Actually, as I thought about this story, the marshal called Matt Dillon really struck my imagination.

"IT involves a famous cowboy sheriff," Rossi said.

"Jesse James?" Bass said, confused that they were on this topic.

"Wyatt Earp?" guessed Jack Orso.

"Wyatt Earp?" Rossi repeated, looking at Dante.

"Wyatt Earp? Maybe it was Wyatt Earp. He's very famous, although I think he's famous in Dodge City, Kansas, or Tombstone, Arizona, not Colorado," Butler said.

"No. Not Wyatt Earp," Dante said.

"Matt Dillon was the sheriff of Dodge City, Kansas," Jack Orso said, "but that was in a TV serial."

"Exactly," Dante said, smiling widely.

"Hold on. Excuse me," Orso interrupted. "Are we talking about Wild Bill Hickok?"

Once again Dante spoke rapidly in Italian, with Rossi providing simultaneous translation.

"Mr. Butler, when you were in Colorado, did you meet the chief of police? On Italian TV they showed a film about this man, and he called my home to tell me to look at it. And how do you call that movie in English—*Wonderful Seven*?"

"*Magnificent Seven.*"

"*The Magnificent Seven,*" Orso said.

"Where they used to dance in that bar. And there is a picture of this—what is the name of this guy?" Dante urged.

"Matt Dillon?" Orso answered.

"Yes, that's it. Matt Dillon," Dante said.

"Let's stop at Matt Dillon," said Bass covering up his annoyance. "We really need to move on. The hour is getting late and we have more to cover—right Mr. Bray?"

"Correct," Bray said acknowledging their dwindling time. He knew the charity lawyers were leaving Italy the next day and it was imperative that a compromise agreement be reached.

—m—

I THINK we should get off this topic.

Mr. Bass is correct. There are more important topics.

"MR. Rosa had died, but all of his sons were there," Dante said, shaking his head sadly. "The sons of Mr. Rosa were playing on the football team—American football—and I was invited to watch, as I was very interested in the sport.

"Good," Bass said. "May we move on. Proceed with other material, Mr. Montepulciano?"

Rossi answered, saying, "Yes that's a good idea, Mr. Bass."

Rossi huddled with Dante explaining their need to move onto new subjects so they could finish the fourth and last evening.

Dante nodded his head vigorously.

Bray immediately asked the other charity lawyers if they had questions.

Orso's hand shot up.

"Mr. Orso has the floor, gentlemen," said Bray happy to move on.

—⚹—

I WAS thinking of how Caprice and I were formally introduced.

A friend, a colonel I knew from my North African war days, agreed to introduce me to Mrs. Taylor during a big party being held for our Olympic soccer team at the Villa d'Este. When I entered the spacious ballroom, he grabbed my sleeve and walked me over to Caprice, who was surrounded by a small group of people in front of dramatic windows that went from the ceiling to floor. They faced out to Lake Como, forming a breathtaking backdrop.

I was in parade dress uniform. My riding boots were polished brown—I could see my reflection in them. My blue-gray uniform jacket dropped to midway between my waist and knees. I had matching riding trousers. My belt and two cross belts were brown. On the right side of my jacket I wore four medals: for valor, for being wounded, for the North African Campaign, and for the King's army regiment—King Victor Emanuel III, even though Mussolini ran Italy at the time. Even if I say so myself, I looked attractive.

When I stood in front of Mrs. Taylor, I took her hand and lightly kissed it.

"Oh my, you're one of the Olympic soccer team coaches," she said with delight in her voice. "I am so pleased to meet you."

"WOULD you tell Mr. Montepulciano that I missed something that came up earlier about the deed to the house in Rifle, Colorado," Orso said to Rossi. "May I ask him a question, please?

"Of course.

"Mr. Montepulciano, I missed the discussion about the deed that is noted as Exhibit Thirteen. I missed the part about the signatures. Were both of your signatures on it—yours and Mrs. Taylor's?"

"Yes."

"May I?" Orso repeated.

"No problem, Sir," said Dante. "Yes. But remember she signed as "Caprice Montepulciano. I did not ask her to do that. She did it on her own."

"And this was the deed to your house in Rifle, was it?" Orso said, holding up his copy.

"Yes."

Orso was being friendly. "Thank you," he said, turning to Guy Bray and indicating that he was now ready to head back to Santa Barbara. Bray indicated that they would leave only when they were done.

—◊◊◊—

I WAS still recalling my first meeting with Caprice.

"You look very handsome, sir," she said.

I will never forget that night. Our eyes met, and that was it—the beginning of our love.

"What medals are those?" she asked. I explained them. Then she carefully touched the scars of my head wound. "That is a serious wound, Mr. Montepulciano," she said, concerned. "But now you are one of the national coaches. You are handsome. May I call you Dante? I like coaches, Dante."

Perhaps I should have worn my formal Sports outfit with the blazer showing Italy's flag.

"Perhaps you will let me be your personal coach, Mrs. Taylor."

"Perhaps," she said, squeezing my hand. "But you also look dashing in your military uniform, Sir."

She turned to her companion, Clarissa and said, "Don't worry, I'll find your goalie, dear."

ROSSI said to Orso, "Mr. Montepulciano says he wants the document to make it clear where it was signed—legally executed."

Orso placated him. "Please, tell Mr. Montepulciano I accept his explanation and confirmations."

"That is the Latin and Italian habit," Rossi said. "When we buy something, we celebrate."

"I see. I see."

"Mr. Montepulciano, do you remember the name of the lawyer who drafted this document?" Butler asked.

"Avvocato," Rossi said.

"Avvocato," Butler repeated.

"He didn't see him many times," Rossi translated, interrupted by Dante who again broke into English.

"I only saw the lawyer a few times. I was more interested in the brokers, and they were very, very patient, because I was taking pictures. Caprice was discussing the thing. And then she would say no. Everybody froze."

"Mr. Bass, do you accept this evidence?" said Bray.

"Yes."

"Mr. Orso?"

"Yes."

"Mr. Lambert?"

"Yes."

Bray concluded that the charity lawyers accepted the document.

—∿—

I WAS thrilled. Her gown was beautiful and her jewelry was spectacular. I told her how splendid she looked.

"Never mind that, Mr. Montepulciano," said Caprice. "Where is that good-looking goalie of yours? Surely he is here."

"Yes, he's over there with the other players," I said, pointing to him.

"Come with me, Clarissa," Caprice said to her companion. "You're about to be properly introduced to that handsome goalie."

ROSSI tugged Dante's sleeve, pulling him closer to discuss something privately. Then Rossi turned to Orso. "Mr. Montepulciano will tell us the name of the lawyer later. He says he knows it, but he can't call it to mind at the moment."

"Mr. Montepulciano, as you said before, the truth is beginning to come out," Orso smiled.

"You must let him tell the truth slowly," Rossi insisted to Orso. "My client must always translate your English to his Italian, then he must consider it. Sometimes he is eager to help you—before he has time to fully consider the importance of his words. He mustn't be rushed. Do you understand, Mr. Orso?"

"I must ask you one question, though—to see if I understand," Orso persisted. "When you and Mrs. Taylor signed the document identified as Exhibit Thirteen, was it at a time when you were Mr. and Mrs. Montepulciano?

"Exacto," Dante said, despite Rossi's cautions.

"And intended to be husband and wife?" Orso said.

"Exactly," Rossi translated.

"I see," Orso said, hoping to demonstrate his growing respect for the fragile Italian.

"Okay. I have got the whole thing. I have got it," Rossi said. "Mr. Montepulciano says he can say *exacto,* because their common-law relationship was public by then, so he can confirm it and affirm it. He is pleased that this is the way we have arrived at the truth. At first, I didn't understand him correctly. But there is another point we would like to make. Mr. Montepulciano considered himself Mrs. Taylor's 'midwife.'"

—⚊—

CLARISSA happily followed her employer.

I followed the two women. I didn't know it at the time, but that was the moment I became Caprice's lover and her teacher of Italian. Her midwife.

"MIDWIFE?" Jack Orso shot back. "What's going on here? What's this midwife all about?"

"Yes, midwife," Rossi confirmed. Dante broke into rapid Italian, with enthusiastic hand gestures.

"He was opening up a new world to her. It was like giving birth. So that's the way, you extract the truth from the facts," Rossi said.

"For example, he was teaching Mrs. Taylor Italian from the first day he met her, because, in his own words, 'I entered her house as a professor of Italian, because all professors by law are professors of Italian.'"

"And I can be a witness to that," said Rossi, "because when I visited Mr. Montepulciano and Mrs. Taylor, he had been putting little slips of paper with the Italian names for things on objects all around the house, so that she could learn them."

"Mrs. Taylor became a good linguist using the Italian language," Dante said.

Rossi agreed.

Butler agreed for what he could contribute.

Guido agreed.

"Originally, Mrs. Taylor thought she might not be able to speak fluently," Dante said, "but she quickly learned that she was good at languages."

Bray encouraged the group to move on.

CLARISSA and her soccer goalie met, and they moved away to dance immediately. Clarissa looked thrilled with her young Italian, and Caprice was happy to have arranged their meeting.

Then Caprice turned around, looked at me and motioned for me to join her. "Come here, Captain, let's dance."

I joined her, and we danced until we were tired. From that moment on, we were a couple. When the celebration was over, we had dinner in her room, which was a well-appointed suite—quite a sight compared to my walk-up flat in my low-rent Milan neighborhood. That night I was in a wonderland, delirious and happy. So was Caprice. We made love all night and talked the way that new lovers do—uncritically and intimately.

"MR. Montepulciano also taught Mrs. Taylor Latin, Greek, and some French in the same way," Rossi added. "At the time he is talking about, the owner of the hotel in which they spent the night—the hotel in front of the railway station—Master Bosco, he says was his name—Master Bosco came back to Italy every six months. He has some relatives in Torino, and that's why he says he's Piamontese, because Piamontese—"

"Do you remember?" Butler asked Dante.

"Did Mr. Bosco understand that Dante and Caprice were living together as husband and wife?" Murray said.

"Yes," Rossi said.

"Did Mr. Ford at the Kenrose Hotel understand that Dante and Caprice were living together as husband and wife?" Murray asked.

"What *was* the hotel? The Kenrose?" Rossi asked, adding, "You have the records in front of you."

"The Kenrose," Murray said.

"Thank you," Rossi said.

"And Mr. Mason and Mr. Rosa confirmed this," Murray said.

"Excellent," Rossi said.

"Then it is true," Orso said.

"They were always selling vegetables to him, and they knew that they were married," Rossi said.

"It was a vegetable garden," Butler reminded them.

"A vegetable garden. They would stop there and ask for something. He told the story many times," Rossi said.

I REALIZED that I had better pay more attention to these American lawyers. They were beginning to ask more and more personal questions about me and Caprice.

I did not want to open too many personal things at this point.

I tugged on Rossi' sleeve and suggested we move on.

He agreed.

I relaxed.

"SO, Mr. Montepulciano, then it's true that during the entire time you were living in Colorado with Mrs. Taylor, you considered yourselves husband and wife?" Murray asked.

"Certainly. Certainly," Rossi said emphatically.

"Even before the record was public?" Butler asked.

"I don't understand," Rossi said.

"He considered himself and Mrs. Taylor married before they bought the property and thereby made the marriage public?" Butler said.

"From the moment they arrived in Colorado," Rossi emphasized. "They wished to be married, but Mrs. Taylor preferred it to be a common-law relationship, which she considered a lawful marriage."

"And that was from the first time the two of you together were in Colorado?" Butler asked.

"Yes, that was from the first time," Rossi translated.

"Until you left to go to go back to Italy in nineteen sixty-six?"

Murray, deciding this point needed clarification, cut in. He knew the charities' lawyers had to accept Caprice's common-law marriage. And it seemed no divorce had taken place. Hell, he thought, there was no such thing as a common-law divorce. Might as well put it into the record. "And then?"

Dante broke in, speaking slowly in English, his heavy Italian accent confusing some of his meaning. "Nothing has changed. Nothing changed. I have always considered myself Caprice's husband. From the moment I met her. All of the telegrams I sent demonstrate our true relationship. All of the postcards celebrating her birthday."

I HAD better pay more attention to these American charities' lawyers.

I asked for a moment to speak with Guido, Rossi, and Lessa.

We talked quietly in the hallway. I mentioned my anxiety that I was saying too much. I asked them to give me signals if they thought the same thing.

Rossi interrupted and said I was doing just fine and he encouraged me to keep doing what I was doing.

"THERE was never a divorce," Dante said. "And the reason she left is not that she was angry with me, but because..." He faltered.

"Because of what?" Bray asked, wondering what in fact came between Mrs. Taylor and Dante Montepulciano and drove them apart. "Did she escape because—"

Rossi interjected, wanting himself to speak, not Dante. "My client says Mrs. Taylor didn't 'escape' from him. She just left—he doesn't know why. Because she got angry with some Italian in Piazza Cavour in the city of Milan regarding the subject of the Fosse Ardeatine Massacre during World War II. Also before in Florence, and in Tucson, where she got in a heated dispute with a sailor over the subject of the Fosse Ardeatine Massacre. One moment while he explains this to me." He held up a hand to silence their questions while he listened to Dante.

—m—

THIS is a sad story.

It shows how hatred happens.

Again, I started to feel bad. It's this kind of stuff that starts my headaches.

I wished Rossi hadn't started the story.

Maybe I should tell this monstrosity of a story.

I suggested to Rossi that perhaps I could tell the story myself.

He looked at me and quietly asked why.

I thought I should tell the story because I was in WWII, not Rossi.

Rossi turned and discussed this change with Guido and Lessa, both of whom supported me telling the story.

Then Rossi asked to speak with Butler, who wondered why the story needed to be entered into the deposition records in the first place.

Butler asked me why I wanted to bring it up.

I told Butler that Mrs. Taylor was bothered by the story.

Because, I said, Mrs. Taylor was appalled by hatred.

This is a story about hatred.

It is also about humankind's worst traits: misanthropic motivation.

"MR. Montepulciano would like to tell the story himself," said Rossi. "It will be easier that way." Then Dante began to speak in English.

"The facts of the Fosse Ardeatine Massacre are these. It was during the last war in Italy, not here in Milan, but in Rome. There is a place called Fosse Ardeatine on the outskirts of Rome, where during the Roman Empire there were catacombs where the Christians held secret meetings. During the war some partisans blew up a German troop transport truck in Rome, killing thirty-three Germans. In retribution, the Germans put three hundred and thirty-three Italian prisoners of war into the catacombs of Fosse Ardeatine, and shot them all to death.

"This is considered one of worst war crimes to take place in Rome. Even today it's still a very sensitive issue in Rome whenever somebody talks about the events of the last war.

"Now, I don't know how it happened that there was a dispute between Mrs. Taylor and some Italians here, and also in Tucson, about the Fosse Ardeatine. What I can tell you is that this is a matter of controversy between leftists and the rightists. Leftists believe that this was a legitimate act of war, and the three partisans who survived it were very brave people. The rightist version is that before killing the prisoners, the Germans asked the ambushers to turn themselves in. But they didn't, and that's why the prisoners of war were shot. So there is great controversy between the two different opinions, right and left, as to whether the partisans were morally responsible for this event. And anytime there is a discussion of the event, it inevitably comes around to politics—wartime politics at that. That's it, right?"

"Correct," Rossi said.

"Good. Thank you," Bass said, growing tired of the subject.

—⚉—

I WAS still uncomfortable.

I did not want to expose the truth—that Mrs. Taylor wanted us to be together from the morning after the celebration for the Italian soccer team and forever on.

DANTE continued in Italian now, and Rossi translated. "At that time, just before Mrs. Taylor left to return to the United States, she quarreled very often with everybody here in Italy. She had an argument with a cook in a restaurant, an argument with a waiter. She sent a bottle of wine back because it was bad; she sent back three or four bottles in succession. She was very nervous about things in Italy."

"Mr. Montepulciano has said that Mrs. Taylor also got into an argument with a woman from Milan?" Butler asked.

"With more than one woman," Rossi said. "According to my notes, Mr. Montepulciano said that Mrs. Taylor went to the apartment of a woman and slapped her across the face—"

Dante interrupted immediately, whispering rapidly into Rossi's ear. "Mr. Montepulciano says that only happened once in Milan. But it also happened in Switzerland. She did that to other people. But he doesn't want to say things like that. You must say them, then he will talk about them—if he can."

"Okay..." Butler said, looking at Dante and Rossi and nodding.

—⚊ℳ⚊—

AFTER that evening in Villa d'Este, Caprice told me her family secrets, which apparently were not so secret. The press had reported several of her family's secrets: that her father was domineering and enjoyed quarrels. It was a family of discord. There was a mysterious house fire. The family blamed Caprice, who was only a child. She always said she didn't do it. In fact, she had a recurring nightmare of fire.

I wanted to stay off this topic until we reached The Golden Pact part of deposition's agenda. So I told Rossi.

He thought this was a good idea.

Rossi discussed the topic with the whole room.

There was general agreement it could wait until the *Atto Solenne* (what I called The Golden Pact) section.

Rossi turned Mrs. Taylor's "slapping" episodes.

"IN other words, you initiate the subject, and Mr. Montepulciano will complete the picture," Rossi said. "He will confirm what you say, and then fill in the blanks. He says she also slapped the accountant who managed her finances in Como. He forgets his name."

"Was the man's name Felisio?" Butler asked, wanting to get the name into the deposition transcript.

Dante shrugged. He couldn't remember.

"I have the name, but I'll have to look it up," Butler said to Guy Bray. Bray assented. Meanwhile Dante was whispering to Rossi.

"Mr. Butler," Rossi said, "Mr. Montepulciano is talking about a friend of mine, Mr. Adam Pederzani, who at one time was a world champion at water skiing. Mr. Montepulciano says that Mr. Pederzani can help by giving a picture of what Mr. Montepulciano was before he met Mrs. Taylor." Rossi stopped speaking, wondering what that had to do with the topic. He was afraid Dante was tired and becoming undone.

"Anyway, after Mrs. Taylor slapped the woman across the face in Milan, she got in a cab and left. She left Italy and never returned."

Bass perked up. "You mean Mrs. Taylor left?" he said suddenly realizing they were close to the end of the deposition. "Is that correct, Mr. Montepulciano?"

"*Corretta,*" Dante said glumly.

"*Corretta?*"

"Correct, Mr. Bass," Dante said in English.

"Sir, I am sorry to hear that," Bass said sympathetically, shaking his head. He looked at Rossi and said that he had nothing more to say.

—⚮—

I REMEMBER with despair Caprice's descent back into alcoholism.

It was a terrible time.

If only we had not celebrated the purchase of the house in Rifle, Colorado. I feel guilty to this day. It was the beginning of the end of our relationship. It didn't happen right away, but as the months went by.

The two of us started going to bars for drinks in the evening.

It was all so subtle. You could hardly pick up on the signs.

"IN the months leading up to the split," Dante continued, speaking through Rossi, "Caprice became a problem: one drink became three, one evening out became every evening. Then came a terrible dependency. Friends got annoyed with us. She had blackouts. Once we even went to a hospital so that she could 'dry out.' The doctors prescribed valium, which caused further problems. I was becoming discouraged, which she sensed, and that made her even more miserable.

"She kept doing things like that. She did the same thing at the La Palma. You can contact the Hotel La Palma if you want to know Caprice left that hotel. I cannot tell it myself. Check the hotel register. You'll find her name there, for room thirty-three. It's the only room she ever used there. There is a good reason for that; but I'm reluctant to give it."

Again Rossi explained, "There are things that he can talk about only after they have been brought up by other people. He doesn't want the responsibility of having done so himself."

—〰—

I DIDN'T like this kind of talk. Yes, Caprice and I experienced such events, but I felt I wasn't supporting her. It seemed wrong.

I tugged on Rossi's sleeve. He turned giving me his attention. I complained that all this stuff involving alcoholism was depressing to me. I asked whether or not we could move to The Golden Pact part of the agenda.

He said no.

I shook my head. This was not doing Caprice any good. That she died from the complications of alcohol was bad, but dredging up that part of her past made me feel badly. Having great wealth brings great temptations.

I asked for a recess, which was granted. I went with Guido to Rossi's office where we could talk privately.

I told him that the direction of the deposition was depressing me. Guido encouraged me to trust Rossi and Butler. He said he felt badly for me but that this was a true part of her life. As for the deposition itself, he said not to worry. Just stay positive.

"BECAUSE the reason for which she chose that room reflects a negative side of Mrs. Taylor's personality that Mr. Montepulciano does not wish to show. He is not happy talking about negative things.

"Anyway, she was very difficult in choosing hotels," Rossi said. "She wanted to see them all first, and she was always touchy about choosing the room she liked."

"Mr. Rossi," Orso said at Bass's bidding, "it's not necessary for you and Mr. Montepulciano to cover all this stuff. I agree it describes Mrs. Taylor's frame of mind and the difficulty of it for him. But lets skip it."

Rossi translated Orso's comments for Dante.

"Mr. Orso," said Rossi, "my client wishes for all of you to hear the truth."

"But—," Orso said. Bray interrupted.

"Gentlemen, I would like to hear this testimony," he said, continuing, "Mr. Rossi, Mr. Montepulciano, and Guido have agreed to the telling of this part of their life. I recommend we continue."

Orso looked at Bass, who shrugged and gestured his permission.

Bray looked at Rossi and Dante and invited them to proceed.

Dante invited Rossi to continue.

Rossi went on, translating for Dante, "She wasn't able to understand all of these difficulties. He would ask, 'Why don't we take the hotel and just sit down?' She said no. She just wanted it her way. And I—Mr. Montepulciano—I could have really slapped Mrs. Taylor herself at those moments. I have a Latin temper."

"Now, thinking about it years later," Dante said through Rossi, "you can see that she was right. Think, for example, of the Pioneer Hotel in Tucson. What happened there? They said she was crazy, but she was right. The true story goes like this: I went into the Pioneer Hotel first, intent on signing us in. Mrs. Taylor stood behind me and let me do the check-in."

—⧟—

WE were quarreling a lot then—always about hotels and her drinking.

Caprice wouldn't listen. I didn't want to be an enabler.

Until our visit to the Pioneer Hotel, I never heard about a problem with the number thirty-three.

"I ASKED the desk clerk if he had a reservation for Mrs. Caprice Taylor. He looked it up and said yes. He said he had a room for us with a king-size bed, and the bathroom had a tub. 'I have you in room thirty-three,' he said.

"Caprice broke in and said to me, but meaning it for the clerk, 'I don't like that room number. Is there another room instead?'

"The clerk looked at Caprice, and said, 'No, we're full.'

"But Caprice wouldn't have it. She said, 'I won't stay in room thirty-three, Dante, love. Let's find another hotel.'

"'Caprice, princess,' I said, 'why don't we just look at the room?'

"'I won't take it,' she said. 'But if you want to look at it, I'll look at it.'

"The clerk handed me the key, but Caprice didn't like that either. 'No,' she said, 'it's important that he shows us.' She said this to me; she refused to speak directly to the desk clerk.

"The clerk was annoyed, but he took the key and asked us to follow him.

"We saw the room. It was big and clean and well furnished. It looked just fine to me."

"The number thirty-three is a bad number, love."

"Why?" said Bass running his hands through his greasy hair.

"The number thirty-three was on the door to the room?" Dante said.

"No, I am talking about number itself," Bass said.

"Number thirty-three?" said Dante.

"Yes, the number thirty-three," Bass said. "I am interested in the meaning of the number thirty-three. Is it a bad number?"

"Yes."

"Why?"

—◆—

I RECALL the room Caprice had at the Villa d'Este at Cernobbio on Lake Como. That room number was eighteen, not thirty-three. This was years ago.

When I think about it, it's odd but until that day we had never had a hotel room with the number thirty-three.

"YOU see," Dante explained, "Caprice was a bit of an occultist. She believed in Satanism, in which the number thirty-three is a mysterious number. For example, she once told me that the Tibetan Book of the Dead refers to thirty-three heavens. And she said the Jewish King David reigned over Israel in Jerusalem for thirty-three years. She insisted that thirty-three is a most mysterious number and there was no arguing with her. She said the room wouldn't do, and that was that.

"The desk clerk asked what was wrong. He said it was one of the better rooms he had—perhaps the very best.

"'It won't do,' Caprice insisted. She said it just didn't feel right. Then she said she was afraid of fire.

"I asked the clerk where the fire escape was; he said it was at the end of the hall.

"'How far is that?' Caprice asked.

"The clerk looked down the hall and said that the fire escape was only five rooms away.

"Caprice hesitated, still not convinced. She looked out the window, down onto the street below and said, 'It's three floors to the street. If there was an emergency, I would kill myself jumping.' Again she asked him to show us another room, but again he said there was none; the hotel was full.

"'Well,' she said, 'you'd better do something, because we're not going to take this room and we have a confirmed reservation.'"

—m—

I SUGGESTED to the desk clerk that he phone another hotel and find an equivalent room for us.

In fact, the desk clerk became upset and lost his manners. But bad things began to happen.

Caprice insisted we be given a room on the first floor.

The clerk understood and said all of the first floor rooms were booked. Unfortunately his voice showed impatience, indicating he just wanted us out of his hotel. Fast.

Caprice was becoming unhinged.

"THIRTY-THREE is a mysterious number," Dante said again. "Jesus died at thirty-three. King Solomon's temple stood for thirty-three years before it was pillaged. There are thirty-three symbols in the Masonic Order; one of those symbols is a double-headed eagle crowned with an equilateral triangle, and inside the triangle is the number thirty-three.

"Caprice told me of these things. She was uncomfortable with the number thirty-three.

"The clerk repeated that this was the only room he had available. I begged him to find us another room.

"Then Caprice interrupted again. Now she wanted to know whether the room was over the kitchen. The clerk said it was, but he said no one had ever complained about cooking odors.

"But she was unconvinced. She put an arm around my waist and addressed the clerk, 'Young man, we want a different room! We reserved a room a month ago, and we want to see another room, one we like!'

"The clerk apologized, and began to say again that this was the only room available, when without warning Caprice slapped the young man's face and shouted, 'Don't you give me a bad time, you young whippersnapper. I want a room, preferably on the first floor, and I won't take no for an answer!'

"The clerk jerked back in surprise, angry, his face flushed. He felt humiliated. He ordered us to leave the hotel. There was *no* room available for us, now or ever. Not at his hotel."

THE CLERK was shocked.

Caprice was angry. There was not going to be any compromise. She didn't even hear his orders.

I grabbed her and suggested we find another hotel.

Then she began crying.

We went back to her car and drove around, look for another hotel.

ROSSI interrupted Dante's account of the Pioneer Hotel. "Excuse me, Mr. Montepulciano, but Mr. Bray has asked what you meant about the hotel *registry*?"

"We went there," Dante said having lost his train of thought about the hotel registry, "and the clerk was not at his station. She was looking at the room. She didn't want that room. She didn't want that one. She drove them crazy. So we went to another hotel.

"A few months later, the Pioneer Hotel caught fire. Twenty-nine people were killed. It was the deadliest fire in Arizona history. And it began in that room, the room where they wanted to put us—room thirty-three."

The charities' lawyers were uncertain what was happening, but they let Dante talk, absorbed by his storytelling.

"What is the fear that you have in California?" Dante asked them.

"Earthquakes," Butler said. All of the American lawyers agreed.

"It's like that. But Caprice's fear was fire. Her family's home fire gave her a lifelong fear of fire."

"Yes, I understand. Excuse me," Butler apologized.

"Mr. Montepulciano, may I ask you another question?" Jack Orso asked. "Originally, I thought we were talking about a registry, a hotel registry. Am I correct?"

—⚬—

REGISTRY? I was forgetting their line of thought.

Rossi spoke to me and suggested we get on another topic.

I was happy to move on.

I began to believe that the American charity lawyers were beginning to empathize with me. I needed all the help I could muster. Time would tell.

We took a short break. During it Butler and Orso came over and talked with me—just to be friendly.

I told them, "You have to understand Caprice was my wife."

Bray called the deposition back to order.

ORSO stopped talking and looked at the eccentric, charming witness. Then he took Bill Bass's tack.

"Mr. Montepulciano, I too have a wife, and I do many things for her. We take walks sometimes. I read to her sometimes. Sometimes we watch television together. We laugh together."

"And we were like that," Dante said, speaking rapidly through Rossi. "We would spend the whole night talking about a word, or things like that."

Now Bass stepped back into the conversation. "I've been married nine years. Sometimes I hold my wife's hand," he said, soothingly. "We go for walks. Sometimes we go to parties. We have friends come to our house. I agree, details are important."

"Mr. Montepulciano wants to give all the details," Rossi said.

"I also would like to encourage Mr. Montepulciano," said Bray interrupting Rossi. "Mr. Montepulciano, we think you misjudge us. We are all married and we understand your sensitivities. We know it is difficult to talk about relationship. We already accept that you were considered "married" under Colorado common law.""

Dante felt appreciated by these statements.

Bray directed the deposition group to stay on subject so that they could conclude the evening, even though they had more material to consider.

Nobody objected.

—◊◊◊—

I REMEMBER my post-war recovery and attendance at university. My professors knew of my head wound, and they were often amazed. They marveled at how well my frontal cortex worked. They agreed I had a prodigious memory, although they were discouraged by my shaking: the war had left me with a tremor, and I had trouble writing. That is why I was allowed to take exams orally.

I was an athlete. I excelled at soccer, and advanced to the varsity team. This eventually led to my being selected as one of the coaches for the Italian national soccer team.

Eventually, the university gave me a degree for my studies in philosophy, education and physical education. Life was good.

"MR. Montepulciano," Bass said, now with a tone of respect in his voice, "were all of the things that I just mentioned part of your love and common-law marriage with Mrs. Taylor in Colorado?" Bass said.

"Yes. Playing golf, doing everything together."

"Frisbee?" Bray asked.

"Yes, we played frisbee too."

"Softball, also," Rossi added.

"Softball also," Dante confirmed. "We played softball in the back yard of the school where I taught."

"Let's go off the record for just a minute," Bray said.

CAPRICE was a good athlete too.

At the beginning, when we lived in Rifle, Colorado, she trusted me and took advantage of my coaching skills.

We also hiked the forest trails, swam in the lakes in the summer, and when the snow came we snow-shoed and skied. Caprice was an excellent skier—the envy of many people. I would let her go first and then chase her downhill.

I gave Caprice massages. She loved my hands, which she said had nice long, strong fingers. She liked the way I kept my nails manicured. She let me give manicures to her.

I admired her legs and bum, and she knew it. When she passed by me in our home, she would brush my front with her derriere.

She often called me coach, because of my background with soccer teams and my love of competition. And in those days, I was still trim and athletic.

We had a hot tub in our home.

We dedicated one room to lifting weights—not like they do today where people develop abnormally large muscles; instead I taught Caprice how to condition her muscles, resulting in good lines.

She was a good student.

Because of her past she was at first a little flabby, but she moved past that and paid real attention to herself.

We were good together and enjoyed building and maintaining our health.

In the spring of love we were joyful and caring.

NOW Rossi produced a document. "Mr. Montepulciano has asked that this be introduced as Exhibit Fourteen, and be part of the official record," Rossi instructed. "It is a journal article describing the benefits of music therapy. Mr. Montepulciano used music therapy to help Mrs. Taylor fight alcohol addiction."

"Thank you. It shall be marked Exhibit Fourteen—or a copy of it will be marked as Exhibit Fourteen," Bray said. "Would you like us to make a copy?"

"Yes, he wants to retain the original," Rossi said.

"Mr. Nelson," Bray instructed, "would you please make a true and correct photocopy of the front and back side of this document, and mark it Exhibit Fourteen, and then return the original to Mr. Montepulciano."

—▨—

MUSIC therapy was important to Caprice's health issues.

We listened to music together. It soothed her, and drew us closer. It helped her. There's nothing very mysterious about that.

I appreciated music therapy because it addresses our physical, emotional, mental, and social needs. I believe it has the power to help heal us. It can help change our moods. It can relax us. It can trigger good feelings. We benefit in so many ways through music. Even Pablo Picasso, who painted *Joie de Vivre*, was attracted to music. I can still see the painting: a blue nubile girl dancing to pipe-playing fauns and dancing figures. Caprice loved Picasso's talent.

I am not focusing. What do I care about these numbered exhibits? In fact, I'm losing interest in the proceedings altogether. These lawyers seem to live on a different planet.

I like the Italian saying about lawyers: "A lawsuit is a fruit tree planted in a lawyer's garden." That about sums it up.

I trust Butler and Murray—even Mr. Bray. I am surprised that I'm even beginning to think that Orso and Bass are believing in my positions.

I am trusting of course of Rossi and Galileo.

EXHIBIT 14 was attached to the deposition record.

John Bray said, "Let the record reflect I am returning the original of Exhibit Fourteen to Guido Montepulciano.

"Let the record also reflect that I am handing the court reporter a card from the American National Red Cross certifying that Dante Montepulciano has completed a course in first aid. Would you please take true and correct copies of the front and back pages of this document, mark it as Exhibit Fifteen, and we will return the original to its owner."

The deposition recorder did so, and Exhibit 15 was entered into the deposition record.

—∽∾∾∽—

IN Colorado I took a course offered by the American Red Cross. My war wound puzzled doctors. Although some things I thought or did were a little strange, my intellectual capacity was not damaged.

At first I hoped to learn more about massage, but the Red Cross did not offer such courses. So I chose adult first aid for coaches: first aid, health, and safety. I thought that would help me be a better coach for Caprice. Later it did help me.

I really wanted to take university courses, but there was no university in Rifle, Colorado. As Caprice would say, "Hey, kid, you're in Kansas now." Actually, I never understood this American saying. Also, Caprice would laugh and say, "You know you're in Kansas if all of the festivals are named after a fruit, vegetable, or grain."

She would laugh at me and slap her sides.

Italians have similar sayings. If I say, *Non tutte le camellia riescono col buco,* it literally means, "Not all doughnuts come out with a hole." But what it implies is that things don't always turn out as planned.

"LET the record reflect that we are returning the original of Exhibit Fifteen to Mr. Guido Montepulciano for placement with Mr. Dante Montepulciano," Bray said.

Roberto Galileo handed Dante an envelope, and said, "Let the record reflect that it is now eight fifty-three P.M., and that Mr. Montepulciano is going to open an envelope, brought here by Mr. Butler and addressed to Mr. Montepulciano in care of Mr. Winslow. It comes from the Santa Barbara National Bank, and contains a letter from the manager of the bank. Its purpose is to disclose—and this is evidence of the fact—that although the bank has continued to send statements to him, he has never touched the funds in the account established for him by Mrs. Taylor."

Rossi asked the lawyers, "Are you aware of the balance in this account?"

"No, I'm not," Orso said, wondering how such a poor man could resist withdrawing at least some of the money.

"Any amount that was withdrawn from that account was spent for the benefit of Mrs. Taylor."

"An autopsy was performed," Butler explained.

"Do we know the day of the death of Mrs. Taylor?" Bray asked.

"The date is recorded in the autopsy. I will try to find it here," Butler said.

"If you can, tell us the date," Galileo said.

I DIDN'T want to hear anything about the autopsy.

I told Rossi that if they talked about it, I would leave the room.

"VENTITRE Giugno," Butler said. "June twenty-third."

"No. Maybe." Dante began to doubt.

"Yes, yes, yes." Butler said, thumbing through the autopsy report. "They found her on the twenty-third. Here, you see: *ventitre.*"

Dante looked at the date on the report. "Exactly. On the twenty-third."

"Ventitre Giugno," Butler repeated. June twenty-third, nineteen seventy-seven.

Dante huddled briefly with Rossi, after which Rossi said, "Mr. Montepulciano would like to have a meeting of this committee, possibly next week. No. Wait a minute. After you've left Milan, please stay in touch with me. I am always in touch with Mr. Montepulciano."

"Right. Yes," Bray said.

"I'm not coming back," Butler said.

"That's the idea," said Rossi. "So let's keep in touch by phone. How old are your boys, Mr. Butler?"

"Ten and two," Butler said.

"And you need to be at home with them. You see, Mr. Montepulciano wants to give help to you, for the sake of your children," Rossi explained.

"Mr. Montepulciano would also like to note a coincidence," Rossi continued. "We started this deposition on the twenty-third—the day of the birthday of my father, *and* the date of the death of Caprice Jordan Taylor. And we are finishing on the twenty-seventh."

"Which is the birthday of his niece, Maria," Guido chimed in, "whom Mrs. Taylor loved very much."

Then, quixotically, Dante switched to old memories. "Is the horse at the Tanque Verde Ranch in Tucson, Arizona, still alive?"

No one knew the answer, so Dante forgot about it.

—⚇—

MY brain is so strange.

IT still remained to read Exhibit 15, the banker's letter, into the record. Bray hurried on, anxious to end this part of the proceedings. He asked John Butler to read the letter aloud.

"'Dear Customer,'" Butler read. "'Our records indicate that more than six months have passed with no activity on your checking account. We have been mailing statements of your account to the above address and would like to make sure that you have been receiving them. It would be helpful to us if you would sign on the line at the bottom of this letter and return the letter to us in the enclosed envelope. If the address shown above is not correct, please change it to show your correct address. We assure you that your account is sincerely appreciated and take this opportunity of thanking you for your continued business.'

"And at the bottom," Butler said, it reads: 'I have received the statements mentioned above, signed—'"

"And what is the current balance in the account," asked Bass.

"Twenty-thousand dollars," Bray said.

"And Mr. Montepulciano never withdrew funds?"

"Correct."

With the letter read in, Guy Bray called for another break. Everyone was getting tired.

—⁂—

I SHOOK my head. These lawyers were still preoccupied with money. They failed to understand that I wanted to make sure the charitable gifts *honored* my Caprice. This is my objective, my duty.

16

Day 4: *Atto Solenne*, the Golden Pact

IT WAS NOW 10:17 P.M. and everyone was exhausted. Only one item remained on the agenda: the solemn agreement made between Caprice and Dante. Dante wanted it placed in the deposition record, but the charities' lawyers didn't particularly want it to become part of the record. They had already conceded that under Colorado law Dante was Caprice's common-law husband. There was little doubt of that. Their main strategy since then had been to try to limit his claim on the estate—which appeared rightfully to be one-half of it, more than thirty million dollars. Somehow they had to find a way to get Dante to take less than that—substantially less.

However, before the deposition was concluded, despite the late hour, Guy Bray agreed to read something called the *Atto Solenne* into the record. Dante referred to it as The Golden Pact.

—⟩⟩⟩—

NOW my head was really aching.

At last we are finally at the Golden Pact—the end of the deposition—and my private shame.

Caprice was clearly sick and unpredictable.

I previously had privately telephoned Clarissa and told her that I could not help Caprice—that her alcoholism was too severe. Clarissa had been her private nurse for years, so I felt I could trust her with this information.

I told Clarissa I had signed an oath to take care of her, but it was increasingly difficult to do that. Caprice was hiding alcohol everywhere and withdrawing from me.

"THE deposition is called back to order," Bray said. "I know it's late. We're all tired. But before we end this deposition, we have one more matter to conclude, one last document. In Italian its title is *Atto Solenne*. Mr. Montepulciano asks that we translate it as the Golden Pact, because he can only make one oath in his life time and as we already know he has done that—to his king.

"Mr. Butler asks that Mr. Montepulciano tell us the background of the *Atto Solenne*, and then read the document himself," Bray said. "After that, we can end the deposition."

"Do we have to go through all this?" protested Bill Bass wearily. "It's all right with me if we just attach it. It's late, Guy. Just attach it as document. I'll accept it. I'm sure *all* of us will." The American charities' lawyers nodded in unison.

"No," said Bray, "this is important to Mr. Montepulciano, and we will extend this courtesy to him," Bray said.

And so the charities' lawyers reluctantly agreed to hear this Golden Pact, this *Atto Solenne*. No one knew where it would lead.

Bray turned to Dante. "Go ahead, Mr. Montepulciano, please tell us about the *Atto Solenne*."

———✲———

I WAS certain that the lawyers were more interested in the sixty million dollars—sixty-eight million now, they had said! Two years ago, when Caprice left us, it had been only about twenty million. Caprice would be happy. But, according to the terms of her will, they had to settle with her husband, and that was me.

Rossi told me that if we were to argue my case in Colorado, at least fifty-percent of the estate would go to me.

I reminded him that I did not want money. I simply wanted each charity to honor Caprice by recognizing her gift with memorial plaques.

Rossi reminded me that I would need to pay his fees.

Then all I needed was enough money to cover his fees.

He also reminded me that such a gift would also be taxable.

Rossi said I should accept a reasonable amount.

I ignored him and asked that we finish with the *Atto Solenne*.

We both agreed to move forward.

DANTE clasped his hands, resting them on the conference table, and stared at them in silence for a few moments. Then he began to speak. He spoke quietly, his voice resonating with dignity and seriousness. Rossi provided simultaneous translation. Everyone listened closely to Mrs. Taylor's proud Italian lover, this man struggling for acceptance of his relationship with Caprice Jordan Taylor.

"Our *Atto Solenne* was written in Lucerne, Switzerland, on the morning of February third, nineteen sixty-eight. It was several years after Caprice and I became common-law husband and wife.

"It was before noon. I don't remember exactly. We were staying at Hotel Wilden Mann. A blizzard had raged for two days. The previous night we had been invited to a party. Mrs. Taylor was drinking again and it was bad. She was out of control.

"The night ended with her breathing out of control—she had collapsed on the floor behind a sofa, unable to get her breath. She took huge gulps of air that seemed not to reach her lungs. Her breathing system—I think the English phrase is autonomous breathing system—was shutting down. She thought she was dying.

"I couldn't get her to the hospital. Fortunately, a doctor was staying at the hotel. It was a bad scene. The doctor gave her some medicine—I don't remember what it was—and we put her to bed. He warned me to keep all alcohol away from her. She was very ill, he said, from advanced alcohol poisoning.

"I was terribly frightened by her alcoholism. It was a terrible thing to see, my wife barely able to breathe.

"After the doctor left, Caprice began to cry. 'Oh, Dante, dearest Dante, I am lost!' she wailed. 'I am dying. This time I know it. I feel it. I'm so sick and so alone. I know you will leave me, not that I would blame you.'

"I went over to her bed and took her hand. 'You are not alone, Caprice. I am here.'

"'Oh, Mary Mother of Jesus, it's terrible! I'm dying! You must swear to stay beside me. I am afraid of dying!'

"The next morning Caprice was wretched. The effects of the previous night's drinking were dramatic: her hands shook, she couldn't eat, her liver was in great pain. She couldn't remember what had happened. There was no memory, a complete blackout.

"Fear gripped Caprice's heart. Her body was ruined by alcohol.

This time she dreaded she would die, and in the way she feared most: alone and abandoned. Most of her friends had already abandoned her. Now she was worried she had lost me. Anxiety gripped her. She feared she would die alone, like a bag lady—maybe even in some unknown alley. She began to cry.

"'Caprice, I am here—now, always,' I told her.

"She sweated involuntarily, her joints and muscles aching. She was in great pain. Every molecule in her body craved alcohol. But she knew that alcohol would kill her. She was certain that this time it would kill her. Afraid she may be dying this very instance, she reached for my hand.

"'You must swear not to leave me, dearest friend.'

"'I will not leave,' I said.

"'I've been so cruel to you—so selfish,' she confessed. She was needy, contrite, dependent.

"'You have my solemn promise.'

"'You must swear it—in writing,' she demanded.

"'My spoken word—as an officer—is enough.' I said.

"'Yes, yes, but write it—swear it in writing. Please, my only love. Do this thing for me, this one thing, now. I beg you,' she sobbed. 'You're the only one who doesn't want my money. Through it all— through all my misdeeds and terrible behavior—you have asked for nothing. You gave your love, and I have killed it.'

"'You have not killed my love for you, Caprice,' I said. 'It survives your sickness. Years ago I gave you the Shakespeare lines: "Love that alters is not love." My love for you is not altered. But you are sick, you must get rest, you must get better—'

"'Dante, quick, help me, write a solemn oath to take care of me. I have become the worst drunk in the world. Do it. Do it now,' she pleaded. She would not be consoled. I must swear this oath not to abandon her."

—⚊⚊—

I COULDN'T make a second oath—I made my one oath to the King, and you can only make one in a lifetime, so I wrote an act.

"THEN I went over to the drawing table, sat in the eighteenth-century antique French chair, picked up a pen lying on the table, and on hotel stationery wrote a solemn pact to care for Caprice. Meanwhile, Caprice lay across the bed sobbing, sick deep in her heart, despondent at being so physically and spiritually miserable.

"I composed this solemn aact, writing in Italian, which Caprice understood and could read."

Thereupon Dante picked up the document lying before him, and began to read.

SOLEMN PACT (THE GOLDEN PACT)

Luzern, 3 February 1968

The undersigned, Dante Montepulciano, son of Pietro and Letizia Montepulciano, born in Verona the 27th of April 1920, makes a formal commitment to Caprice Jordan Taylor, with this solemn pact or *Atto Solenne*, and on his honor as an officer: to continue to assist with maximum care, constancy, expertise, prestige, devotion, love, and diligence; to be with her at any time everywhere in any country of Europe and of the world, and as long as she will want it.

Moreover, in case of sickness he shall stay always beside her at home, in a private clinic, or in a public hospital. Furthermore, in case of calamity he shall provide her hospitality at home among relatives of the undersigned. Well understood according to his and his relatives possibilities.

Written, read and undersigned on the above date,

Dante Valentino Caesar Montepulciano

"I prayed this would help Caprice. She was shaking involuntarily and taking huge gulps of air.

"'There, Caprice,' I said, showing it to her. 'It is finished—my solemn pact to take care of you. You have nothing to fear. I, Dante Montepulciano, will care for you in health and in sickness.'

"Caprice read swiftly, and thanked me profusely for each promise to care for her."

Dante set down the document gently and fell silent. Rossi handed copies of the document to the lawyers, "Here is a copy of their pact, in the original Italian."

ATTO SOLENNE

Luzern, 3-2-1968

Addi ventun givano millenovecentosessantotto il sottoscritto Dante Montepulciano fù Pietro e di Letizia Bortolameazzi nato a VeDonalda il ventisette Aprile millenovecentoventi, si impelna formalmente con il presente atto solenne, sotto il vincolo del givramanto e sull'onore di ufficiale, di continuare ad assistere com Massimo zelo, costanza, perizia, prestigio, devozioniz, affecto, diligenza di seguiria in dani momento dovunque, in ogni nazione d'Europa e del Mondo e per quanto tempo ella vorra'. Inoltre in caso do malattia di rimanere sempre vicino in casa, in clinica privata o ospedale pubblico. Inoltre in caso di calamita ad assicurarle un post. Nella casa e fra I familiari del sottoscritto. Be intes. Nei limiti delle possibilita proprie e dei parenti.

Redatto, letto e sottoscritto nella data do cui sopra

I fede

Dante Valentino Caesar Montepulciano

Dante took a deep breath, and continued his story. Rossi translated.

"The next days were wretched. Caprice did not respond well to medicines. She remained miserable, dependent, always fearful that I would grow tired of her—disgusted even—and go away. She couldn't bear the thought of being alone. Nightmares caused insomnia; not a night passed without nightmares of desertion, frightening her into wakefulness.

"Three days later she changed our Golden Pact. She inserted an addendum.

"Late that night she got up, got the *Atto Solenne*, and added something. Afterwards she woke me, and showed it to me. She had added a paragraph at the end—"

Dante put on his reading glasses and read.

"*Sicomme questa dichiarazione e stata fatta con l'idea e intenzione che Montepulciano deve starmi vicino per tutta la vita e anche di piu.*

"*C.J.T.*

"*3/6/68*"

"Translated verbatim," Rossi said, "the addendum reads, 'By this declaration is the idea and intention that Montepulciano must stay close to me for all his life and even longer.'"

—∞—

I COULD not help Caprice. By the time of our Golden Pact, she was out of control. She was slowly killing my love for her.

I would not let her do that. I still remembered our noticing each other, our formal meeting, the long nights of romance and our early travels.

I decided I must leave before my love for her died.

She needed the care of a hospital and Clarissa, her nurse and companion.

This stage of alcoholism was heartbreaking. Caprice wasn't drinking for enjoyment, she was drinking because her body craved it. Caprice was drinking to avoid the painful symptoms of withdrawal, like tremors, nausea, headaches, and vomiting. She often experienced hours of insomnia.

She began drinking early in the day. In social situations she annoyed friends and strangers alike. Caprice began to lie about her drinking.

Blackouts became a common occurrence.

Worst of all, I became an enemy and, for me, this was the worst part because I was deeply in love with her.

She had stopped taking hikes, stopped all sports, and began to lose weight.

And her face was turning red.

Everything had taken a wrong direction.

My only relief came from Clarissa who began to prepare to come and help her dear friend.

DANTE paused, looked up, and said, with Rossi translating, "Caprice should have signed C.M. after her addendum—Caprice Montepulciano, not C.J.T., Caprice Jordan Taylor. And so I realized that the days of Caprice Montepulciano were ended. She no longer called herself by my name, which she once so eagerly adopted.

"That date, February sixth, nineteen sixty-eight is important. It was on that date that I decided to leave Caprice to return to my home near Tremezzo. This is the only document that records our parting. It is a very sad date, a date that requires explanation, especially since there is no doubt that we were still common-law husband and wife in Colorado—'for all our lives and even beyond,' as the addendum put it."

Dante's voice faltered. He showed obvious distress from deep in his heart. His eyes flooded with emotion. But he continued.

"Until February fifteenth, Caprice and I stayed on in Luzern. You see, she was very sick. She visited the hot springs and the doctors there, trying to repair the tremendous damage caused by her alcoholism. I stayed with her. I nursed her as I best I could. I tried to help her get better. It was my solemn oath to do that. It was my duty. Besides, I loved her and she was my wife."

Rossi glanced over to Guy Bray and indicated with his eyes that they should take a break and let his client gather himself. Bray immediately suggested they do so. The American charities' lawyers were deeply moved and quiet.

I WAS crying, sad and broken-hearted. I felt foolish crying in front of the lawyers. But as they left the room each came over and patted my back.

When the room was empty, Guido and Lessa came over to me, sat down, and comforted me. Even Rossi stayed, saying, "Dante you don't have to disclose your secret.'

"No, I must," I said. "Even Caprice would approve of me telling the truth."

"It's up to you," said Rossi, patting my back.

"I know. It's up to me."

17

Day 4: Offensive Acts

AFTER THE BREAK, Guy Bray brought the deposition back to order for the final time.

He explained that Dante wanted to discuss personal privacies. "It is an important fact, one we need to hear before our returning to America."

John Butler invited Dante to tell his story himself. "Mr. Montepulciano, please tell us *why* and *when* you left your wife. Tell us what happened. Tell us why, despite your great love for Mrs. Taylor, you left. Tell us why you never reconciled."

—⚬—

I HOPED I would tell my story of offensive acts fairly.

It would affect us all.

I did not sleep well last night. But I woke up feeling that—at last—I should tell this part of my story.

Caprice is dead. The love of my life is gone.

Only she can tell her story, but here I am with lawyers asking me to tell my story wanting a settlement with me so that each of their charities can receive their gift from Caprice as stipulated in her will.

How interesting.

I never wanted her money. I only sought to share her heart.

Now I have to expose her sickness and my pride. Will I be understood? Will I be able to get through my story? Will I destroy her and me and our once great love for each other? Will these lawyers keep this record private?

DANTE had already told his story to John Butler—alone, weeks ago in private, but he had omitted one aspect of the story. Mr. Butler agreed with Dante's decision to tell the story. And he thanked Dante for telling the complete story to him.

Dante composed himself and told the story of when and why he left Caprice. Rossi translated.

"On February fifth, the second day after the Golden Pact, I discovered that Caprice was still drinking—secretly and heavily. She drank enough to pacify her addicted, trembling, craving body. Convulsions periodically seized her. She was sick in body, brain, and soul. Her closet drinking filled her with guilt and remorse, with even greater shame and self-loathing. But despite her desire to exert self-control, she remained out of control. Her physical craving for alcohol was overpowering, beyond psychological control. She knew she must hide her drinking from me. I was the last person she wanted to know.

"I had been reading books about alcoholism and alcoholics, looking for advice on what to do."

"Who were they written by?" said Lambert wondering.

"The main one was famous," said Dante. "His name is Franco Basaglia. He was the psychiatrist who abolished mental hospitals in Italy, which indulged in terrible practices on their patients. Anyway he also dealt with alcoholics."

"Why don't we let Mr. Montepulciano continue his story?" said Bray.

THIS was terrible for me too.

Caprice was self-destructing. Our relationship was being destroyed.

I was no longer an inspiration in her life. She kept secrets about the extent of her drinking. If I went shopping or traveled, she would buy alcohol and hide it from me. To my own shame, I would find it and remove it.

She had become a periodic drinker—from two to six P.M.

I had become a judge of her life.

We both hated our roles.

We were bankrupting our romance.

"I HAD gone to the pharmacy to get a prescription filled. It would take me an hour or so. It was a sunny morning, and I wanted to get out and walk a bit and enjoy Luzern's brisk winter air. Taking care of Caprice had become exhausting.

"I left the hotel and turned right, and walked toward the park on the shore of the lake, one of Luzern's most enjoyable public spaces.

"I saw Caprice peering through the white lace drapes of our first-floor suite as I walked down Mont Blanc Strasse. Later she told me that she wondered how long I would stay with her. How long would I stand for her drinking?

"As I learned later, she phoned room service as soon as I was out of sight, and ordered a bottle of Château Fille Pommard."

"Who told you?" said Bray feeling the record should reflect Dante's source of information.

"The hotel manager," Dante said.

"So this part of your story was provided by a third party?"

"Yes, it involved room service."

—⁂—

I CAN tell this story because the hotel manager told me later what happened.

It helped me to prepare for these lawyers.

At first, the manager was hesitant to tell me his experience about what happened after I left for my walk and to go to the chemist—Americans say pharmacy.

When he realized who I was (Mrs. Taylor's husband), he carefully described what had happened. He pleaded with me not to tell my wife. Also, he did not want his story revealed to any of the hotel's executives. He would be fired, and he had a family who were dependent on him.

I understood and told him not to worry.

I did not want anyone to lose his job. I assured the hotel manager that this was not a thing he had to worry about.

ALONE in the suite, Caprice called Room Service. "I want two bottles of French wine for this evening. A Pommard, a Premier Cru, will do. Please send it up immediately. In the next ten minutes. Do you understand?"

"Yes, Mrs. Taylor."

"Immediately. Don't be slow," Caprice demanded. Then she went back to the window and made sure that Dante was out of sight. He was. A ringing phone broke her reverie.

"Mrs. Taylor?"

"Speaking," Caprice replied, recognizing the hotel manager's voice. She felt a tug in her heart. Why would the hotel manager be calling back? she wondered.

"Madam, I wish to be most respectful, but your doctor has asked me not to send alcohol of any kind to your room," the hotel manager said. He spoke with the greatest solicitation and caution, cringing in expectation of a reprimand. He knew of his guest's mercurial temper and her dreadful language when provoked. To say nothing of her reputation for slapping hotel help. At least she couldn't slap him over the phone.

— ⁕ —

I LIKE walking along the promenade. I knew now that I had to leave Caprice. I wondered where I might go.

Money was not a problem. Caprice often gave me more than enough to shop or gas up her car. She was a generous woman with me. She knew I do not abuse money; she knew I can live on very little.

I thought about returning to Milan, to get a teaching job and resume coaching. My degrees and coaching record would help me.

It was difficult to even think about leaving Caprice.

But she was ill and I wanted to help her. Besides, we had mutually written the *Atto Solenne* (the document we called The Golden Pact).

I had promised to be by her side.

This was a serious confirmation of intentions.

I needed to finish my story.

"PARDON me?" Caprice said, stung to the quick, feeling controlled, stripped of her secret. Her drinking would now become a matter of public gossip, as she never doubted for a moment. But mostly she was filled with deep shame and guilt. And yet those emotions were overcome by her urgent need for alcohol. She held the phone with a shaking hand.

"Madam—" the manager began.

"No. You listen to me, you impertinent, self-righteous son-of-a-bitch," Caprice screamed. "You get that Pommard up here to my suite—*now*. If you have the slightest common sense—and I doubt you do—you will do what I say, Sir."

"Madam—"

"Goddammit, don't you 'Madam' me."

"But—"

"The only but will be your butt," she screamed into the phone. "I will sue you for personal insult—personal defamation of character and injury. I will cause you to spend all of your savings—including your pension. Now, you send that Pommard—no, two bottles of it—up to my room this minute!"

Caprice slammed down the receiver. She was shaking with rage.

—m—

I WATCHED the lawyers' reactions. They did not appear upset. In fact they were leaning into the table, fascinated.

I felt relief, but not comfort.

Even Guido was leaning forward, listening, fascinated. I had never told him of the offensive acts that caused my break up with Caprice. He was a sympathetic brother, did not interrupt, and respected my truths.

Even Bass didn't interrupt. He appeared to understand that I was sincere, baring my soul, and unprotected.

The deposition clerk kept his head down and just quietly kept typing.

Orso listened, took a few notes. That was about all.

Butler was learning about these events for the first time, looked at Rossi from time to time. No response.

Even Rossi and Galileo had never heard this information.

WITHIN ten minutes, the suite's doorbell rang. Caprice composed herself and opened the door. The hotel manager stood holding two bottles of Pommard. His face was ashen, troubled by this confrontation with his wealthy and powerful but unlikable guest. He knew he shouldn't be doing this; but he had to protect his job.

"Madam Taylor, your wine," he said, and he held the bottles out to her. "Please forgive me. I didn't intend to be rude. I—"

"Come in, come in," Caprice said. "I shouldn't have gotten angry. I don't know what's come over me today. Come in, come, come. Please open one of the bottles, so when my husband returns it will have breathed."

With trained flair he opened one of the bottles, then retreated backwards, reaching for the door, wanting out.

"No, no. Wait. Please allow me, Sir," Caprice said, and she hastened to get her purse. He paused and watched her take out a one-hundred-franc note.

"That is not necessary, Madam Taylor."

"I know, but I want to thank you—and to apologize for my bad behavior. Now, please, take it."

"Excuse me, Mr. Montepulciano," said Lambert, Did you say this tragic story came from the hotel manager—in this detail?"

Dante confirmed the source and detail of his story.

"Mr. Bray," said Lambert, "is it necessary to hear the story?"

"Yes," Bray said. "Since it is important to Mr. Montepulciano, it's important that we hear it. It all links to The Golden Pact—the *Atto Solenne* document, which we've just heard. At the end of his story this deposition will conclude."

"I see, thank you, Mr. Bray."

Rossi turned to Dante and encouraged him to continue.

—∿—

THESE personal secrets are difficult to tell. When I fought in Africa, I learned an African proverb: Until the lion learns how to write, every story will glorify the hunter.

I think about this.

THE manager took the money, mostly just so he could get out. He opened the door and backed into the hall, keeping an intent eye on her every move.

"And, please," Caprice added with a wink, "let's keep this just between ourselves."

"Madam, I assure you. I will mention it to no one."

Caprice heaved a great sigh of relief and poured herself a full goblet of wine. What satisfaction, what physical, what psychological relief. She downed the wine in one long unbroken gulp. Next she hid the second bottle of wine inside one of her suitcases, one Dante would never bother to open. Then she moved a chair to the window and slowly drank the rest of the opened bottle of Pommard.

"When I returned from the pharmacy," Dante continued telling the lawyers, "I went straight to our suite. I felt refreshed. My walk through the lakeside park had revived me. My spirit had picked up. I was ready once again to care for Caprice, whom I still loved deeply. I unlocked the door to our room and walked into the room, my key in hand.

"Caprice rose from her chair, startled. She had a glass of wine in one hand, and the bottle in the other hand. I stood looking at her, my jaw open, unbelieving. Another empty bottle lay on the rug."

—✺—

I LOVED walking, and this walk had helped me clear my head.

At the moment Caprice needed Clarissa—not me. I realized this. Thank God Clarissa was in Luzern and in the hotel.

Clarissa was important to Caprice's recovery. First, they had a long friendship, she had seen Caprice through many recoveries, and she knew what to do. I did not. Despite my coaching background, I could not help. I didn't understand alcoholism. In fact, I only made things worse—despite The Golden Pact.

Caprice needed Clarissa.

I needed Clarissa.

"'CAPRICE—' I managed to say.

"'It's not what you think, love! I'm better. I've only had a sip. Just a sip—to calm my nerves. I'm much better now. You'll see,' she said, aware of her voice. It had pleading, whining, begging tones, and she became angry with herself and at me.

"'Caprice, this is very bad for you. The doctor said not to—' I moved toward her and reached out to take the bottle.

"'Stay away from me, you son-of-a-bitch!' Caprice snarled.

"'But the doctor said you could die—'

"'Stay away! What does that quack know?' she said, her voice rising.

"'Caprice, give me the wine. Where did you get it?' I demanded.

"'None of your business!"

"I gently twisted the bottle from her hand, and without warning, she slapped me viciously across the face. I stood rooted to the spot, frozen by surprise, my hand holding the wine bottle in midair.

"'Caprice, you don't know what you're doing,' I said. 'You must be drunk.'

"She slapped my face a second time, only harder, sending me reeling sideways, my face contorted with rage."

—m—

I WAS shocked.

I was momentarily paralyzed, not sure what to do.

My heart turned to ice, hating Caprice for her rudeness. This was not something that would turn out well. She was killing my love and respect for her.

Before the alcohol, we were great together. We laughed, we loved, we exercised, and we had good friends. She had loved not being hounded by the press, and she had insisted on being my wife, Mrs. Montepulciano. I was the light of her life. Caprice was my Picasso's *Joie de Vivre*.

Everything had collapsed.

I only felt rejection.

"'YOU bastard!'" she screamed. 'You can't tell me what to do. Don't ever tell me what to do again, you self-righteous little Italian shit.'

"I moved toward her, reaching with both hands to hold her arms. She backed away.

"'Get away! In fact, get out of my life! Get out of my room,' she shouted at me. 'I don't need you. You're only here for my money, anyway. That's it isn't it? Money, money, money! For years you've lived off me. You're like all the others—money, money, money. You dago! You *guappo*. Hit the road, mister!'

"'Caprice—'

"'I said get out. Go. I don't need you.'

"'Caprice, you're drunk,' I said, holding her arms, pinning her helplessly against the wall.

"Unable to slap me again, she spit in my face. I let go of her arms. Shocked, I wiped her spit from my face. That was when she slapped me a third time.

"It was the last time Caprice would ever slap me. I turned and walked to the door and left, but not before saying, 'Caprice Jordan Taylor, you are a very sick person. But you have said things and done things to me that are very bad. I will not let you destroy the love I have for you. I have always—in every moment—loved you with my complete heart—in my soul. You cannot destroy that. I will not let you do that.'

"Then Caprice changed. She broke down.

"'Oh, Dante, I'm sorry, truly,' she said. But it was too little, too late."

—ఐ—

THIS was a terrible ending.
    And she has shamed me.

"'I APOLOGIZE. I shouldn't have done that to you," Caprice wailed. Anger drained from her. She dropped to her knees, crying, her shoulders convulsing. Desolation washed over her.

"'No. I am leaving,' I said.

"'But you promised—in *Atto Solenne*,' Caprice said.

"'Forever. I am leaving—'

"'But you signed the Golden Pact,' she pleaded.

"'*Exacto*. But I am leaving. I intend to take my love for you with me, Caprice, and protect it. I will not let the sunshine of my love for you be destroyed and ruined by the dark storm clouds in your life. You should never have said those things. You should never have slapped me—an Italian officer. You've made a serious mistake. Those are not actions I will allow you to take back.'

"Then I walked out, closing the door behind me, leaving Caprice pale, shaking, mute but crying. I walked out of the hotel and walked to the train station. I took the next train across the Italian Alps back to Cernobbio, where I boarded a bus and went to Tremezzo.

"After that date—February fifteen, nineteen sixty-eight, Caprice and I never saw each other again. Neither of us found the will or a way to mend broken fences. But my love for Caprice remained unbroken, undiminished, unaltered. As for Caprice, love was always clouded by the twin tragedies of great wealth and alcoholism. She called me her husband. Except for her will, she simply said 'my husband.' I remained husband to Caprice. Thus the American charities' lawyers must settle with me."

I FELT cleansed. At last my secret was shared.

Since I left, I sent postcards on every one of Caprice's birthdays, sent my love and best wishes. She never returned my greetings.

Now Caprice is gone—no more gossip, no more hassle.

Our journey together was like a shooting star.

And all shall be well and all manner of thing shall be well.

IT was after midnight by the time Dante finished his story. The assembled lawyers, tired though they were, were deeply moved.

After declaring his responsibility as an officer of the Italian army to keep certain matters between a man and a woman private, Dante stopped talking. He folded his hands in front of him on top of the conference table. He had nothing more to say. He felt sad.

Silence filled the room, except for the sounds of the lawyers breathing and the court reporter typing. Eyes shifted guardedly, each person wondering what might be a next appropriate action. Was it time to end the deposition?

Bray felt now was indeed the time.

"It's after midnight," he said. "These proceedings are concluded on this twenty-seventh day of October, nineteen seventy-nine."

Then he addressed the court reporter. "Mr. Montepulciano's account of his break-up with his wife is not germane to this deposition. It will be kept private, and is not to be included in the deposition records." Nelson nodded his assent.

As a final act, Dante signed a statement declaring, under penalty of perjury, that his testimony had been true and correct. And with that, the deposition came to an end.

Guy Bray rose from his chair, went over to Dante, thanked him. He embraced the old man, and whispered, "Mr. Montepulciano, I do believe you are the legal husband of Mrs. Caprice Jordan Taylor."

Dante let the tall American lawyer hug him. In fact, he hugged him back, saying, "*Grazie, Signor* Bray. Watch out, you may become like an Italian yet. You may visit my home anytime—just like Mr. Butler."

The two men smiled at each other and shook hands.

IV: Finali

18

A Compromise Agreement

ONE WEEK AFTER their return to the United States, the charity lawyers met to discuss the deposition of Dante Montepulciano. They agreed, unhappily but unanimously, that he did indeed have a legal claim to the estate of Caprice Jordan Taylor. He could prove that he was Mrs. Taylor's common-law husband under Colorado law. A Santa Barbara judge had earlier threatened that should the charities dispute Dante's claim, he would send the case to Colorado. If that happened, the result would most likely be unfavorable to the charities: Dante would likely get at least fifty percent of the estate's worth, some thirty-four million dollars, and perhaps more, drastically reducing the amount left for the charities—doubtless reducing the lawyers' fees proportionally as well.

Dante and his Italian lawyers had held the charities' feet to the fire. The charities had been forced to concede that Caprice Jordan Taylor and Dante Valentino Caesar Montepulciano were married by common law; that they were not subsequently divorced; and that Dante was the surviving spouse. Further, the charities had agreed to proclaim her good works with appropriate memorial plaques.

They must honor her gifts.

In turn the charities asked Dante to sign a quit-claim. It was important to them that the estate be unencumbered, so as to be able to distribute the entirety of the estate to the charities, as provided in the will. But for this they knew they must pay. If Dante would renounce his rights to the estate, then in turn the charities would agree to pay five million U.S. dollars to him—and he would have no rights or claims to the rest of the monies.

Based on the Charities' consent to accept Dante as Caprice's husband, and on their agreement to place memorials appropriate to designated gifts, Dante agreed. Subsequently, the executor distributed Caprice's sixty-eight million dollars as follows:

To Pueblo Hospital: 60%.

To the Art Museum: 20%.

To the Botanic Garden: 10%.

To the Fleischmann Museum of Natural History: 10%.

To Dante Valentino Caesar Montepulciano: $5,000,000.

Separately, the Society for the Prevention of Cruelty to Animals received $100,000. This was a specific dollar grant and was dealt with accordingly.

Over time, these grants and payments were made according to everyone's consent. Thus, finally, after two and one-half years, the Compromise Agreement was distributed.

19

A Visit to the Taylor Memorial Garden

SOME YEARS LATER, Dante, in the company of John Butler, arrived in Santa Barbara to complete, finally, the Golden Pact. The two-hour drive up the California coast from Los Angeles had made him tired. Sleep had evaded him the night before, and he was so anxious to see the Memorial Garden that had been built in Caprice's honor that he had insisted on leaving their Beverly Hills hotel at five o'clock. For Butler it was an ungodly early hour, but as Dante's host he was determined to let Dante visit America and Caprice's memorials on his own terms.

Butler parked the car on Santa Barbara Street, a relatively quiet palm-lined street of mostly Craftsman-style bungalows, in front of the Caprice Jordan Taylor Memorial Garden. Dante stepped to the curb and stretched his arms languidly in the golden early morning sunshine, then walked slowly to the low, ungated sandstone wall that surrounded the park. Beyond it, he could see a spreading lawn surrounded by trees, and at its center a gazebo next to a pond on which ducks floated lazily. Butler came up to join him, and they went up the sandstone steps into the park.

There was more to the park than Dante had expected. It was spacious, covering an entire city block. In the 1920s, it had had been the grounds of a popular two-story hotel in the Italianate style, where East Coast socialites came by train to rest and play. But years of abuse and neglect had relegated the romantic old structure to the wrecking ball. The land had come into the hands of the Art Museum, which briefly considered building a new facility there. But Caprice had purchased the land from the museum, with the intent of donating it anonymously to the city for a park. The Santa

Barbara City Council had accepted the gift on December 9, 1975; but Caprice's name was not mentioned until her death two and a half years later, when it was decided to build this memorial park in her name.

Well, Caprice, Dante said inwardly, *you always sought the highest value for your money, and—even in death—your estate is completed.*

The two men, one tall and strong, the other old and frail, passed a small sign at the entrance that read CAPRICE JORDAN TAYLOR MEMORIAL GARDEN. They immediately came upon expansive green lawns, colorful flower beds, and wonderful rare trees and shrubbery from around the world, all planted along winding pathways. Tall Canary Island date palms with long, graceful fronds stood sentinel throughout the park, providing welcome shade and noble perspectives for the park's ingenious plantings. It was late May, and the dirt pathways were littered with dates.

Then they strolled to the edge of the park's central pond. Was this Caprice's Walden Pond? Colorful carp, gray trout, and black catfish swam in the clear, shallow water. A family of pond turtles was sunning on large rocks. A small sun-bleached wooden gazebo jutted out over the north shore of the pond.

Leaving the quiet solitude of the pond, they retraced their steps to the street, to read the plaque inset in the sandstone column at the western entrance. They leaned over to read the simple bronze memorial. John read the inscription aloud in clear, slow English. It was written in plain, honest language.

CAPRICE JORDAN TAYLOR

ESTABLISHED IN HONOR OF CAPRICE JORDAN TAYLOR, BY THOSE WHO LOVED HER SOARING SPIRIT. THE CITY OF SANTA BARBARA PARKS DEPARTMENT GRATEFULLY ACKNOWLEDGES THIS GENEROUS GIFT OF THE CAPRICE JORDAN TAYLOR ESTATE. THIS PARK IS DEDICATED TO THE ENJOYMENT OF THE CITIZENS OF AND VISITORS TO SANTA BARBARA.

Tears filled Dante's eyes, but he smiled through them, because he knew the real story—the real Caprice, a wonderful woman destroyed by great wealth and alcoholism. A great sadness welled in his heart, gripping the core of his being. His love for her remained: steadfast, true, always.

Now Butler fully understood the integrity of this old man, his great love for Caprice, and his dedication to the Golden Pact.

Yes, Caprice, thought Butler, *your memorial is beautiful, a garden of repose in the middle of this romantic city.* The morning's golden light illuminating the beauty of the park moved him to the mysteries of his very being: *What am I? And what are you? And what are we? And why?*

Dante slowly walked back up the path to a bench that looked across the lawn to the pond and gazebo. Butler followed. When they reached the bench, Dante turned to Butler and said, "I would like to just sit here for a while and remember Caprice and our life together. If you don't mind, please leave me here. I would like to be alone. When I'm finished, I will walk to your office and meet you there."

Butler objected. "I can't let you walk all that way by yourself, Dante."

"No, I can walk. In Milan I walk everywhere. That is why I am still healthy, despite my age. No, you go on. I will join you later."

Butler left, and Dante eased himself slowly onto the bench and looked at the lawns, the trees, the pond, the gazebo—Caprice's gift to Santa Barbara and to all of Santa Barbara's visitors. And he grieved. He grieved for her life's tragedies, sorrows, loneliness, and unacknowledged contributions.

Then he remembered a verse from the one American poet whom he revered as great, Walt Whitman. Caprice had introduced him to Whitman's writing in Colorado. Dante recalled Whitman's lines,

> *I play not marches for accepted victors only, I play marches for conquer'd and slain persons....*
> *I beat and pound for the dead*
> *I blow through my embouchures my loudest and gayest for them.*
> *Vivas to those who have fail'd!*

In the end, Caprice had failed. She had failed tragically to put her life together. She hadn't been burnt by the sun; rather, she had lost her way on the dark side of the moon.

But never mind. This memorial to Caprice's memory had

integrity. Yes, definitely it had integrity. Every corner of it appealed, with great integrity and great design.

Having journeyed through two continents to find Caprice, having searched out her secrets, having talked with people who knew her, and now at last having arrived here, on the ground of her memorial, Dante was moved to introspection. A great pride arose within, and he acknowledged it. It was so real, so deep, personal, loving, respectful. "Oh, Caprice, to have held so closely such a perfection for a few precious moments, only to lose it," he lamented. "To have experienced such rare friendship, only to lose it. I will always love you."

As Dante lapsed into reverie, memories of Caprice led him to journey into himself. He visited his dark places, and deplored what he found—and, especially, what he did not find.

20

A Memorial for Dante

DANTE MONTEPULCIANO DIED on April 12, 1997. He was seventy-seven years old.

He was buried in Milan's Cimitario Maggiore, in a section dedicated to veterans of World War II. His brother, Guido Montepulciano, had preceded him in death two years earlier in a fiery automobile accident.

Therefore, the sole mourner to brave the rain was Adam Rossi, who watched from beneath a black umbrella.

Dante's modest tombstone bore a carving of the Medal of Valor, and this inscription:

DANTE VALENTINO CAESAR MONTEPULCIANO
BORN 1920 — DIED 1997
WOUNDED IN NORTH AFRICA IN 1943
WHILE SERVING HIS KING

While settling Dante's affairs, Rossi was surprised to discover what Dante had done with the money he had received from Caprice's estate. Other than Galileo & Rossi's legal fee, $500,000, he had donated the entire amount—$4.5 million—to Italy's national pension fund for teachers.

Rossi stood in silence for several minutes.

So it was true: Dante had never loved Caprice Jordan Taylor for her money. It meant nothing to him. During all their years together, and for the remainder of his life—and even longer, as he had sworn in the Golden Pact—he had shown that he loved Caprice for herself, and herself alone.

Caprice never fully believed it. She had misjudged the full measure of Dante's integrity. Or had she? Perhaps she had never completely lost her love of Dante. Didn't her will prove that?